"I w...   e
why you are come."

Susanna spoke the words gently.

But Hugh only replied, "No, better not."

She persisted in a soft and urgent voice. "It is only that I think you are very worried and sometimes it is better to share a care. I think we are friends. Surely you can trust me?" She put out her hands to him in a gesture of sincerity.

"You have a true heart," he said in answer. "And if you admit me to your friendship then I am indeed honoured."

"But..." began Susanna just as Hugh reached for her hands and turned her palms upward.

"I cannot read your hand," he said ruefully, "but if I could, I would wish to read much happiness in it. I hope you will always be happy, Susanna."

But Susanna knew she could never be happy as long as this man remained a mystery to her.

Books by Ann Hulme

HARLEQUIN REGENCY ROMANCE
8–THE UNEXPECTED AMERICAN
40–A SCANDALOUS BARGAIN

FALSE FORTUNE

ANN HULME

Harlequin Books

TORONTO • NEW YORK • LONDON
AMSTERDAM • PARIS • SYDNEY • HAMBURG
STOCKHOLM • ATHENS • TOKYO • MILAN

First published in Great Britain 1989
by Mills & Boon Limited

Harlequin Regency Romance edition
published May 1991

ISBN 0-373-31149-4

FALSE FORTUNE

CHAPTER ONE

THE GREEN PLUSH CURTAIN across the doorway on the far side of the room moved aside and a plump, balding man in a grey coat entered. He was closely followed by a mirror-image of himself.

The man who had been waiting, pacing impatiently up and down the room for some ten minutes, blinked. He did not think there was anything wrong with his eyesight, nor had he drunk much the previous evening. He wondered briefly if seeing double was the result of being cooped up in a place he detested. He glanced mistrustfully at his surroundings, the bare walls and solid but unlovely furniture, and his expression, already uncompromising, grew even more truculent.

"I see you are surprised, sir!" said the plump man, beaming delightedly at his visitor like a mischievous baby. "Took aback, I dare say. People often are. May I present to you my brother, Tobias Clay, my business partner and, as you see, my twin."

His identical shadow bobbed his head but said nothing, increasing the uncanny effect.

"People often cannot tell us apart," chuckled the balding man, rubbing soft white hands. "When we were children we played many a trick on our nursemaids, ain't it so, Toby?"

"Indeed, yes," said the shadow at last.

"But if you will observe us closely, sir," the speaker sidled up to the visitor who drew back with marked distaste from the offer of closer contact. "You will mark that I am just a shade taller. Thereby you can tell that I am Josiah and he is Tobias. Ain't it so, Toby?"

"Indeed, yes," echoed the shadow.

"As it happens," continued Mr. Josiah Clay, "I am also the elder by a full eleven minutes, ain't I, Toby?" He made this appeal to his twin as if Tobias might have some clear recollection of their joint birth and be able to confirm the delay between their arrivals from memory. Tobias, obviously a cautious man, only nodded.

A silence fell on the room. In it, the twins observed their visitor as curiously as he observed them. They had, thought Josiah to himself, all sorts in here. But this was a rum one. A gentleman for sure. But with a skin burned as walnut-hued as a gypsy and hair flecked at the temples with an early grey though still abundant and black. Probably in his thirties, calculated Mr. Clay, six-footer in his stockings and with shoulders like a coal-heaver. Tough customer, very.

"You have it?" the gentleman demanded testily, breaking the silence.

Josiah started. "Yes, sir. Toby!"

Tobias Clay sidled out from behind his twin and could now be seen to be carrying a flat ebony box. He placed this reverently on the table and opened it.

"There now," said Josiah fondly as Tobias stepped back into the shadows which he seemed to haunt by preference. "What do you think of that, eh? Ain't that a fine piece of workmanship?"

"Wrap the box up," ordered the visitor without bothering to reply to this comment. "I have to leave at once for the country and I shall take it with me."

"Wrap it up?" exclaimed Josiah in unfeigned horror. He reached out a pudgy hand and touched the box protectively. "You can't mean, sir, to put it in your pocket and just ride off with it? It ain't the way Toby and I do business.

Suppose it should fall into the wrong hands, sir? Very embarrassing."

"Let me worry about that!" said the customer, his impatience breaking through his voice. "Wrap it up and be quick about it."

"I suppose," said Josiah resentfully, "something might be done with waxed paper and string. But mark me, sir, we ain't responsible, Toby and me."

"I don't ask you to be. Only to hurry up. I haven't all day!"

A few minutes later the disconcerting visitor pushed his way out of the front door and set off down the quiet street. It was late December, cold and grey. The twins watched his departure from the window. They saw, as he left, that a small wiry man quitted a nearby doorway in which he had obviously been waiting and scuttled along crab-like in the wake of their man. The contrast between the man who strode out briskly in front and his diminutive follower scurrying along behind would have caught most eyes. But the most important thing about the scene to the watching brothers was that the man following did so openly—which caused Josiah to heave a sigh of relief.

"After all, Toby," he remarked to his twin. "It wouldn't do if he was to get knocked on the head straight off—not outside our door, if you take my meaning."

"No, Josh," said Tobias.

"Not but what knocking him on the head might be difficult," went on Josiah. "Since he's built like a brick wall. A difficult customer, that, Toby—in both senses of the phrase, if I might venture a small witticism."

"Very droll, Josh," supported Tobias.

"Hope he don't come back," said Mr. Josiah Clay thoughtfully. "I can't say that doing business with him was a pleasure. A deep one, that, very. Wish I knew what he was up to."

"No good, if you ask me," said Tobias, venturing at last his one and only independent comment.

"You're right there, Toby," said Josiah, reversing their roles. "Oh, yes, indeed . . ."

"I ABSOLUTELY REFUSE! You shan't bully me into it, Suky, and you shan't wheedle me into it, either!"

"It's traditional!" exclaimed Susanna Harte in some exasperation.

"Devil take tradition!" said her cousin briefly.

They glared at one another. The young man was planted before the carved surround of the fireplace and warmed his nether regions unashamedly at the flames by tucking his hands under the skirts of his coat and presenting the seat of his inexpressibles to the heat. He appeared to have been out riding and still wore mud-splashed breeches and topboots. His fair hair fell over his forehead in straight damp locks and his thin, clever, handsome features were set obstinately.

"See here," he grumbled, "I'm chilled to the bone already, riding all the way into Newbury on a dozen errands for Viola for which I doubt I'll get much thanks. Now you want me to turn out at dead of night and hang about outside in the rain catching my death, just so that on the stroke of midnight I can appear, half-frozen and clasping, if you please, a lump of coal!"

"It's a tradition on New Year's Eve!" Susanna said crossly. "A stranger must come over the thresh-hold bringing a piece of coal. It ensures that there will always be a fire in the hearth for the coming year. Which, considering the way you are hogging that fire, is something you should want to ensure!"

"Right!" said Leo Drayton, letting the skirts of his coat fall back into place and shaking a finger at her. "I can demolish all that argument, my girl! Firstly, it's supposed to be a dark stranger—and I'm not dark. Nor, may I point out, am I a stranger! I've lived here four, no five, years."

He paused to take count of the points he had made. Susanna bit back the observation that he had indeed lived with them for almost five years and done very little for it, apart from appear once a year at midnight with a lump of coal. It seemed little enough to ask in return for his keep for the past twelve months. It was true, however, that he had ridden all the way into Newbury today at the behest of her stepmother. It had not stopped raining all day and he could not really be blamed for not wanting to turn out again.

"Thirdly," Leo said, pursuing his argument, "there's little chance that there won't be a fire in the hearth in this house for years to come! It may make sense to a cottager to arrive with a lump of coal—it's a piece of arrant nonsense to play out such a silly charade here at the Hall!"

"You've done it every year, Leo," she persisted, altering her tone to a coaxing one.

He was unmoved. "But I ain't doing it this year. Lord, Suky, it's raining cats and dogs! You can't have overlooked it! I'm soaked to the bone!"

"No, you're not. Your riding cape was, but you are fairly dry. Don't be mean, Leo. I particularly want us to see the New Year in as we always do. There have been so many changes of late—" she fell silent and a look of gloom crossed her countenance.

Leo shifted uneasily. "I know what you mean, Suky. We have just to get used to it, I'm afraid."

"She intends to wear them tonight," Susanna said. "She told me so. She does it to spite me. Oh, Leo—it's not that I mind because I want to wear them myself. They look far more splendid on Viola than ever they could look on me. But Father bought those for Mama and to see another woman wearing them—"

"Look here," he said hastily, seeking to distract her, "I'll arrange something about your dark stranger and piece of coal, since it means so much to you. Leave it with me."

"You'll do it, then?" she asked hopefully.

"No! I said, I'll arrange something! Now then, I'm going to change." He walked past her, but at the door of the room hesitated and turned back. "Don't be downhearted, Susanna. Cheer up, the coming year may be full of surprises."

"So was last year!" came the sharp response.

"Well, yes," he admitted. "But I meant, nice surprises, you know..." He went out and could be heard whistling as he ran up the stairs.

Susanna sighed and sat down by the hearth to stare into the crackling flames. The firelight threw a rosy glow over her oval, pensive face. She was not a conventionally pretty girl, but she had regular features and a good skin and the simplicity of her dress and of her hair, twisted into a knot on top of her head, suited her. Leo sometimes said she looked like a Quakeress. She did not mind his teasing. Leo meant well. In his own inconsequential way he had supported her over this last, difficult year. But now it was New Year again. In a few short hours—Susanna glanced up at the clock ticking remorselessly on the mantelshelf—1816 would be gone for ever and 1817, with whatever it chose to bring, would be upon them.

It was almost a year ago now that her father had arrived home with a new bride on his arm. He had taken the whole family by surprise. Sir Frederick Harte was member of parliament for his native heath, a responsibility he discharged to the best of his limited ability. He had quitted them at the end of the last Christmas recess and returned to London to fulfill his duties, only to return, a mere matter of a few weeks later, with a handsome and fashionable wife almost half his age on his arm.

Viola, the new Lady Harte, could not be more than five and thirty. Sir Frederick was well into his sixties. He was a bluff, kindly man, essentially a country gentleman and certainly no follower of fashion. What on earth had possessed him to marry after a whirlwind courtship such a dashing wife—and even more puzzling, what had brought such a beautiful and fashionable woman to marry him, well, that was something no one could fathom.

Over and over again, Susanna told herself she had no objection to her father remarrying, in principle. But to someone suitable, a lady of his own age and interests. The new Lady Harte liked parties and routs and cards and little dinners. All through the summer the house had been filled with her friends, some of them of very rakish appearance and conversation, who descended upon the Hall on the pretext of the popular race meetings at nearby Newbury. They sat up all night, they almost drank Sir Frederick's cellar dry and half of them departed with bills unpaid in local taverns and eating-houses or with merchants who supplied the wants of such gentry.

With the winter, these summer starlings had all migrated elsewhere. Thank goodness, thought Susanna. Even good-natured, hospitable Sir Frederick had begun to look distinctly harassed at seeing so many new and unknown faces at his table. Now New Year was upon them and at least they were to celebrate it en famille. Just Sir Frederick, his wife, his daughter and his nephew.

Yet there was still something which destroyed Susanna's pleasure at the thought of a little peace and quiet in the house again. By way of a wedding gift, Sir Frederick had presented his new wife with the remarkable diamond necklace which he had originally had made for his first wife. He had always declared this should be Susanna's some day—but he seemed to have forgotten his promise. The new Lady Harte had accepted the gift without the slightest hesitation or appearance of embarrassment and Susanna supposed she could not be blamed. The Harte necklace was not to be sneezed at—to quote Leo on the subject.

"All the same," said Susanna aloud to the crackling hearth. "Flaunting it under my nose shows a certain want of tact! But I suppose it is what Papa wants and it makes him happy to see her wearing it. In any case, I shan't let her see I mind, so there!"

Fortified by this resolution, she went upstairs to dress for dinner.

UPSTAIRS LEO WAS SOAKING in his bathtub with his fringe of fair hair tied up in several rag knots to achieve the romantic curled effect. He was also thinking about Lady Harte and not very kindly. She had given him a list of errands, "as long as my arm!" said Leo aloud, extending one soapy arm out of the water and surveying it. "Sent me out in the sort of weather a dog wouldn't want to be out and about in, can't be bothered to say, 'Please, Leo!' and probably won't say 'thank-you,' either, has upset poor Suky and is altogether a dashed awkward woman!" He hunted for the bar of soap which slithered elusively around his feet. "But a very attractive one, there's no denying. The thing is..." Leo fell silent and brooding, the bath water growing cold about him.

The thing which so worried Leo was, quite simply, that this still-young Lady Harte might declare herself at any moment to be in an interesting condition. Leo supposed, after consideration, that his Uncle Frederick wasn't altogether past it. The old fellow was sixty-odd, but older men had fathered sons. "To say nothing of any one of those fellows who came visiting in the summer," muttered Leo. "And with whom she appeared deucedly friendly. You're going to have to watch out, Leo my boy!"

When Leo came downstairs again later, suitably spruced up and dressed for dinner with his hair miraculously trans-

formed into quite a riot of Byronic curls, the weather had
not improved. Rain lashed against the windows and the
wind howled in the chimneys. The fire flickered and hissed
as raindrops found their way down and pattered onto the
coals. The drawing room had an unpleasant atmosphere of
smoke about it, as it always did when the wind "blew the
wrong way."

Leo seized the fireirons and rattled them energetically in
the bowels of the hearth.

"Do leave it, Leo!" said a woman's voice behind him.
"You're making things worse! That chimney has to be
swept. I've told the house-keeper a dozen times and she's
promised the chimney-sweep will come directly New Year is
over."

Leo straightened up, wiping his hands carefully on his
handkerchief. "Dear Lady Harte, you look delightful. And
you are right, of course, about the fire. I shall leave it alone
and let it smoke us all like kippers."

She smiled at him, not only because of the compliment
but also because he was, after all, a very good-looking
young man, and held out her hand for him to kiss.

As he straightened up he observed just a shade maliciously, "And you are wearing the Harte necklace."

Viola touched the glittering jewellery with the tips of her
slender fingers. "Yes. Does it become me, Leo dear?"

"You become the jewels, Lady Harte, you become them.
You would make a piece of string tied round your neck look
like pearls."

Anyone else, thought Leo unkindly, would tell him immediately he talked nonsense. But it was impossible to flat-
ter Viola too much. She lapped it all up as a cat does cream.
She folded her fan now and tapped him on the arm.

"You're a wicked fellow, Leo, and I shall let you take me
in to dinner. Freddie will be down shortly and I suppose
Susanna will not be long."

"Isn't that a new gown, dear aunt-by-marriage?" he asked.

"Yes. Do you like it? I kept it by for New Year. I think it lucky to wear something new at New Year." She twitched at the silk skirts of the rose pink gown she wore.

She was one of those women who possesses an ivory complexion with jet-black hair such as are more often seen in Mediterranean countries. In an unguarded moment she had told Leo that she had Italian blood but she had not been specific about it. Viola was always very vague about her family. But there was no denying the diamond necklace showed to its best advantage on her lovely bosom. He could not help giving her a look of frank admiration. She saw it and liked it. He was rewarded with another tap of the fan on his sleeve.

"You must be as superstitious as Suky," he said. "I mean, you believe that one should wear something new at New Year. Suky believes someone must come in the front door at midnight, a dark stranger for preference, bearing a lump of coal. She quite insists on it. The last four years I've done it, but I've adamantly refused this year. Listen to that rain beating on the window!"

"She will be disappointed," said Lady Harte in rather offhand tones. Clearly she had little interest in her stepdaughter's odder notions.

"No, she won't. I've fixed it all up, bribed a footman. Simple sort of fellow and quite happy to turn out in a howling gale and come stumbling in with a lump of coal. He's got dark hair, too, so it will be all quite right. Suky shall have her dark stranger and I shan't get pneumonia."

As he said this, the voices of Sir Frederick and his daughter could be heard as they approached the drawing room together.

"Don't tell Suky what I've set up!" Leo hissed. "I want it to be a surprise!"

"If you like," said Viola, bored with the subject and peering at her own reflection in the looking-glass. Satisfied, she turned to face the newcomers, ready to receive their approbation.

The first sight to meet Susanna's eyes on entering was that of her step-mother, cool, elegant and devastatingly beautiful, dominating the room. The Harte diamonds glittered and flashed around her throat like points of white fire as she moved forward beneath the overhanging chandelier.

"My dear," said Sir Frederick, kissing his wife's hand in his old-fashioned way. "You look very fine, upon my soul, you do!"

Leo, standing a little to one side, caught Susanna's eye and grimaced. She frowned at him to put him in his place. Leo's sense of humour occasionally got him into scrapes. Besides which, his sympathy was not altogether welcome. It was only a step from that to feeling sorry for her. Susanna turned aside.

She would not have been human if the sight of her step-mother had not upset her at all. It was not merely Viola's poise and beauty, nor was it the wearing of the Harte diamonds, although both these things depressed her and she was honest enough to admit it. I am no beauty, thought Susanna, nor could I ever be fashionable like Viola or cope so brilliantly when surrounded by admirers as she was all summer. I won't be jealous, because that's a mean-minded and stupid thing to be. But try as I might, I can't like her. I'm sure she dislikes me. I can't believe she loves my father, and it was no way to behave, having so many male friends visit her—nor did papa like it much. If she truly cared for him, she would have chased them all away!

Her father, that was the nub of the matter. Her father's remarriage had changed her view of him and her relationship with him forever. Previously she had seen him only as her father or, from time to time when she had acted as his secretary, as a member of parliament. Loyally she had transcribed his notes and written out his letters. She knew him to be incorruptible—a rare thing amongst politicians of the day—and an honest, kindhearted, reliable man, hitherto a rock in her world, something unchanging and immovable.

That her father could still entertain a weakness for young and charming women had never occurred to her. She found it essentially shocking although she forced herself to admit that it was only natural. But the sight of her father making a fool of himself—Susanna tried not to use this phrase but it forced itself forward now as it had done from the first—over a woman half his age struck her as acutely embarrassing and disturbing. She loved him dearly. It pained her that behind his back people might now gossip unkindly about him, even make jokes at his expense, jokes of the kind people always make when an old man takes a young bride. And she feared for him, because she was sure that in the end he would be made unhappy.

Perhaps if Viola had been a different kind of young woman, her age would not have mattered. But a more ill-assorted couple, thought Susanna ruefully, than Viola and Sir Frederick would be hard to imagine.

She became aware that her father stood at her elbow. Leo and Viola were talking together some little distance away.

"She's a beauty, isn't she?" said Sir Frederick unexpectedly. His gaze was fixed on his wife and he seemed to look at her as he might have gazed at some recently acquired work of art or antique statue.

Susanna flushed. "Yes—she is, very beautiful."

Sir Frederick seemed to recall that it was to his daughter he spoke and that his turn of phrase had not been altogether fortunate. He cleared his throat. "You look very handsome, too, my dear!" He pinched her cheek affectionately.

"Thank you, Papa."

He seemed to have some matter on his mind. He shuffled his feet and cleared his throat again. "I have wanted to have a word with you, Suky...concerning your late mother's diamonds. I know I said you should have them, and so you will, one day, no doubt."

Susanna said nothing, but if Sir Frederick thought the Harte diamonds could easily be wrested back from Viola, he was surely sadly deluded.

"The thing is," he said, lowering his voice even more and sounding urgent as if he wanted to convince not only her but himself. "The thing is, they are more suited to Viola. You are still very young, Susanna."

"I am twenty-six, Papa," she said calmly.

He paused and frowned. "Are you? I suppose you are, by Jove." His look of displeasure increased. He glanced again at his young wife, as if he made a comparison between her age and that of his child, and disliked the mere nine years difference between them—especially when taken in consideration with the thirty years difference which lay between himself and his wife. "So you are," he repeated more stiffly. "I tend to forget it, since you ain't wed."

He moved away. He had been made to feel unsure of himself. Susanna saw him glare at Leo who was making Viola laugh. She felt a wave of pity for her father. Poor Sir Frederick. "Marry in haste and repent at leisure" might prove his epitaph yet. He was beginning to suspect, very faintly, that he might just have made himself ridiculous in the eyes of all his acquaintances. It was not a situation he was accustomed to be in. He looked around for someone to blame it on and paradoxically blamed it on anyone who was younger, on Susanna and on Leo.

Viola was not insensitive to her elderly husband's morose looks. She left Leo's side to tuck her arm through Sir Frederick's and say playfully, "Come now, Freddie! Such a glum face! Will you see the New Year in looking so gloomy?"

"No, no, my dear," he said, cheering. He patted her arm. "No, no, now let us go in to dinner." He bore his wife away in the direction of the dining room.

"I was supposed to have that honour!" said Leo, not looking particularly downcast. "Viola promised I should take her in!"

"You will have to make do with me, Leo!" said Susanna, smiling at him.

"Lord yes. Come along, Suky." He took her arm. "I say," he said, leaning down to whisper in her ear. "I've got a capital surprise lined up for you!"

"What have you done?" she asked, immediately suspicious.

"Shan't tell. But you'll have your dark stranger and bits of coal with all the trimmings!"

Leo could no more keep a secret than he could fly. He both wanted to surprise her and could not bear not to tell her what he had arranged. He struggled manfully with his inclinations and finally declared, "Wait and see—but I got it all set up!"

DESPITE EVERYTHING dinner passed off very well. Leo was in excellent form, at his most amusing and evidently highly pleased with himself. Viola was all attention to her husband and Sir Frederick had mellowed between his wife's teasing and a bottle of good wine—one of the few the summer visitors had left him.

When dinner was over, they retired to the drawing-room and played whist whilst they waited for midnight.

"My father always maintained card-playing wasn't what it was in his day," said Sir Frederick reminiscently. "Fellows fought duels over cards then. Why, even when I was a boy, it wasn't unknown. But we are more civilised nowadays. I made much of that in my speech on law and order in the last session . . .'

"Do hurry and put down a card, Freddie!" urged Viola.

But Sir Frederick was not to be hurried. "In my late father's day, that fellow, Beau Nash ran the assembly rooms in Bath. He used to keep an eye open and if some silly young devil was getting in too deep, he'd step in and put a stop to it before blood flowed. Of course, they said Nash was a rogue himself, but Bath was never the same after he quitted it. All kind of riff-raff appeared who would not have got past the doors in Nash's day. Now that set has taken itself off to Brighton where it is sadly encouraged in its dissipated ways by those who should know better!"

"Nonsense, Freddie!" said Viola. Her face seemed pinker than it had been and she added crossly to Leo, "Do put the screen in front of that fire, Leo! What with the heat and it smoking so vilely—the chimney must be swept this week!"

"It's not nonsense at all," said Sir Frederick obstinately. "Nash was deuced strict. Why, on one occasion, to my father's certain knowledge, he prevented an elopement. He whispered a word in a lady's ear. 'Madam,' he said, 'You should go home at once!' She saw he was in earnest and left the card-table directly to return to her lodgings. What do you think she found there, eh?"

"I have no idea, Papa," said Susanna who had heard this story several times before.

"A carriage before the door and her own daughter about to climb into it with a fortune-hunter!" Sir Frederick chuckled. "She put a stop to that! But Nash was to be thanked."

"He sounds a very tiresome man," said Viola firmly. "And very much inclined to meddle in other people's business! I should think most people were glad to see the back of him! Freddie, you have revoked!"

"I most certainly have not!" he protested.

"You have, you were so busy telling us about Nash that you played a spade just now when hearts were led and see, now you have put down a heart!"

"Bless me," said Sir Frederick. "Well, if you say I have, my dear, I suppose I have. I do beg the company's pardon!"

"It is almost twelve!" said Leo hastily. He glanced up at the clock.

As if in response there came the sound of some commotion outside the hall. They could hear the voice of the butler and then of one of the maids. A cool draught seeped into the room beneath the door which indicated that the outer front door of the house had been opened. The fire puffed fresh smoke crossly in response.

"Hah!" exclaimed Leo, rubbing his hands gleefully in anticipation. "It's my surprise!"

"What's that?" asked Sir Frederick.

The door opened and the butler appeared looking slightly non-plussed. "I beg your pardon, sir, but there is a gentleman here."

"What—at midnight?" exclaimed Sir Frederick, rising to his feet.

"It's all right, Uncle!" Leo jumped up. "It's all arranged—I arranged it—for Suky, you know. The piece of coal and all that. Show the gentleman in!" he ordered the butler.

"Yes, sir," said the butler, giving him a look of some misgiving.

Booted feet tramped on the parquet flooring outside. The butler stood back and as they all waited with eyes fixed on the doorway, a complete stranger strode into the room.

For a moment they all stared at him in stunned silence. He was a very tall, strongly-built man who wore a heavy military riding cape by way of travelling dress. His topboots were also mud-splashed and he gave the appearance of someone who had journeyed considerable distance. Nevertheless, when he threw back the cape, a coat of very fashionable and expensive cut was revealed. He pulled off his gloves and handed them to the expressionless butler in an assured manner.

Susanna, slowly recovering her powers of thought, felt a movement of anger because it seemed that just when they thought they had seen the last of Viola's disreputable friends until the next summer, here was one who had the effrontery to turn up unannounced in mid-winter. And yet, this man was not quite like the usual run of Viola's admirers. There was something about his manner, both capable and determined, which made a deep impression and the military cape also had a well-worn old-friend look about it, as if it had accompanied its wearer on a few adventures and hazardous journeys, unlike the civilian coat which looked brand new and anonymous as if perhaps its wearer really didn't like it. Susanna thought, "This one has been a soldier!"

She looked again at his face, more closely, and noted how weather-beaten was his complexion, markedly at odds to the dandyish cut of the coat, far more in keeping with the cape and now that she considered him again there was a certain aggressiveness in his air and a truculent set to his jaw.

"Good heavens..." breathed Leo, echoing all their thoughts.

Sir Frederick was more blunt and to the point. "Leo!" he exclaimed, "Who the devil is this?"

Leo looked startled and dismayed and his mouth gaping open foolishly, stammered, "I—I really have no idea, Uncle!"

"You said you have arranged some tomfoolery!" roared Sir Frederick. "Is this it?"

"No, Uncle, I swear—I don't know who this—this gentleman is!"

The unknown gentleman advanced on their huddled group. "Sir Frederick Harte? I beg your pardon, sir, for intruding at such a late hour. I was delayed upon the road. There is a little snow falling over the downs." He paused as if he expected some comment and receiving none, frowned, crinkling his thick black eyebrows. For some reason she could not explain, Susanna felt an odd nervous trembling in the region of her diaphragm. "You had my letter, sir?"

"To my knowledge, sir," retorted Sir Frederick angrily. "I have never had any kind of communications from you in my life! Do you mind telling me who you are, and why you have seen fit to invade my house?"

"I can answer that, Freddie!" To everyone's surprise it was Viola who spoke up. Her voice had lost its assured and playful tone. She sounded like a frightened child. Susanna stared at her in surprise and some dismay. All colour had fled from her step-mother's face which was now as white as a ghost's. "This gentleman, Freddie, is Major Hugh Russell. He—he is my nephew."

"What?" roared Sir Frederick.

"My—my nephew, Freddie. My eldest sister's son. Much of an age as myself, I know, but—but that is the way of it."

They all remained as if frozen in some tableau. It was shattered by a further scuffle of feet and the sudden appearance in the doorway of a rustic youth with a shock of dark-brown hair, dressed in a curious travesty of mediaeval garb including crossed thongs around his shins and a hat with a feather in it.

"What the—?" howled Sir Frederick, his already plum-coloured complexion turning dusky purple.

"Here I be, Master Leo," said the apparition, obviously pleased to see he was making a great impression. "I'm sorry if I be a bit late. I had to come round the back way so as them girls never saw me, the maids—Cook she saw me and laughed fit to bust her stays!" He searched in some hidden pocket in his jerkin and produced an object which he held up clasped in his palm. "I wish you good cheer, gentle-folk," he declaimed loudly, frowning and obviously re-peating some speech he had been taught. "I wish you—oh, I done that bit. A happy New Year and a prosperous one. May you have fire in your hearth and meat in your belly—"

"Upon the spit," said Leo hollowly, "Meat upon the spit..."

"Sorry," apologised the speech-maker. "Tis same thing, anyhow." He opened up his raised palm. "What do you want me to do with this here lump of coal, Master Leo?"

CHAPTER TWO

REFLECTING ON IT all afterwards, it struck Susanna how very well-trained they all were. Leo recovered his lost presence of mind instantly. He pressed half-a-crown into the hand of the harbinger of New Year and bundled him out of the room, shutting the door firmly on him and on the other servants who had gathered in a curious group outside in the corridor.

Sir Frederick stepped forward, extended his hand and said, "I fear your letter has gone astray, Major. But you are more than welcome as a relative of my wife."

"Thank you," said the newcomer, adding after a moment's hesitation, "I have brought my man along with me—he is still outside."

"Oh, yes, of course," exclaimed Sir Frederick. "Leo, my boy, go and tell Merrihew to see about accommodation for Major Russell's man! Now then, come to the fire, Major. You must be near frozen! Snow on the downs, you say? I'm not surprised. It usually comes earlier and we have been remarkably fortunate with the weather this year. But a glass of brandy wouldn't come amiss, I dare say?"

"Indeed, it wouldn't!" confessed Major Russell with a rueful grimace.

He looks a perfect rascal! thought Susanna grimly, studying the arrival's windswept and travel-stained appearance and slightly Mediterranean good looks enhanced by the growth of midnight stubble on his jaw. And if he is her nephew, I'm the Empress of Russia! But even she was so well-schooled in receiving a guest that none of this showed on her face and she smiled welcomingly upon him.

Viola, too, had quickly recovered her aplomb. "Goodness, Hugh!" she said. "What a surprise you've given us all! If we had known, we should have waited dinner on you."

"Dear Aunt Viola, I wouldn't have you starve to death on my account!" he said and kissed her hand with a bow. The bow brought his nose to within inches of the Harte necklace. Susanna, still scrutinizing him intently, saw an extraordinary expression cross his face. It was fleeting, but it was so thunderstruck that she almost stepped forward to ask him what was wrong. But in an instant the expression had vanished to be replaced by one she could not quite interpret. That, too, was wiped from his face as quickly as it had appeared, leaving her feeling uneasy, almost afraid. Russell straightened up and asked politely, "How are you, aunt?"

"Very well, thank you, Hugh. Have you—have you seen any of our family recently?"

"Oh, I haven't been long returned from Paris," he said, it seemed to the listening Susanna, a little evasively. In explanation he turned to Sir Frederick and added, "I have been with the army of occupation in Paris, following upon our recent successful campaign. But I've bought out, as you can see from the way I'm newly turned out in civilian dress, and all set to lead a more peaceful life!"

"You were present at the engagement of Waterloo, then, sir?" cried Sir Frederick. "Then you are doubly welcome! And you shall tell us all about it, tomorrow naturally, when you are rested and recovered! I shall be more than pleased, sir, to have a first-hand account of that notable battle! But as Lady Harte says, we should have waited dinner on you, if we had known—ring the bell, Susanna, and have them bring a tray for Major Russell!"

Bemused, Susanna stretched out a hand and did as requested. In due course the tray arrived, laden with cold ham and turkey. By this time Major Russell was settled in the best position in front of the fire and seemed perfectly at home. He appeared to have stepped into the role of guest of honour with complete ease and no indication of any embarrassment, even the fire stopped smoking as if it wished to be obliging. Leo had retreated to the back-ground where he sat biting his nails and looking very much put out, scowling at the newcomer when he thought he was not observed. Viola on the other hand had adopted a brittle air of gaiety and fussed about her relative in a way, thought Susanna rather unkindly, which would have fooled no one but Sir Frederick. Her step-mother was as upset as Leo about it all, more so, in fact, but she had chosen her own way of disguising it.

As for Susanna, she found herself pushed forward by her father to do her part in making the guest feel welcome and sat beside him as he demolished the cold meat with increasing feelings of frustration which it was hard to conceal. She suspected her smile was becoming rather fixed.

"That was excellent, Miss Harte," said Major Russell approvingly, as the tray was removed and wiping his hands briskly on his napkin. He gave her a little nod.

"You're sure you've had enough?" demanded Susanna a little tartly.

"Yes, indeed! I did stop at an inn just on the other side of Newbury, but it was very poor fare, only a boiled chicken and some not very good apples in pastry and half a pint of sherry."

Just so long as you paid your bill there! thought Susanna, mindful of the habit of Viola's other friends, who were apt to overlook this small matter.

But the visitor was graciously allowing the butler to refill his brandy glass. "Well," he said, rising to his feet. He

towered over them all, even Leo who was by no means short.
"May I wish you all a very Happy New Year!"

"A Happy New Year!" they all chorused obediently and
drank the toast.

SO ONE WAY AND ANOTHER they fussed around Major Russell until the early hours and finally took themselves off to
bed not long before the dairy-maids would be getting up to
see about the milking.

"I suppose," said Susanna to herself as she climbed at
long last into bed, "we shall find out what he wants sooner
or later, if not today then tomorrow. But I for one shall be
watching Major Russell very closely and he needn't think
he's going to pull the wool over my eyes!"

She shivered as she snuggled down into the cold sheets
and wished she had thought to bring a hot brick up to bed
with her.

In various other rooms about the house, others made their
belated way to couches long grown cold from earlier appli-
cations of warming-pans.

"Well, Charlie?" asked Major Russell of his valet. He
dragged his cravat from his sinewy neck and tossed it carelessly onto the bed. "What's your opinion of the billet?"

Charlie had retreated to the dressing-room with his master's coat. He now re-emerged, a small wiry figure sidling
back into the room in cautious, crab-like fashion. He
glanced about him judiciously.

"Very fair as billets go, Major. Very fair. You and I have
seen worse!"

"We have that," agreed Hugh, throwing himself down on
the nearest chair. "We shall bivouac here for a while,
Charlie. Get my boots off, there's a good fellow."

Charlie obligingly turned and stooped to grasp one
booted leg whilst his employer planted the other foot against
his manservant's broad rear end. What with Major Russell

bracing himself in this fashion and Charlie tugging, the boot suddenly shot off and propelled Charlie, purple-faced, across the room as if he had been shot from a cannon. A repeat of the process divested the gentleman of his other boot. Charlie clasped both boots to his bosom and stood upright—or as upright as he ever stood. At that moment there came a peremptory knock on the door.

"Hugh?" demanded Viola's voice through the panels. "Are you still decent? I want to talk to you!"

Major Russell removed his watch from his waistcoat pocket and observed the hour. He smiled slightly. "Four in the morning..." he murmured. "My, my Viola... you are growing careless!" he nodded towards Charlie who deposited the boots and went to open the door.

Lady Harte appeared precipitously in the room and at the sight of the manservant, stopped dead in her tracks. "Oh— I came to see if there was anything you needed, Hugh."

He smiled again and glanced at Charlie who promptly disappeared, closing the door behind him.

"Who is that odd little man?" demanded Viola, now that she and her nephew were alone. "I never saw a more peculiar valet! Where do his particular talents lie, Hugh? In marking cards or in switching loaded dice for good ones?"

"He was my batman, Aunt Viola," Hugh told her. He had risen to his feet and towered over her as he offered her the chair he had vacated. "We campaigned together for several years in war and so thought we might try our luck together in peacetime. His name is Charlie Treasure. As the name, so the man. He's perfectly honest, I do assure you, and I find him indispensable."

"Hah!" declared Viola, seating herself and twitching nervously at her skirts. "Don't call me Aunt Viola, Hugh! You know I can't abide it. I'm very little older, that is, you and I are much of an age. You have always called me Viola since we were children together."

"Yes, I know, but I thought your husband might prefer it," he said. "And speaking of your husband, Viola, isn't this a very late hour to come calling, especially on a bachelor in his bedroom?"

"Freddie is an innocent," said Lady Harte briefly. "And will be snoring his head off by now. Anyway, I don't mean to stay long. I just want to know what you mean by it, Hugh!"

He sat down on the edge of the bed which sank alarmingly under his weight, and eyed her thoughtfully. "Mean by what, Viola my dear?"

"Don't act the simpleton with me!" she stormed, clapping her slender beringed hands together in annoyance. "You understand me perfectly. What are you doing here? What do you want? And don't, please, repeat that taradiddle about a letter. You know you wrote no such thing. What has brought you, Hugh?"

"Now see here, Viola," he said reasonably. "Your imagination is running riot. All right, I confess I wrote no letter—but I had no time. I've been less than two months back in England and had a great deal to do. I've been a soldier for twelve years and settling back into civilian life has been worse than any engagement against the French! However, I finally got things settled and knowing you had remarried, I thought, well now, I'll go and see Viola in the bosom of her newly-acquired family. Is that all of it, by the way?"

"All?" she asked sharply.

"Yes, your husband and the girl and the young fellow. No one else?"

"No one." She hesitated, then continued, "The girl is my step-daughter as you have already learned and the young man is a cousin of hers, Leo Drayton. He's a worthless rattle and lives here because he has run through his own fortune and sponges off Freddie. So you can forget any notion you may have, Hugh dear, of fleecing him at cards. Leo hopes,

I dare say, to marry the girl eventually...if she is fool enough to have him. I dare say she might grow desperate enough in this neck of the woods to accept him." Viola shrugged elegantly. "But there, it's not my business. She is Freddie's only child."

"And his heiress? That is, until you came along, Viola." Hugh rasped a thumbnail across his rather blue and bristly chin. "Put the cat amongst the pigeons, hasn't it? After all, you are still a young woman, as you have just reminded me, and could present Sir Frederick with a bouncing son and heir!"

"It is highly unlikely," said Viola icily.

"Oh, I see," he said and a mocking gleam showed in his dark eyes. "Bad luck, Viola. However, there are obviously compensations to being Lady Harte. That is a remarkably fine necklace."

She started and put up her hand automatically to touch the diamonds which glittered at her throat. "Yes—it is known as the Harte necklace and was Freddie's wedding gift to me."

"I hope you keep it under lock and key," he said.

"Yes, I do!" Viola rose to her feet. "You may stay for a week or two, Hugh. Then I want you out of here and I don't want you to return! Nothing much ever happens here anyway and you will be bored to tears. And tell that manservant of yours that in this house we count the silver spoons!"

"As I dare say you counted 'em, Viola, metaphorically anyway, before you accepted poor Freddie!" he retorted.

Lady Harte advanced on his seated form and pushed her lovely face close to his, almost spitting with rage. "You are an adventurer, Hugh! You always were and always will be. How you must miss the military life! Always moving on like a gypsy and leaving your debts and your ladyloves behind you! I really don't know what you will do now that they have packed Napoleon off safely to St. Helena.''

"No more do I, Viola. I dare say most of what you say is true. In fact, all of it is true. But we are somewhat two of a kind, you and I, don't forget that! I haven't. I know you very well, my dear."

"Two weeks, Hugh!" she said sharply, drawing back. With a swirl of silk skirts she was gone.

A scuffling at the door announced the return of Charlie Treasure. "Will that be the lady, Major?"

"That's the one, Charlie," he said softly.

"Ho!" said Mr. Treasure gloomily. "You wants to be very careful, Major, my opinion, if you asks it."

"I don't, Charlie, not on that matter."

"Very well," returned the valet serenely. "But you knows it, anyway."

NOT SURPRISINGLY everyone slept in late the following day and when Susanna came down it was almost noon.

"Shall I set out a luncheon, Miss Susanna?" asked the housekeeper. "There's plenty of cold fowl."

"Yes, set out something in the dining room," Susanna agreed. "The gentlemen certainly will want to eat when they arrive."

"One of the gentlemen is down already, Miss. The gentleman who arrived so late last night. He's been down since before ten this morning and I believe he's now in the library."

Major Russell. He had taken advantage of their tardiness to prowl about the house all morning unobserved. Susanna's expression froze.

"Thank you, Mrs. Merrihew. Oh, Lady Harte is complaining of the chimney in the drawing room and it really doesn't draw well. I think it must need sweeping."

"Yes, Miss. Bundy the sweep will be here tomorrow early. I'll see everything is dust-sheeted up first thing and by the evening you will be able to use the room again."

Susanna thanked her and made her way to the library. Before the door she paused and after a moment, unashamedly put her ear to the panels. There was no sound on the other side. She frowned and opened the door.

Major Russell was standing on the library steps at the far end and consulting a volume he had taken down from a high shelf. He looked up quickly as she entered and returning the book immediately to its place, jumped down from the steps, which creaked and rocked, and came to meet her.

"Good morning, Miss Harte!" He looked perfectly recovered from his journey, was freshly-shaven and showed no sign of lack of sleep. He looked, in fact, extremely dashing and much less of a brigand despite his dark hair and sunburned skin. Susanna drew upon her moral armoury and met his eye unflinchingly.

"Good morning, Major Russell. I hope you slept well?"

"Oh, excellently," he said. "But I'm accustomed to rise early, even if I turn in late...so you see I've been up and about some time."

"Mrs. Merrihew is getting out a cold luncheon for us," Susanna informed him. "Major Russell, I am glad to see you alone. I should be glad of a word privately."

A slightly wary look entered his eyes but he said courteously, "Of course, Miss Harte. Though perhaps you would call me Hugh. We are, after all, related."

"Are we?" she returned coolly. "Are you really her nephew? I find it hard to believe."

"But it's true, I swear it." He sounded quite sincere. He saw she still looked doubtful and propped himself on the edge of the library table. "My mother was the eldest of a very large family, eleven children surviving, and Viola the youngest. As sometimes happens in such circumstances, my own mother was married and raising a family of her own when my grandmother was still caring for children of *her* own in the nursery. Viola, I'm sure she would not mind my telling you this, is two years older than myself.''

So he was thirty-three. He looked a little older but, thought Susanna, surveying him, that was probably because his skin was so weather-beaten and his hair had early become flecked with grey. Viewed closely, however, and at more leisure, the face was clearly that of a young man. She relaxed slightly.

''Thank you. I dare say you think it odd my questioning your story—'' She began to sound embarrassed.

He interrupted her. ''No, I think it's perfectly natural and sensible. Tell me, Susanna—you will allow me to call you Susanna, won't you?—how do you find Viola?''

She flushed deeply. ''She is very—very charming. But I'm not sure I should discuss my step-mother with you!''

''Yes, of course, step-mother...'' he mused to himself. ''I'm sure Viola don't like that and I shouldn't think you do!''

He glanced up and saw that the girl was glaring at him again. She didn't trust him. He could not blame her for that. But finding her here was an added complication and one for which he had not allowed. She struck him as an intelligent young woman and in her own way, he thought, she is extremely attractive. Not pretty. That would be the wrong word. But she had very fine grey eyes and a straight little nose beneath a rather untidy fringe of hair which fell in curling strands across her forehead. Despite that, and despite her present obvious unease, there was a natural dignity about her such as he had seen on the faces of some Spanish girls of good family. He dragged himself back to matters in hand.

"I should apologize to you again for arriving as I did. When I see Leo, I shall apologize to him for spoiling his surprise."

"Oh, that," she said. "That is one of Leo's bits of nonsense. Leo is always thinking up practical jokes and so forth."

"He's a cousin, I understand?"

"Yes," she said uneasily.

"Forgive me—you see I am a stranger so I have to ask all manner of peculiar questions otherwise I don't know what's going on... But is he—" Hugh broke off and gestured vaguely with his right hand. "Do you and he have some kind of understanding? Is he here courting, I mean?"

"No, he isn't!" she replied angrily. "And I don't see why that should possibly concern you!"

He made what he immediately realised was a serious mistake. He was tempted into gallantry. "On meeting an attractive young lady, the first thought of almost any man would be to ascertain what rivals, if any, he might have!"

She did not turn a hair, other than a scarcely perceptible deepening of the rosy flush on her cheeks. "Allow me to set your mind at rest, Major. The question of rivals does not arise. If you hope to help pass a tedious stay with a mild flirtation with me, you will be disappointed. I have neither the inclination nor the talents for such nonsense!"

She turned away and walked down the long narrow room towards the windows at the far end.

"Ouf!" thought Hugh, wincing metaphorically. "That's me set in my place and no mistake!"

He watched her go thoughtfully. The pale winter sunlight falling through the panes struck her hair and revealed unsuspected auburn depths in it. She turned now and faced him and because the light was now behind her, he could not make out her expression, whereas she had an excellent view of his features since he faced the window and the light fell full on him.

He felt a movement of admiration. She was a very clever girl. He had been right. She meant to ask a few more questions of her own, and she had manoeuvred their respective positions to give herself the advantage.

"Major Russell!" she said, "Or Hugh, if you prefer. It really makes no difference to me. You spoke just now of not knowing what was 'going on'—to use your own phrase. I suspect that *I* do not know what is going on, and I am sure my poor father doesn't! I don't know why you have come, but there is some trickery afoot and I believe my unfortunate father to be the object of it!"

He pushed himself away from the table and walked slowly towards her. She stood her ground until he came right up to her. "I promise you," he said in a low, quiet voice, "that I mean your father no harm. Nor you. I can only ask you to believe me. I cannot prove it."

She found it difficult to meet his dark eyes watching her so seriously and looked away. All this was proving very difficult. The wretched man had the ability to set her all of a dither. "Pull yourself together!" she admonished herself severely. She sighed and rubbed her hand over her forehead, disarranging her fringe of hair in a way which brought a smile to his face which fortunately she did not see.

She did not know what to think. All this was completely beyond her experience. She could not prove anything. All she had was instinct and instinct told her Hugh Russell had come to this house with some purpose in mind. He was Viola's relative and that in itself roused suspicions. Viola, however, had seemed dismayed to see him when he first arrived. She had disguised it quickly but could not manage to look pleased.

"I think," he said gently, breaking in upon her thoughts, "That you dislike this marriage your father has made."

"I don't think it suitable," she admitted unwillingly. "But he is very fond of her. I wish, I wish I could believe she was as fond of him."

"Hmm," he muttered. "Viola isn't bad at heart, you know. A little impetuous, perhaps, and extremely self-centred and sometimes foolish. But none of those things are crimes."

"If you saw her friends!" burst out Susanna fiercely, causing him to start with her vehemence. "I never saw such a—such a disreputable crowd in my life! All summer they came and went, making free with our house, behaving in a quite disgraceful manner amongst themselves and going off leaving unpaid bills behind them, half of which my father has been obliged to settle for the sake of the good name of the Hall!"

"I can imagine that," he admitted. "Viola never chose her friends wisely. But, you know, it is for Sir Frederick to regulate his own household. If he didn't like them, he should have thrown them out!"

"He would do nothing to cause her a moment's unhappiness!" she replied bitterly. "He didn't like her friends, but if that company is what she wants and makes her happy—"

No fool like an old fool, thought Hugh. Yet he felt less sympathy for Sir Frederick than he had done. The old man had no business to make his daughter so unhappy. He should have thought what he was doing! But then, reflected Hugh ruefully, few of us do that, especially when in the grip of passion for anything, for a woman, for cards, for horses...

His companion said in rather stilted tones, "There is cold fowl set out in the dining room. I dare say you are hungry."

"Could eat a horse," he confessed so spontaneously that she was hard put not to laugh, despite all her misgivings. "Will you come too?"

"Later," Susanna said evasively.

He made her a bow and walked out of the library. When she was sure he had gone, she pulled out the library steps and carefully climbed to where he had been searching amongst the books. The steps were old and not much used. They rocked insecurely and she grasped nervously at a projecting cornice to steady herself. Whichever maid had the task of dusting here, she was a lazy worker, or perhaps she understandably did not wish to entrust herself to the rickety steps. The shelves up here were thick with dust except for a clean patch where a book had obviously recently been removed and replaced. Susanna silently gave thanks for the indifferent cleaning efforts of the maid concerned. She took out the volume Major Russell had been consulting and opened it curiously.

"The properties of minerals," Susanna read aloud. She frowned. "How very odd. What did he possibly want with this?"

HUGH, MEANTIME, HAD arrived in the dining room to find Leo already established there and eating very heartily of a plate of thickly sliced boiled ham. He was a little surprised because he had imagined the young fellow was the sort who found it difficult to drag himself out of his bed before the afternoon. Leo, however, hailed him boisterously.

"Good day to you, Russell! Slept all right, I hope? Sit down and have some ham. Have some of Mrs. Merrihew's mushroom pickle with it. There's no beating her mushroom preserves. Cucumber is very good, too."

Hugh smiled and took a seat opposite him. He nodded at the servant to indicate he would have a plate of the ham and when it had been placed before him, took up a fork and asked, "Do you think I could borrow a horse? My poor brute is sadly in need of a rest after the journey. I'd rather like to ride out. I'm accustomed to take exercise and don't care for sitting about all day."

"Of course you can!" replied Leo indistinctly. "Just carve me a wing of chicken, Brown, will you? I'll see to it. Mind you, I should have thought you were in need of a rest yourself, but you military men are all as tough as old boots, I dare say. If you want to view the park, I'll come with you. Be glad to show you round the place."

"Thank you," said Hugh, ignoring the less than flattering comparison drawn for him.

THE TWO MEN rode across the expanse of parkland surrounding the house, and then through a gate and out over the gently rolling swell of the downs. During the early hours of the morning the rain had indeed turned to snow as Hugh had told them. But it was wet snow and had not lasted. The pale winter sunlight had been enough to disperse it and now, past mid-day, it was no more than a faint white dusting across the downs, like icing on a cake. Bare earth showed through and only here and there, under bushes or walls, was any amount of snow left.

"I'm sorry I disturbed your plans last night," Hugh said. "About the New Year messenger, I mean."

"Oh, that," Leo shrugged. "I just arranged that to please Suky. She's rather down in the dumps these days, what with one thing and another."

He broke off abruptly and pointed across the downs. In the distance an exercise string of horses cantered sedately along, wary of dangerous ruts in the frozen ground.

"Racing country," said Leo. "But you'll know that."

"And does this land belong to Sir Frederick?"

"Some of it—as far as that line of trees down there. But the old fellow ain't interested in horseflesh. A pity." Leo put a hand up to shield his eyes and squinted into the pale clear sunlight towards the distant string of racehorses.

Hugh, watching him, asked casually, "Gambling man, are you?"

Leo shrugged. "I usually don't say 'no' to a modest wager. But modest is the word! I'm somewhat light in the pocket these days, you understand."

And something of a lightweight generally, I should think! thought Hugh unkindly. Within twenty-four hours this boy will touch me for a small loan and I'll wager my last guinea on that!

"Mind you, I'm no card-player," said Leo. "But I know something about horses."

He dismounted as he spoke and Hugh followed suit. The string of racehorses had disappeared over the horizon. Leo looped the reins over his arm and began to walk across the frozen turf, leading the horse. By a small growth of hawthorne bushes, he stopped, threw the reins over a projecting branch of scrub and turned to face Hugh.

"I owned a good horse once," he said. "Used to ride him myself."

"Did you?" Hugh was surprised and could not help it sounding in his voice. Leo noticed and grimaced.

"Had to sell when I ran out of funds, of course. See here, Russell, what do you want?"

The question was sudden but not unexpected. Hugh stroked the nose of the bay horse he had borrowed and answered slowly, "You are the second person to quiz me this morning." He saw Leo raise his eyebrows and added, "Miss Harte has already interrogated me in the library and very efficiently, too. I can only say to you what I said to her. If I have business here, it is not to make mischief for your uncle or your cousin."

"It's to do with Viola, then," said Leo calmly. "Between you and me, I like Viola even though she can be difficult. But then, I'm a bit of a family black sheep myself, so I don't go criticising others. I won't have you making a fool of my uncle, Russell. Not in his house and certainly not in his bed."

Hugh's mouth set grimly. "I'll excuse you, lad, because your interest is to defend your family—but if you make any such remark again I'll knock you into the middle of next week! The lady is my relative, my aunt, to be precise!"

"Oh, I know that," returned Leo, unabashed. "Or you say she is, and frankly, it doesn't matter to me one way or the other whether she is or not. I told you, I like Viola. I'm not questioning her honour. I'm questioning yours."

"You idle young rogue—" Hugh almost choked on his words in his ire. "You're lucky I don't confounded well call you out!"

"You'll blow my head off," said Leo. "I don't want my brains splattered all over the downs here. If you call me out, I shall refuse. Duelling is a dashed silly business to my mind."

"I don't know," said Hugh seriously, "whether you are simply without any guts or quite mad."

"Neither, I'm honest. I'm not a ruddy hero. Nor am I quite an idiot. I leave guns and swords and so forth to splendid chaps like you. But I mean what I say about my uncle. I won't have you cuckolding him and before you set about me, I ought to tell you that I saw Viola leave your room in the early hours of this morning. She wasn't in there long and I don't suppose you could have got up to much. But you were dashed lucky only I saw her and not Suky or a servant—and God forbid my uncle! To me your arrival here looks more than odd. I'd say it looks damn suggestive."

He let out a sudden squawk as Hugh's hand shot out and grasped the lapels of his coat. "Now you listen to me, lad!" Hugh snarled, jerking Leo towards him and almost off his feet. "I'll mind my business and you mind yours! And I'm not accustomed to be told what mine is by a young whelp who curls his hair and snoops round corridors—and I ain't about to start!"

He released Leo who staggered back and then straightened his coat with as much dignity as he could muster as he struggled for composure.

"Fair enough. I don't want to know your business. As I say, my concern is for my uncle."

"Yes," Hugh said slowly and meaningfully. "You won't want that boat rocked, would you?"

Leo's face turned ruby-red in the cold air and a sudden warlike gleam entered his eyes.

"Well, well," said Hugh casually, turning to remount. "So there is something which stirs you up, lad, after all. Glad to see it. I was beginning to despair of you."

"Go to hell!" said Leo savagely.

"I MIGHT SAY," said Mr. Treasure appreciatively, "what I'm something of a connassewer of the pickle. I've eaten pickles in Germany—they make a very fair pickle, them Germans. I've eaten pickles in Flanders. I've eaten pickles in France, though to my mind them Frenchies don't understand how to make a good pickle. But this pickle, Mrs. Merrihew, is a Queen of Pickles. A veritable royal pickle, this."

"You want to try the cucumber, Mr. Treasure," said Mrs. Merrihew, blushing. "And the onions will take the roof of your mouth off!"

"Ah!" said Charlie appreciatively. "That's how a pickle should be. Bit of cheese—Cheddar by preference—and a plate of hot pickle. But right now, ma'am, I couldn't eat another morsel. Bust me buttons, I would!"

"Go on!" said the housekeeper, gathering up his plate and knife and pushing them into the hands of the kitchen skivvy. "You go and wash those, my girl, and stop gawking!" She patted her hair and returned her attention to the visitor. "You'll have travelled a lot, then, Mr. Treasure, from what you was saying?"

"Oh, yes," said Charlie, settling back in his chair. "Done a few miles, the Major and me, together. Seen a few sights, too. That wouldn't be ale in that cask over there, by any chance?"

He was duly supplied with ale.

"I've always thought," said Mrs. Merrihew, "as it would be nice to see the world. But there, somebody has to stay at home."

"Well, now," said Mr. Treasure expansively. "If home was a fine house like this'un . . . You been here a long time, ma'am? Although when I sez a long time, a young female like you can't have been here that long!"

"Get along!" said Mrs. Merrihew. "You're a bit of a card, you are, Mr. Treasure! I've been here since I was a girl. My late husband, God rest him, was butler here but I buried him five year back. I was Cook's helper and then I was Cook and then housekeeper. Lady Harte depended on me. I'm speaking of the former Lady Harte." Mrs. Merrihew grew slightly mournful. "Poor dear lady. I cried buckets when she passed on. We all did. Sir Frederick was that cup up. I never thought he would have got over it, but there, in no time at all he came back here with a new wife! Between you and me, Mr. Treasure," Mrs. Merrihew leaned forward and lowered her voice, "I was a trifle shocked. I know my place, I hope, and don't criticise my betters. But a man that age, you know, it's not right. Hardly put aside his mourning, too. And him such a steady sort of gentleman. Not what you'd think of as fickle. And her so young and—and lively. You'd think she'd fancy a young man better."

"Still," said Charlie, sipping at his ale. "Better an old man's darling than a young man's fool, eh? That's what they say!"

"She's his darling right enough!" said Mrs. Merrihew with a snort. "Everything's done the way she wants. And the presents he gives her!"

"Oh, ah?" said Mr. Treasure idly. "Bits of rings and things, I expect."

"Rings? He gave her my poor late lady's diamonds! The Harte necklace. She wore it last night! Those diamonds were meant for Miss Susanna, after her dear mama passed on. But the new Lady Harte, she got her fingers on 'em straight away!"

"Did she, indeed?" murmured Mr. Treasure. "Likes to wear 'em, I suppose."

Mrs. Merrihew sat back and frowned. "Funny you should say that, Mr. Treasure. But first off, she didn't wear them much. In fact, I don't think we saw them for weeks. I even overhead the master ask her why she didn't wear them and she said, it was on account of Miss Susanna and she didn't want to upset the young lady. But this last month or so she's wore them several times, so I reckon she's got over her scruples—if she had any!"

"Is that a fact?" said Mr. Treasure. "Fancy that, now."

CHAPTER THREE

THE HOUSEHOLD was all hustle and bustle early the following morning because the sweep was expected. Viola, of course, did not concern herself with such matters, but Susanna was downstairs at an early hour and together with Mrs. Merrihew supervised the dust-sheeting of the drawing-room furniture and the removal of paintings from the walls and any other valuable or breakable articles. The chandelier was shrouded in a vast bag and curtains taken down. It was altogether a work of considerable labour but it was all carried through efficiently and they were ready for the sweep when he arrived.

Mr. Bundy, the sweep, put in his appearance at nine. Susanna saw him from the window trudging up the drive with a bundle of brushes over his shoulder, followed by a small child similarly laden. She had never liked Bundy, who frequently smelled of drink. He was a big burly fellow with a cast in one eye and yellow uneven teeth which he would bare in a travesty of a smile. The smile never reached his eyes which despite being bloodshot were as unexpressive as those of a fish, even if one did look in upon the other which made matters worse.

A little later Bundy was ushered into the drawing room by a disapproving Mrs. Merrihew and stood before Susanna sucking his yellow teeth and breathing noisily.

"Morning, Miss!" he said hoarsely and made his unattractive grimace in an attempt at an ingratiating smile. "Bit of a nip in the air this morning."

It was pretty obvious that the nip in the air was not the only nip with which the sweep had acquainted himself that morning. The usual aura of alcohol hung about him and the top of a gin bottle stuck out of one capacious side pocket. He was warmly wrapped up against the cold in a heavy coat and woollen stockings. The same could not be said of his minute helper who wore ragged clothes obviously all handed down from someone older and larger and odd boots. The child did not appear very old. Susanna suspected he was not more than eight or nine. There was an extraordinary un-childlike air about him which both touched her heart and made her curiously apprehensive. He neither smiled nor spoke, but put down his bundle of brushes and squatted down on his heels wrapping his stick-like arms around his knees, to await Bundy's instructions and all in total silence.

"Now then, Mr. Bundy!" said Mrs. Merrihew briskly. "It's not a year since you were last here and that chimney's been smoking as bad as ever it did. Lady Harte has complained particular. The smoke ruins the curtains and the carpets and the portrait of Sir Frederick's late father which hangs above the mantelshelf had to be sent to be cleaned. It had fair turned yellow all over. It's not satisfactory, Mr. Bundy."

Mr. Bundy looked aggrieved. "I dare say it ain't, ma'am. I dare say it ain't. But you won't go blaming me for that, I hopes? That there chimbley—" The sweep jabbed a dirty forefinger towards the chimney breast. "That there chimbley must be what, all of a hundred year old or more, and they didn't build then like they does now. That there chimbley is crooked and that's why it don't draw proper and the soots lies up in it. That there chimbley is a fair—" Mr. Bundy's straight eye rolled round and observed Susanna standing by the door. "That there chimbley is a very difficult 'un to get the brush up. I lorst a brush in there two year ago, if you remembers."

"Yes, we most certainly do!" snapped Mrs. Merrihew vigorously. "It fell down two weeks later of its own accord and frightened the maid who was sweeping the carpet out of her wits. It was a lucky thing it didn't come down of an evening when the gentry were sitting here, and mess the ladies' gowns!" Mrs. Merrihew turned to Susanna. "The stupid girl thought it was a hobgoblin and come screaming out of the room. Give me a turn, I can tell you, Miss Susanna."

"Yes, yes," said Susanna hastily. "Please do your best, Mr. Bundy."

"Depend on it, Miss. I allus does a good job. Joe Bundy stands by his work. It's me reputation, is that." He wiped his nose on his sleeve. "Right, then, best get to work. You, Sammy, let's get the big brush fixed up. Best be off out of it, ladies! There's going to be a pile of soot come down there in a matter of ten minutes or so!"

Susanna and Mrs. Merrihew retired. "I don't care for that man at all!" said Susanna with some feeling to the housekeeper as they parted company.

"Nor more does anyone, Miss Susanna," returned Mrs. Merrihew. "He's got a bad character, has Bundy. Especially since his poor wife died. Used to knock her about something cruel, he did, and everyone knew it. But there, as sweeps go, he is very good and it's right as he says, that the chimney is an awkward one. It's got some sort of a kink in it half way up. That come about when they made the alterations to the house in your grandfather's time. That chimney has never drawed well since. But don't you fret, Miss. I'll see to it all and keep an eye on Bundy. You go and have yourself a bit of breakfast. When you come back next it will all be cleared up and cleaned!"

This turned out to be an optimistic forecast. However Bundy was best left to his work. Susanna went into breakfast and found Hugh already there together with Sir Frederick and deep in discussion on the restored monarchy in France.

"I agree, sir, that it is the best solution," Hugh was saying. "But depend on it, it cannot be popular for long. One cannot trust the Bourbons not to repeat all their old mistakes. Besides, in a few years people will forget all the trouble Bonaparte caused them and remember only his victories, depend on it!"

"Dashed fellow..." muttered Sir Frederick. "But they say he is a sick man, you know. The Bourbons will see the Emperor out, mark me!"

"The sweep is here, Papa," said Susanna after exchanging morning greetings.

"Bundy, isn't it?" demanded Sir Frederick. "Another dashed bad character!" Hugh blinked and looked mildly amused at this comparison between Napoleon and the sweep. "The last time he was here," continued Sir Frederick wrathfully, "he did a dashed bad job, too, if I recall!"

"He blames the chimney, Papa, and says it is crooked."

"Well, make sure he does a proper job this time!" said Sir Frederick. "Now, excuse me, both of you. I've letters to write on parliamentary business and I don't want to be disturbed." He wiped his mouth on his napkin and stomped out leaving Susanna and Hugh looking at one another across the table.

"Your cousin doesn't appear to be an early riser," observed Hugh, helping himself to coffee.

"Leo? Oh, he won't come down before noon. He hardly ever does." Susanna toyed with a piece of toast. "I think you will find your stay here very boring. There's little here I'm afraid to amuse a man of the world."

"Which is what you take me for?" He twitched his thick black eyebrows at her comically.

Susanna felt herself blush. "I mean, someone who has travelled and seen so many interesting places. Besides having had so many adventures."

"Adventures?" he asked, startled. "Oh, I see what you mean. Battles and so forth—that sort of adventure!"

"Yes—oh!" She paused and frowned. "I didn't mean the other sort. Though I dare say you have had your share of those as well."

"Miss Susanna," said Hugh seriously, leaning across the table towards her. "I begin to fear you have the lowest possible opinion of me!"

This was uncomfortably true, but she was spared having to reply by a crunch of running steps on the gravel outside the window. Both looked in the direction of the sound and saw through the panes Sammy, Mr. Bundy's boy, run past and onto the lawn where he stood staring up into the air. Somewhere near at hand a window opened and the sweep's unmelodious voice bellowed, "Can you see it yet?"

"No!" squawked Sammy.

Mr. Bundy swore roughly and Hugh's black eyebrows met in a threatening scowl. He got to his feet. "I think I shall just go and have a word with that fellow. Perhaps he doesn't realise he can be overheard."

"You had best not go into the drawing room," said Susanna in practical tones. "You will only get covered in soot. Ignore Bundy. As for not knowing that he can be heard, I believe he knows it perfectly well and does it on purpose."

Hugh sank down again unwillingly. "You are more tolerant than I am. If the fellow doesn't know his manners, someone should knock his head against a wall a few times and teach him some!"

"And is that your way of dealing with most problems, Major Russell? With violence?"

He shrugged. "I'm a soldier, not a parson. And you are back to calling me Major Russell."

She sighed. "Oh, very well, Hugh, if you insist. I keep forgetting."

"Do you know?" he exclaimed suddenly. "You are the most devastating female. You totally destroy any temptation I might have to form a fine opinion of myself! You set me down quite ruthlessly. My confidence is reduced to shreds!"

"I'm very sorry," said Susanna with a genuine pang of conscience. "I really don't mean to be rude. But I have—I have other things on my mind. You must excuse me."

A further burst of profanity from Bundy was heard at this point.

"Now see here!" said Hugh fiercely. "If that happens once more I shall go and tell that fellow to mind his language, soot or no soot!"

They sat for some minutes in silence, Hugh grimly drinking coffee and Susanna making an unsuccessful attempt to finish her toast before abandoning it. As she rose from the table, Hugh got to his feet also and they left the room together.

Mrs. Merrihew was scurrying along the corridor looking very vexed. "I don't know," she was muttering to herself. "I don't know, I'm sure!"

"What's wrong, Mrs. Merrihew?" asked Susanna sharply.

"That Bundy! I know it's not his fault the chimney is crooked, but he's had experience of it before and I did tell him to be careful! Last time he got the brush stuck up there and this time he's got the boy stuck!"

"What!" exclaimed Susanna and Hugh together.

"He sent the child up because the brush wasn't coming through on the roof, now the lad is stuck—"

Hugh strode past the housekeeper, leaving her in mid-speech, and threw open the drawing room door.

The dust sheets about the room were plentifully covered in soot which also filled the air making Hugh cough and causing Susanna to clasp a handkerchief to her nose. Bundy knelt on hands and knees before the grate and peered up the chimney.

"Sam? You useless little tow-rag! You get down here this minute or it will be the worse for you! You hears me, Sam? I'll take my belt to you, I promises!"

"Out of the way!" ordered Hugh brusquely, seizing Bundy's shoulder and hauling the sweep away from the fireplace. He quickly shrugged off his coat and handed it to Susanna and then going to the fireplace, he put a hand on the marble supports to either side and stooped to call up the chimney.

"Sam? Can you hear me, lad? Give a shout if you can, and don't be afraid! We'll have you out of there in no time!"

There was a pause as they all listened. A faint muffled whimper sounded from somewhere distant.

"Boy is about fifteen feet up," said Hugh, coming back from the fireplace and dusting his hands. His shirt was plentifully smeared with black streaks as were the knees of his breeches. He fixed Bundy with a look which made the sweep shuffle uneasily. "What do you mean by sending the boy up there?"

"He's trained for it!" said Bundy defiantly. "He oughta be able to shin up there like a monkey. I trained him meself. It ain't easy, training a climbing boy. You has to harden 'em off, elbows and knees in particular. You rubs 'em with alcohol and even then it takes a long time before they hardens up proper. Keeps skinning and making scabs and the scabs comes off and they has to be rubbed again and the kid starts screeching and kicking up. Go nearly mad they do. It ain't easy. I sent that boy up on account the chimney is crooked and I can't get the brushes up there. Housekeeper will bear me out, and the young lady! I lorst a brush in there two year ago. I always have trouble with that chimney. As for the kid, it's gluttony, that's what it is. They eats too much, them kids, if you let them and then they gets fat and then they gets stuck! Gluttony, that's what, and that's a sin, that is!" concluded Bundy virtuously.

"Gluttony!" cried Susanna angrily. "Why, there is nothing of the child!"

"You has to keep 'em thin, Miss. It's in their own interests. They don't know it, but they has to be taught it. Taught not to keep eating. That boy up there in that chimney, he'd eat all day if I let him. Even steal food, he will. I has to keep reminding him. You has to keep their weight down, Miss. If not they gets stuck. But don't you go worrying. I know how to get him down." Bundy nodded.

"How?" demanded Hugh in a low, dangerous voice. He had been listening to Bundy's regime for raising chimney boys with increasing and ill-disguised fury.

"We lights a fire," said Mr. Bundy with some satisfaction. "Smoke him out. When he feels the heat on his feet he'll start to wriggle and shift himself."

"Good God, man!" roared Hugh. "That will send the child further up, if it doesn't cause him to crash down into the flames! Besides, he could be seriously burned!"

"If he can't get down," said Mr. Bundy patiently, "he has to go up! Makes sense. It's the law of gravity, that. What can't go down, goes up. He goes up and he comes out at the top."

"Or he suffocates in the chimney! No one," said Hugh in a steely tone, "is lighting a fire under the child! Is that clear, Bundy, or whatever your name is?"

Mr. Bundy's straight eye rolled alarmingly. "Just like you says, guv'nor. But he has to be got down. But perhaps you knows a better way, being eddicated?" Mr. Bundy's voice grew sarcastic.

Hugh turned to Mrs. Merrihew. "Fetch Charlie Treasure along here, will you?"

"Yes, sir!" said Mrs. Merrihew and promptly disappeared in a whisk of skirts.

Hugh went back to the chimney and crouched in the open grate to call up into the blackness again, watched sardonically by Bundy.

"Sam? Don't panic, lad, and listen to me! Can you move at all?"

There was a scraping sound from within the chimney and with a rush, a small fall of soot cascaded down, deluging Hugh who retreated coughing and spluttering. A broad and unlovely smile split Mr. Bundy's face. The sweep folded his arms and stood back, obviously anticipating more entertainment when the gentleman with the penchant for interfering next put his head up the chimney.

Hugh, face blackened and with his hair full of soot, went back to the fireplace. "All right, you can move a little! Listen, Sam, don't try and go any further up. Do you understand me?"

There was a silence and then a small, distant, tearful voice wailed, "I'm afeared of the fire!"

Susanna's hands tightened convulsively on Hugh's coat.

"No one is going to light a fire, Sam!" Hugh called up encouragingly. "We'll get you out of there, just wait a little and don't be scared!"

There was a scurrying footstep behind Susanna and Charlie Treasure bustled into the room. "What's amiss, then, Major? Cor!" He stared at his blackened employer with some awe.

"Take your coat off, Charlie, and get up on my shoulders," said Hugh briskly. "I reckon the boy is about fifteen feet up but with luck he might be a little lower. The chimney is wide enough down here to let you reach up. I don't know at what point it gets narrower, probably at the level of the ceiling and that's where the child is."

This manoeuvre led to Hugh disappearing into the chimney from the waist up and Charlie disappearing altogether.

"Can you touch the boy's feet?" came Hugh's voice, muffled.

"He ain't here, Major—hang on. There's toeholds here and I can get a bit further up."

"For God's sake, Charlie, don't get stuck as well!"

Mr. Bundy chuckled. Susanna turned a furious glare on him and the sweep hastily assumed a straight face.

"Allo!" came in Charlie's muffled voice suddenly. "I got him, he's here—"

There was an almighty rush of soot and a shout. Susanna leapt back and so did Bundy as a black cloud enveloped the room. From the fireplace came a horrific crash.

"Hugh!" shrieked Susanna in alarm. "Are you all right?"

"Lord—yes!" came in choked tones from somewhere in the cloud of soot. "Get off me, Charlie! Are you all right?"

"Yus, guv'nor, and I got the whippersnapper... Hold up, young'un! You're sitting on me head!"

The dust slowly settled and three figures became distinguishable, entangled like Laocoon, his sons and the serpents. They slowly untangled themselves and sorted themselves out into one large form, a smaller one and a very small one. All were completely black and reminded Susanna irresistibly of the three bears.

The largest bear, revealing himself to be Hugh, appeared out of the soot haze holding Sam by the hand. Sam was totally soot-covered except for two grey-white strands where the tears had run down his cheeks.

"Mrs. Merrihew?" asked Hugh hoarsely. "Do you think you could take this child away and clean him up?"

When Mrs. Merrihew had taken away Sam, and Charlie had taken himself off for a similar reason, Hugh turned to an apprehensive Bundy.

"Clear all this up!" he ordered in a way which brooked no argument. "And later you and I will have a talk!"

Bundy muttered, "Yessir!" and began assiduously to sweep up the soot.

"Oh, Hugh—" exclaimed Susanna. "Thank you so much! I am so pleased you got the child down! And you are—" She paused and stared at him, conflicting expressions on her face. "You are so very dirty!" For all drama of the situation, she felt a tremor of laughter rise in her throat.

He looked quite extraordinary, begrimed from head to toe. He made an ineffectual attempt to dust himself off and shake soot from his hair and then grinned at her, his teeth gleaming white in his soot-stained face. "I think I should go and wash!"

"I'll have them fill a bath for you!" Susanna promised, turning to carrying out this intention.

"No, no, it will take too long. I'll go out in the stable-yard and wash down under the pump. It won't be the first time!" He strode past her and disappeared leaving a trail of black footprints to mark his progress.

Susanna left the room more slowly and stood for a few minutes in the hall deep in thought. Then she gave a nod of resolution, threw Hugh's coat round her shoulders and went out of the house. She walked round to the stable-yard. It was cold and crisp and she was glad of the coat. She could hear the noise of splashing water and the squeak of the pump handle before she reached the yard. At its entry, she stopped.

The pump and horse-trough were in the middle of the yard, surrounded by the stable-blocks. Hugh had stripped down naked to the waist. He was stooped over the horse-trough and as the stable boy energetically worked the pump,

sending a shower of water over Hugh's head, so Hugh
scooped up water from the trough and rubbed down his
arms and chest. He appeared impervious to the icy chill of
the water and as she watched, Susanna was seized by a
strange mixture of emotions. She was both fascinated and
alarmed. Fascinated because she had never seen a half-
naked man before and alarmed because of the power of that
muscular body, shining with the silver sheen of the water,
and also because sight of it aroused curious feelings inside
her which she could not identify. She bit her lip.

She ought to go back. Women had no place in a stable-
yard at any time, and certainly not at this. It was a man's
world. The language spoken here was the language men used
when they were amongst themselves. The sights were such
as would not bother a man, but might certainly bother a
lady.

She had of course seen paintings and statues of partly-
clothed Greek gods and other. But the reality of human flesh
was somewhat different. She supposed she was embarrassed. But if she were, she would already have turned and
fled. So if it was not embarrassment, what was it? If that
were Leo, she thought, I would not be feeling so muddled.
But it was not Leo, nor was it conceivable that it could be
Leo. Leo, washing down in cold water from a horse-trough?
Leo set up a commotion if his bath-water was tepid. Nor had
Leo that Herculean build. And yet it was still something else
which set up that curious trembling in the pit of her stomach. She thought, perhaps he is, after all, a man of action
and we see few such here. In battle, he must have been terrifying. Then a little voice in her brain whispered, "Perhaps he is simply a man, and that is what is so terrifying?"

Susanna took a step backwards, but in that instant the
stable boy saw her. He ceased his exertions at the pump
handle and said something to Hugh. Hugh looked up.

What he saw was Susanna with his coat draped about her and almost completely enveloping her slim form, standing by the yard entrance in a shaft of winter sun and staring at him. He dismissed the boy with a word and stood up, wiping the water from his forearms with his hands and narrowing his eyes against the glare of the sunlight. He half thought for a moment that she was some kind of apparition because she was the last person he would have expected to see there. She came a little way towards him, moving uncertainly, her fingers gripping at the lapels of the coat.

The closer she came to him, the more curious Susanna felt. Her knees were like jelly and her throat seemed to have closed up so that she was afraid she would not be able to speak at all. She ought to have made good her escape when she could. Now it was too late. She thought wildly, Oh my goodness, what a lot of hair he does have on his chest! Men never do in paintings...

"The water must be very cold," she croaked at him.

"No worse than a Pyrenean mountain stream!" he replied.

"No, of course not," said Susanna weakly. "I suppose, you are used to all manner of hardship. I—came down to say..." She drew a deep breath and looked up to meet his eye directly. "This morning, at breakfast, you said I had a very low opinion of you. And so I did. It's true. But that was wrong of me and ignorant. I wanted to come and tell you, now straight-away, that I know I was wrong, and should apologise, and tell you I think you are, after all, a very—a very nice man."

He was listening closely. She did not understand the expression on his swarthy face, but he did not look as if her words had particularly pleased him. "No, Susanna," he said quietly. "Not at all a nice one, I'm afraid. I was born into respectable enough family and I don't believe I've ever quite disgraced its name. Yet I have run close to it once or twice.

None of the professions I've ever followed has been noted for niceness. I've been soldier of fortune, or better adventurer perhaps. Sometime a gamester, sometime a rake and sometime cannon-fodder, I suppose you would call it!'' He smiled now for the first time and ruefully.

"Leo would not have got so sooty or clambered into the grate to rescue a climbing boy!'' she said frankly.

"Leo was not there so we can't say.''

"I can,'' she said briefly. The breeze blew across the yard and touched her face with its chill fingers. "How cold you must be!'' she exclaimed. "You will catch pneumonia. You must take your coat!'' She pulled it from her shoulders and held it out towards him.

"Keep it!'' he said brusquely. "You are more likely to catch cold than I!''

"Nonsense!'' She was regaining some of her aplomb. "Put it on at once! I shall go back and make sure they have made up the fire in the morning room and I'll tell Mrs. Merrihew to make hot toddy!''

She thrust the coat into his arms and turned and ran out of the stable-yard. Hugh stood for a moment in thought, then threw the coat over his broad shoulders and set off slowly towards the house.

"I AGREE it is very distressing,'' said Sir Frederick. "I shall of course do something about it, Susanna. You have no need to get into such a fret!''

"What do you mean to do, Papa?'' insisted Susanna, leaning over her plate.

Sir Frederick looked regretfully at his plate of mutton, growing cold. "I understand Bundy got the child from the parish. The child was a foundling. If it can be shown, as evidently it can, that Bundy has been beating and starving the child, then the parish will take the boy back again! It is not the intention of the parish officers, in placing a child

with an employer, to have that child ill-used! The boy shall
be returned to the parish forthwith and I shall insist that no
more parish orphans be apprenticed to Bundy. There!" Sir
Frederick picked up his fork.

"It's not good enough, Papa!" said his daughter vigorously. "What will the parish do with the child, when it gets
him back?"

Her father sighed and put down his fork again. "Dear
girl, they will find him a new master, but someone more respectable and some more congenial work. In a shop, perhaps?" He set about his mutton determinedly.

"And Bundy will get a new climbing boy from somewhere else!"

"I can't help that!" said Sir Frederick indistinctly. "But
it shall be made clear to him that there are to be no more
tricks such as lighting fires beneath a boy if he's stuck!"

"Bundy already understands that!" said Hugh quietly.

Susanna glanced at him. "It is not only Bundy. It concerns all sweeps and their boys. It is an intolerable practice.
Papa, you must bring in a private member's bill outlawing
it."

"What?" exclaimed Sir Frederick, startled. "Outlawing
sweep's boys? How is a fellow to get his chimney swept?"

"With better brushes. Surely someone can invent a better chimney-brush?"

"How about one activated by a steam engine?" asked
Leo, captivated by the thought. "Get that fellow Stephen-
son onto it."

"Be quiet, Leo!" said his cousin unkindly. "You must
lobby support, Papa!"

"I doubt that it would be forthcoming, child. The house
is much taken up with reform—"

"Then let it reform its law on children's labour."

"I don't believe," said Sir Frederick thoughtfully, "That
there are any laws on children's labour, unless you count

that Factory Act Peel put through in 1801 and which for all I know has sunk without trace like a stone thrown in a pool. Mind you, Peel is agitating about putting through another one."

"Sound him out about chimney sweeps!" urged his daughter. She sighed. "I wish I could sit in parliament, I know what I would do!"

"Women in parliament?" said Leo. "Lord! Like a lot of old hens clacking. Not that it doesn't already sound like—" He cast an eye at his uncle and thought better of what he was going to say.

"A private bill might make your name, Freddie!" said Viola unexpectedly.

Sir Frederick's patience ran out at last. "Am I to be allowed to eat my dinner in peace or not?" he demanded testily.

"Yes, of course, Freddie," said Viola. "I'm sure it wasn't I who started all this."

Susanna opened her mouth but caught Hugh's eye. He shook his head imperceptibly. She sighed and cast her own eyes back to her congealed dinner. He was right. Sir Frederick had been pushed to action as far as he would go. The practice of climbing boys would remain with them for a while yet. It was something that young Sam had been rescued from it. She thought again of Hugh's part in that and made a resolve to be extremely civil to Major Russell for the rest of his stay. The rest of his stay.... Yes, he would indeed soon be going away again. It suddenly seemed a thing to be regretted.

IN FACT MAJOR RUSSELL took himself off—temporarily at least—sooner than Susanna expected. The very next morning when she came down it was to find he was gone.

"To Newbury..." said Leo, unusually early up and about himself. "Gone to visit some military acquaintance or other who lives in the town. Won't be back tonight."

"Oh," said Susanna blankly. So much for her decision to be pleasant. One cannot be pleasant to a person who isn't there. She felt vaguely annoyed, because Hugh had said nothing to her of intending to go off for twenty-four hours. But then, why should he?

"I hope it doesn't snow hard before then," she said. "He will be stuck in Newbury and not able to get back."

"Best thing!" said Leo shortly. He glanced at her sharply. "Why—would you mind?"

"Not for myself!" she retorted quickly. "But all his baggage is here. Has he taken his manservant with him?"

Leo pursed his lips and scowled. "No, now you come to mention it, he hasn't. Funny little fellow, Treasure. He snoops about, you know, and chats to the maids and so forth. I wouldn't be surprised if Russell hasn't left him behind here on purpose. To keep an eye on us."

"Whatever for?" Susanna exclaimed in surprise.

Leo shrugged. "I don't know. But you won't persuade me Russell only came here to present his compliments to his Aunt Viola. If, of course, she really is his aunt."

"I don't think he would lie to us!" Susanna said firmly. She fiddled absently with the silk cord securing a curtain as she stared out of the window down the empty main drive. "Did he tell you the name of his military friend?"

"No—oh, I take your meaning!" Leo gave her a knowing wink. "Probably a lady. Wouldn't be at all surprised. Some dashing Amazon who has followed the regiment and whose husband is prepared to turn a blind eye to a little gallantry!"

"I didn't mean any such thing!" said Susanna indignantly and turning bright red in the face. "That's unkind of you, Leo, and quite unjustified! You don't know anything of the sort!''

"Dear cousin…'' Leo walked across to her and took hold of her hands. "You are a sweet innocent. You've spent your entire life buried here in the country. What on earth could you possibly know about a man like that? How he spends his time, or about his morals—or lack of 'em! Look at him! Don't tell me, women don't—look at him, I mean. And like what they see!''

"That is uncalled for, Leo!'' exclaimed his cousin angrily, a scarlet flush invading her cheeks. She snatched her fingers free from his grasp.

"Ah, you see? Now I've offended your sensibilities!'' returned Leo, unabashed. "And that just goes to show what a dear unworldly girl you are! A real little country mouse with such high notions of how everyone should behave!'' Leo's expression suddenly became serious. "Suky, my dear, do stay away from Russell. He cannot be relied upon to behave as a gentleman. And before you bite my head off, I am sure that he would be the first to agree, if he were to be asked, and if he were to be honest!''

Not at all nice, was what Hugh had actually said.

"I suppose you are right, Leo,'' admitted his cousin in a down-cast voice.

"Depend on it. Now, cheer up. I'll take you out driving. It's not a bit muddy, frozen hard rather. But as you say, it may snow and then we shan't be able to get out at all. So run upstairs and wrap yourself up warm and we'll drive out over the downs and watch the racehorses at exercise.''

As an entertainment watching horses had more appeal for Leo than for her. But Susanna put a good face on it and tried to look enthusiastic as she went off to prepare herself for the outing.

Leo, who was by no means as addle-pated as some people supposed him, was not fooled. "She ain't seen anything like him before, and it's turned her head!" he muttered. The answer was to keep her occupied and not to let her mope about the place. She was sensible and the mood was temporary. In due course, Russell would take himself off for good and she would forget him. "Good riddance!" growled Leo, adding in country fashion, "and bad cess to him!"

AS LUCK WOULD HAVE IT, Susanna was in the hall the following morning when Hugh returned, a little after ten. He came in stamping hoarfrost from his boots and rubbing his hands briskly.

"Good morning!" he said cheerfully.

"Good morning," she said and for some reason the day, which had appeared gloomy, suddenly seemed much brighter. "Did—did you enjoy your stay in Newbury?"

"Excellently, thank you!"

He looked very pleased with himself and her heart plummeted. Perhaps Leo had been right.

"Your—your military friend, was he well?"

"Broughton? Lord, yes, in fine fettle. I hadn't seen him since Quatre-Bras. He was wounded in the engagement and sent back behind the lines and after that, sent back to England. I went on to Paris, as you know, so I didn't see him again. But now he's bought out, as I have, and settled in Newbury."

As he spoke Susanna's heart had been rising like a lark. Not a lady-friend, after all, but a genuine soldier, campaign medals, battle wounds and all. "I hope Mr. Broughton is quite recovered?"

"Fit as a fiddle. He always had the luck of the devil."

"You will have had much interesting news to exchange."

"Oh, yes..." said Hugh growing thoughtful. "Broughton was always a mine of interesting information and this time was no exception."

He obviously did not intend to expand further and share any of Broughton's interesting news, but it had probably been gossip concerning mutual acquaintances. It occurred to Susanna that perhaps they had been quite mistaken in thinking he had any sinister motive in coming to the Hall. If he had other acquaintance in the neighbourhood besides Viola and if he had last parted from one of those friends amongst the shell-fire of Quatre-Bras, then he had plenty of reasons for coming here and all of them above reproach.

"And now you would some breakfast, no doubt!" she said briskly. "I'll tell Mrs. Merrihew."

But he was shaking his head. "Thank you but please don't bother Mrs. Merrihew on my account. I did in fact breakfast this morning at six on beef and brandy, after sitting up all night at cards with Broughton. What I need is my bed!"

Cards. Her heart sank again. Gambling. That was the link which bound the friendship of Hugh and Mr. Broughton. Not just comrades in arms, but fellow devotees of the card table and the wild life style it inspired—the loss of a fortune or the dubious gaining of one, the drinking, the quarrels and the duels. That men did frequently lose their fortunes she knew very well because Leo had lost his—admittedly more through wagers on unsound nags than on the whereabouts of an elusive ace. But Hugh did not appear to be in need of funds so he, presumably, had more luck or was shrewder than Leo. He looked in very good humour at this moment, so she supposed he had risen from the card-table at dawn this morning the winner. She wondered how much money had changed hands. The better opinion she had formed of him since his rescue of Sam from the chimney, had received a severe set-back. But there again, perhaps she had been foolish to revise her first impression, solely on the basis of one kind action.

Hugh suddenly delved in his pocket. "Take a look at this—" He produced a small silver and enamel box and handed it to her.

She examined it curiously. At first she thought it was a snuffbox, but it was too large. A patch box, perhaps, from a previous generation? The workmanship was exquisite. The enamelled lid depicted some scene of Grecian merrymaking and the colours were delicate and clear.

"Why it is beautiful!" she exclaimed in unfeigned plea-sure. She opened the lid and gave another cry of surprise and delight as the tinkling notes of a pretty tune filled the air. "Why, it's a musical box!" She looked up at Hugh, her eyes shining.

He had been watching her and now smiled. "Attractive piece of nonsense, isn't it? Probably French, although Broughton picked it up somewhere in the Low Countries, so he says. I won it off him about three this morning."

The musical box suddenly lost much of its charm. Susanna closed the lid and held it out to him, the enthusiasm fading from her face. "Mr. Broughton must be sorry to lose it."

"Lord, he don't care! He probably won it in the first place. Nor do I care much about it. It's hardly my sort of thing! I brought it back because I thought you might like it."

"I?" she cried, startled and not best pleased.

"Yes. I spoiled the surprise Leo had planned for you on New Year's Eve so I feel I owe you some reparation. I thought it might amuse you, and you could keep buttons or something in it . . ." Hugh concluded vaguely.

Susanna struggled with disappointment and outrage. To accept a gift would be, in any case, inappropriate. She hardly knew him. But to have a valuable trinket tossed in her direction on a vague excuse, because he didn't want it, was humiliating and an insult.

"I don't want it!" she said vehemently. But he had probably meant well and other women of his acquaintance would have had fewer scruples. He wasn't to know how she felt. She added more calmly, "I really couldn't keep it, although it is very pretty."

But Hugh was already walking past her, ignoring her protests and her outstretched hand holding the box.

"Then do what you like with it, if you don't want it yourself. It's a lady's trinket and it's no use to me. And now, I'm off to my bed!"

He ran up the staircase and disappeared from view. Susanna was left standing with the musical box in her hand and an expression of despair on her face.

"Hullo, what now?" asked Leo, coming into the hall and seeing her there.

Hastily she thrust the box away in her pocket before he could see it. "Nothing at all!" she said fiercely.

"Russell back?" He jerked his head towards the staircase and the suspicion crossed her mind he might have been eavesdropping.

"Yes!" she said vehemently. "And I wish he had stayed away!"

CHAPTER FOUR

IT WAS PROBABLY as well that Major Russell was not unduly sensitive because it was fairly obvious that his return pleased few. Sir Frederick was occupied with parliamentary business and took little notice of anything else so he was probably the least put out of them all. But Leo was barely civil, Susanna avoided the guest and Viola, who ought to have been pleased to have her relative return, was nervous and fidgety, snapping at both Leo and Susanna and directing barbed remarks at Hugh himself.

The atmosphere within the house was so tense with undercurrents of unease that Susanna became desperate to escape from it, besides wanting to avoid Major Russell for reasons she was not altogether able to put into words, so she dressed warmly, pulled a pair of inelegant but practical galoshes over her shoes, pinned up her skirts and set out to walk to the village and call on the Vicar and his family.

The Reverend Mr. Lucas was a married man and father of a large and boisterous brood. The vicarage was a rambling and untidy dwelling. All the furniture showed sign of having been climbed over by numerous small children and the carpets were worn down to the threads. Susanna knew that Mr. Lucas found it very difficult to provide for his large brood—thirteen of them in all—on the modest income of his living so she took care to arrive bearing a gift of a cake baked by the Hall cook. A shoal of little Lucases danced around her filled with glee at thought of the treat. Susanna was conducted into the parlour and installed on a worn sofa out of which bunches of horsehair protruded through holes in the upholstery. As always, she was treated with the deference due to the daughter of a gentleman from whom Mr. Lucas held his living, mixed with the delight of the children at seeing a favourite courtesy "aunt."

Miss Harte was a great favourite with them all and soon had the baby enthroned upon her lap and was listening to tales of the exploits of various young Lucases who talked across one another loudly in an effort to secure the visitor's attention. Mrs. Lucas, with her lace cap askew and wearing a dress which had obviously been turned, presided over tea whilst small children climbed on and off her lap and tugged at her skirts and upset the sugar bowl.

"I understand," said Mr. Lucas, making himself heard with some difficulty. "Thomas, don't tug at Miss Harte's gown like that and William, kindly don't speak when I am trying to do so! I understand, Miss Harte, that the—ah—military gentleman has returned to the Hall."

News was scarce and anything which happened at the Hall was of interest. This past summer there had been enough happening there to satisfy the most curious of village gossips. With the coming of winter, things had become quieter and Major Russell's visit noticed the more because of it. She agreed that the guest had returned.

"I did not see him at Matins on Sunday with Sir Frederick and yourself," observed Mr. Lucas delicately.

Sir Frederick, when he was at the Hall, never missed divine service of a Sunday in the little grey village church. Susanna also always attended. But it had to be admitted, other dwellers at the Hall were less scrupulous. Leo seldom turned up, usually because he was still in bed when the church bells rang out and Viola appeared to have little interest in setting a good example to the village. So Sir Frederick and his daughter generally attended alone. Mr. Lucas, holding his living from Sir Frederick, was shy of expressing too much

criticism, but he was a conscientious shepherd of his flock
and he did feel he should say something. Last summer, for
example, when the Hall had been filled with visitors, not one
of them had shown his face at church. Although, thought
Mr. Lucas grimly, a more rakish set of people he would have
found it hard to imagine and he could not honestly say he
had expected to see any of them.

"I—I don't know Major Russell's views on religion,"
confessed Susanna. "I dare say when he was in the Penin-
sula, you know, regular observances of that sort rather fell
by the way." Being obliged to apologize for Hugh rankled,
and she did not know why she should feel that she should.

"Probably," agreed Mr. Lucas regretfully, although to
himself he was thinking that the army was not, as far as he
was aware, short of chaplains and church parades.
"Thomas! You will cause Miss Harte to spill her tea!"

Despite the mild criticism of the lack of enthusiasm to
hear Mr. Lucas's sermons on the part of some the company
at the Hall, Susanna enjoyed herself thoroughly amidst all
the hubbub and confusion and left for home in much better spirits than she had set out.

The weather was cold and there were few people about.
Susanna climbed over a stile and set off along a footpath
across the fields. The ground was soft and muddy and she
soon began to think that she would have done better to have
gone the longer way round by the road. About half way on
her journey the path led by a small pond. It had originally
been formed by water collecting in an indentation in the soil
and over the years had gradually become bigger. In summer the sun shrank it back somewhat but in winter the rains
fed it and it expanded onto the low lying field around it.
Rushes grew at deeper points around its banks and it had
even been known to play host to a small number of wildfowl. Leo had occasionally come out here with a gun and
potted a brace of duck. There were no birds to be seen to-

day but there was something alive and moving down by the
edge of the pond, a small black shape which squirmed and
wriggled. Susanna paused and squinted beneath her hand.
As she did a desperate yelp reached her ears.

The creature was a small dog, some sort of terrier mixed
with hound. Where it had come from she could not imagine
but it was obvious what a fix it was in now. It had gone
running down to the edge of the water, perhaps chasing the
now absent wildfowl, and become stuck in soft mud. The
more it had struggled, the more it had sunk in and now it
was lodged fast, wet, cold and miserable. Seeing Susanna it
set up an imploring bark and wagged its straggly mud-
encaked tail.

"Poor boy!" called Susanna. "I'll fetch you out of
there!"

Brave words, but not easily fulfilled. Susanna looked
about her. Not a soul. She put down her basket and took a
few cautious steps towards the pond. The ground was horribly soft and her feet began to sink. The little dog whined
and wagged its tail again, flattening its ears beseechingly.
Susanna retreated, found some sticks and threw them down
ahead of her to make a primitive causeway. Slowly and uncertainly she squelched nearer to the trapped animal. By
now her galoshes were just two lumps of mud, her stockings were wet through and smeared grey-black and the hems
of her pinned-up petticoats soaked and stained.

The dog obviously saw her as his saviour. His joy at every
step she took nearer was so pathetic that despite her own
difficulties, she did not think of giving up and abandoning
the poor creature. She managed at last to reach him and
patted his head consolingly as she tried to see how she might
free him. He wore no collar she could grasp so in the end
she was forced to wrap both arms around him regardless of
the damage to her clothes, and haul him bodily out of his

muddy trap. It was not easy. he began to struggle in her arms. Susanna gave a mighty heave.

The little dog came free with a great squelching noise and so suddenly that Susanna lost her balance. She fell over backwards and sat down abruptly in the mud. The dog, freed, now showed a fine disregard for all her sacrifice, bounded across the muddy ground towards firmer turf and disappeared across the fields towards the village.

Susanna had no time to reflect on her protégé's ingratitude. She was forced to put down both hands to push herself up out of the ooze, only to find, to her complete dismay, that now she was stuck as firmly as the dog had been. She tried to lift one foot out of the clinging mud and it came out free of both galosh and shoe. Hunting in the morass to retrieve at least the shoe, her stockinged foot went down on the ground and sank in. The mud stuck horribly cold and clammy on her foot and she gave a cry of distress.

At that moment a voice called out distantly, "Stay where you are, Miss Harte! Don't try and move—you'll sink in further!"

There was a thud of hoofs and she looked round to see Major Russell cantering towards her across the field.

"Oh, bother it!" mumbled Susanna crossly. It was bad enough to be stuck. It was worse to have to be rescued. It was extremely embarrassing and annoying to be rescued by Major Russell. She glanced down at herself in horror. She was completely smeared in mire from chest to the ground. She had lost a shoe. She must look a complete idiot.

Hugh drew rein a little way from her on solid ground. He called, "What the devil are you doing there?" His face was serious but there was a distinct tremor in his voice which she suspected was laughter.

With as much dignity as she could muster she retorted, "I am trying to get out! If you mean just to sit there and look at me, I'm sure I can manage without you!"

"Hold on," he said. He urged the horse forward. It walked unhappily but steadily through the mud towards her. Hugh leaned down from the saddle. "Put your arms round my neck."

"What?" She gaped up at him.

"Come along!" he ordered impatiently. "Just warp your arms round my neck and hold on!"

"I—I am very muddy..." she stammered, unwilling to do as he asked, even if it meant rescue. "Your—your coat..."

"My dear young lady, I can see that for myself! I never saw such a mudpie in my life! Come along now, do as I tell you!"

With despair she recognised that she was between the proverbial Scylla and Charybdis. She wanted to escape the mire but she did not want to put her arms anywhere near Major Russell, let alone around his neck. He was leaning down from the saddle, his swarthy handsome face, flushed with the cold wind, showing some sign of impatience. He was probably used to young women throwing themselves about his neck and could not understand the reluctance of this one to do so.

He said brusquely, "I won't let you fall!"

"Indeed, no..." mumbled Susanna. With very bad grace she stretched up, resting her forearms on his broad shoulders and linking her hands at the back of his collar.

"Hold tight!" he advised. He wrapped both strong arms firmly round her waist and hauled her up and out of her prison and onto the saddle in front of him.

"I have lost my shoes!" she gasped. She could not let go of him for fear of slipping from her insecure perch and was obliged to remain clinging to him in the same highly affectionate manner whilst he still kept his arms tightly about her waist, crushing her against his chest.

"I'm afraid they're lost for good," he replied. "You shall have to ride home with me."

"Oh, no!" she said hastily. "Please try and retrieve my shoes and I can walk!"

"And catch pneumonia whilst you do! You are quite wet through, Susanna. Do have some sense!" was the less than gallant reply. "I'll set you down over there and you can remount pillion." He turned the horse towards safer ground.

She had never been held so tightly in a man's arms nor so close. Her face pressed against Hugh's coat buttons, Susanna prayed no one would come along and see them. All the same, it was not an altogether unpleasant sensation. Embarrassing though the situation was—and of course she would much rather it had been Leo who had found her since Leo didn't matter at all—to be held firmly and in close contact by Major Russell was a strangely comforting thing. When he set her down, she slid to the ground with a pang of real regret which both surprised and annoyed her. Be sensible, Susanna! she told herself sternly. Remounted behind him, they set off again. This time she had to put both arms around his waist to hold on, but oddly enough was far less reluctant to do so.

"I suppose," he said over his shoulder, "you are not going to tell me how you came to be in such a fix?"

"I went to rescue a little dog. The poor creature was stuck but after I got him free, he ran off very ungratefully and then I was stuck too."

"You're an intrepid young lady," he said, "and I don't know many who would muddy their clothes in such a cause. But you should not have done it. You should have walked on home and sent out a groom to rescue the animal."

It is extremely annoying to be told what you should have done when you just made yourself ridiculous following your first instinct. Susanna snapped, "I dare say I should, but I didn't!"

"Now how would it have been," continued Hugh severely, "if some great lump of a country bumpkin had come by and you had been obliged to let yourself be rescued by him?''

''I expect,'' said the goaded Susanna, ''that he would have pulled me out and not gone on moralising at me afterwards!''

''No, he would just have gone to the nearest tavern and been regaled by all and sundry with free beer for the entire evening on the strength of his story! You have a position to keep up in this part of the world, Miss Harte!''

''If you go on like that!'' shouted Miss Harte into his ear, ''I shall get off this horse and walk home in my stockinged feet!''

He glanced back and grinned at her. ''Yes, I do believe you would.''

They rode on a little way in silence and then Susanna asked more quietly and rather nervously, ''Hugh? You won't go telling everyone at the Hall, will you? Leo will laugh himself sick, Papa would be cross and Viola sneer.''

''True. I shall have to smuggle you in by some means.'' Hugh paused. ''I'll ride round to side of the house and set you down in the garden. You hide the bushes and I'll go in and open up the window in the morning room and you can scramble through. Do you think you can climb through a window?''

''I can certainly try!''

''Good girl!'' said Hugh encouragingly.

This manoeuvre was carried out. Susanna hid shivering behind the box hedges until the sash window in the morning room was pushed up and Hugh's head appeared. He gave a low whistle. She darted out of her hiding place, ran across the gravel path and scrambled through helped by Hugh's guiding arm.

''Well!'' he said cheerfully as she landed breathless in the room. ''This makes a change. Helping a lady to climb in, I mean. I have several times climbed out of a window helped by a lady!''

Susanna, panting and in some disorder, could not miss the implication of this statement. But now she was safely inside the house her annoyance at the whole ridiculous episode grew stronger than any gratitude she ought to have felt towards her rescuer. This mildly risqué remark, on top of everything else, was the last straw.

''That was a most ungentlemanly remark, Captain Russell! Boast of your exploits to others, but kindly don't refer to them before me!''

''Ungentlemanly, am I? Well, my dear, I've sadly muddied my coat on account of you. Moreover, ladies, I might remind you, don't get stuck rescuing stray dogs nor are they reduced to returning home through the window! Perhaps you would have preferred I left you there and rode home to send out your cousin, Leo? He wouldn't muddy his coat for you!'' Hugh snorted.

''And that is unfair!'' She almost stamped her foot but realised in time that she had no shoes.

''It's true!'' he retorted quickly. ''Next time you need rescuing or want to send someone up a chimney, find another. Or is it possible that unpolished fellows like myself come in useful occasionally?''

''I am most grateful for your help on both occasions!'' said Susanna through clenched teeth.

''But not enough for you to express an unprompted word of thanks?''

She felt the hot tide of crimson rise up her throat and suffuse her cheeks. ''I did not mean to lack manners! I thank you, of course!'' She turned and walked out with as much dignity as bare feet and muddy garments allowed her and ran upstairs to repair the damage to her clothes and to her composure.

To HIS CREDIT and her relief, Hugh kept his word and made no mention of her escapade. She was forced to admit to herself that she had been exceptionally rude to him. He had indeed behaved in every way as a gentleman and been quite right to take offence at her churlishness. This made her feel a little awkward in his presence. She supposed she ought to apologize but perhaps he didn't expect it. He certainly acted as if the whole matter were forgotten. She felt an obscure gratitude towards him for this but her unease had not left her. They were all polite but no one behaved as though they enjoyed having him there. He was either totally thick-skinned or staying on for some purpose.

Others had the same idea. Anyone watching Lady Harte since Hugh's return from Newbury, would have realised that Viola was working herself up to some confrontation. Two days later, Viola cornered her nephew in the drawing room in mid-afternoon, closing the door and putting her back to it to prevent anyone else interrupting.

Hugh, who was seated by the fire scowling at the newspaper, looked up. His initial expression was of a fleeting disappointment as if he had hoped to see someone else. Then it was replaced by a certain look of dry curiosity.

"What's the matter, Viola? You look as though you're about to impart some desperate message."

She darted across the room and hovered over him, her lovely face flushed and her eyes sparkling with anger. "You've been here over a week, Hugh. I told you, you might stay for two, so you have very little time left here!"

"That's blunt enough, dear aunt. Are you showing me the door, by any chance? What have I done to offend you, eh?"

"Don't try and tease me, Hugh! I'm in no mood for your nonsense! My life has been a misery this past week, a perfect misery! Ever since you came! And don't pretend you are unaware of it! You know perfectly well what you are doing to me. You have no right to torment me like this! I know you have come on some mischief. What is it you want from me?'' Her voice rose on a cry of such real anguish that the bantering tone left his manner and he reached out and took her hand.

"Sit down, Viola. You're quite right and it's time we had a long and serious talk. But don't fly into fits of hysterics because I can't be doing with it. So pull yourself together and act like a sensible woman—for once in your life!''

"You see?'' She threw herself down on a chair near to him, her bosom heaving with emotion. "You mean to throw every mistake I've ever made in the past in my face! You've come here to ruin me, Hugh, I know it!''

"On the contrary, my dear!'' he said sharply. "I've come to save you from yourself, if such a thing is possible!''

Viola sat biting her lip and staring at him mistrustfully. She began to twist her hands together, in particular twisting the gold wedding band round and round on her slim finger. "I know I've been foolish in the past, Hugh. But I am—I am thirty-five, as you are so fond of reminding me, and this is the last chance I shall ever have to make a decent life for myself. Do you think I want to throw it all away? Do you think I'll ruin it?'' She leaned forward and held out her hand pleadingly. "Oh, Hugh, don't ruin it for me, please!''

He shifted in his chair and crossed his long legs, otherwise seeming unmoved by the agony on her face and in her voice and the expressive gesture. "That's a heart-breaking speech, Viola, and anyone who did not know you as well as I do, would be moved to tears by it. But I am not. Every scrape that you have got into, and which I and others have been obliged to get you out of, has been followed by a scene like this one. Every time you have wept small lakes of tears, promised to behave yourself better in future, asked us all to be patient and forgive you. And so we have, every time. And every time, Viola, you have let us down. If we no longer believe you, you can hardly be surprised.''

She let her hand drop back onto her lap and a wilful jutting of her lower lip and a hardening of the expression in her eyes told him that she was about to put up a fight. But that he had expected. Cornered, she would use every weapon in her not inconsiderable arsenal. She was a redoubtable foe. "Then you have seen the family!" she said spitefully. "Have they made you their messenger, then, Hugh? Are you running their errands? Is it your concern for me which brings you? Or their concern for the family name?"

"In my case, both!" he retorted. He got to his feet and began to pace up and down the room, his hands clasped behind his back. "I'll put my cards on the table, Viola, and be frank. I like this errand of mine no better than you! I didn't ask to be sent here—in fact I put up quite an argument against it, but in the end I was persuaded it was my duty."

"Duty!" she said mockingly. "Did the army teach you that, Hugh? I think there must be as many blots upon your copy-book as on mine! Much you've ever cared for our family!"

"I'm a man," he said frankly, "and the sowing of wild oats is allowed me. You are a woman and the same thing is not. You may believe that unfair, my dear. But it is a fact of life. If I decide to turn over a new leaf and become respectable, everyone will be so kind and indulgent as to forget my misdemeanors. But a woman's reputation, once lost, is gone forever. I am sorry about it, but there it is." Hugh walked over to the fire and taking a paper spill from a tub on the mantelshelf, stooped to light it at the flames. It flared up suddenly and he blew on it, extinguishing it. "Just like this twist of paper, Viola, used only once and then finished..." He dropped the charred spill into the grate.

"How cruel you are..." she said softly, almost with wonder. "Now I understand why they chose to send you."

He gave a little exclamation of impatience. "Perhaps they also sent me because they know I have a genuine affection

for you, Viola, but that I won't let it addle my brain." He
paused and added more soberly, "And perhaps they chose
me because I know the shadowy world of your unsuitable
friends so well on my own account. I am not likely to be
misled."

She sat back in her chair, suddenly relaxed. "Well,
Hugh—and what do you propose to do? Denounce me at
dinner to the assembled family? The boy will be delighted
and the girl. They both want me out of this house forever!"

"Don't be so foolish. There is no reason whatsoever that
they should know of your past mistakes—provided you
don't set about repeating them here! But it seems you have
already done so!"

Her eyes gleamed dangerously. "For example?"

"For example," he said calmly, "I hear you filled the
house with riff-raff during the summer. How do you think
that looked to the surrounding community? What impression do you think local society gained of you? Didn't you
consider the embarrassment to your husband? He's a man
of some consequence, a member of parliament, for goodness sake—he cannot afford any scandal!" Hugh suddenly
strode forward and stooping, gripped Viola's shoulders and
shook her. "Think of it, Viola! Whatever you have done
before, it's been a nine day wonder, a titbit of gossip to be
passed around people who don't matter, until some other
item of scandal replaces it! But what you do now involves
Sir Frederick! My dear, the gentlemen of the Press would
seize upon it—all those scribblers for daily news-sheets who
like nothing so much as to throw mud at the government
and its ministers! Your husband would be obliged to resign
his seat—which he has served loyally for almost forty
years—and on whose account? On yours, Viola!"

"That is to say, on account of a nobody, like me," she said icily. "Perhaps Freddie has a better opinion of me than you do, Hugh."

"Then you have so much more to lose, Viola."

She started and then looked away. "I am well able to take care of Freddie, Hugh. I don't need to be lectured."

"Freddie has certainly been taking good care of you," he said sharply.

"And what does that mean?" she demanded vehemently.

"You seem to have been the recipient of a great many expensive gifts." Hugh's dark eyes swept over her appraisingly. "Well, that is Sir Frederick's prerogative. He may load his wife with jewels if he wishes. By the way, Viola, I should very much like to view the Harte diamonds closer to hand. They do constitute a remarkable necklace."

A new light entered her eyes, wary and calculating. "Yes, they do, Hugh. You may see them tonight at dinner when I shall be wearing them."

"I should very much like to see them before that," he said courteously but there was a touch of iron resolve in his voice which made her fidget uneasily.

"I keep them perfectly safe, Hugh! They are locked in a drawer in my dressing-room!"

"Then let us go there and take a look at them," he said easily. "Do you have some objection to my seeing them, Viola?"

"None at all!" she exclaimed furiously, leaping to her feet. "Come along, then, if you must! But this is the first and last thing I shall do to oblige you! After this, I don't want to hear another word about my marriage or any of the presents Freddie has given me!"

She swept out of the room and he followed her up the main staircase and along the corridor to the door of her dressing-room. She flung it open. The maid was sitting on a stool in the middle of the room, engaged in mending her mistress's linen.

"Get out!" ordered Viola brusquely.

The girl dropped her work, bobbed a curtsy and scuttled away with a curious, sidelong glance at Hugh, who stood aside in the doorway to let her pass.

Viola had produced a key from her pocket. She went to a small walnut chest of drawers in the corner and unlocked the top left-hand compartment. Hugh still stood in the doorway, filling it with his burly frame, one hand raised and holding the door frame above his head. Viola pulled out the drawer and took out a flat box.

"Well, then, Hugh—here it is—the Harte necklace!' She put the box on the dressing table and opened it.

The necklace lay on a bed of purple velvet. Even in the dull light of the little dressing-room, a white fire seemed to burn in the heart of the stones as they nestled in their sumptuous cradle.

Hugh moved slowly forward and came to stand over it, looking down at it. He said nothing but his eyes narrowed and he stared down at the necklace as if mesmerised by it.

"Yes," he said softly at last. "It is ... very beautiful."

He stretched out a hand as if he would have picked it up out of its velvet nest, but before his fingers could touch it, Viola had snatched up the box and slammed it shut ruthlessly.

"You wanted to see the Harte necklace, Hugh, and you have seen it! I have done as you wished. If you want to see it again, you will have the opportunity tonight and tomorrow night as well. I intend to wear it every night this week! Freddie likes to see me wear it." She returned the box to its drawer in the walnut chest and locked it, dropping the key into her pocket. "There, Hugh! Now I hope you are satisfied! You can write and tell the family that I take good care of the Harte diamonds!"

He ignored this to lean back against the wall with his arms folded. "How much does Freddie actually know of your past, Viola? Does he know about your previous marriage?"

"Of course he does!" she snapped. "When I met Freddie I was Mrs. Devaux. He knew from the first I was a widow."

"And does he know what kind of a man Harry Devaux was? Or how he died?"

She turned visibly paler and a nerve twitched at the corner of her mouth. "He knows Harry was killed in a duel, if that's what you mean—and that it was over a quarrel at the card-table."

"Does he know Harry squandered his fortune and yours before someone obligingly blew out his brains?"

"Freddie is well aware I have no money of my own!" Viola stamped her foot. "I won't be quizzed any further, Hugh! It's intolerable! Whatever has taken place between Freddie and myself, whatever arrangements he has made concerning me, what I have told him and he has told me— all of this is no one's business but mine and Freddie's!"

"And does Freddie know," continued Hugh inexorably, "that Harry was helped in squandering two fortunes by his wife and that the card-table had almost the same lure for you as for him?"

Viola came forward. Her manner had changed completely. She now had an air of dangerous calm and when she spoke, her voice was cold and steady. "If you try to turn Freddie against me—if you do anything, anything at all to harm my situation here—then I shall ruin you, Hugh! We shall go down into perdition together! Remember that! I can do it—and I will!"

She pushed past him and disappeared down the corridor. Hugh listened for the sound of her retreating footsteps to fade and then he went to the walnut chest and tugged experimentally at the brass handle of the drawer which housed the Harte necklace. It was securely locked. Hugh pulled out the lower drawer directly beneath it and slid in his hand to feel around the base of the drawer above, but there was no way of gaining access to the locked drawer and its contents without the key. He reclosed the lower drawer and stepped back.

"What are you doing?" asked a clear female voice behind him.

Hugh swore softly and swung round on his heel. Susanna stood framed in the doorway. "I asked, what are you doing here?" she repeated, hostile and suspicious.

"I—I had something I wished to say to Viola," he said awkwardly. He moved away from the walnut chest.

"But she isn't here."

"No—but she was!" He heaved a sigh. "We—we had a quarrel, Viola and I. There, now you know!"

Susanna flushed. "I wasn't prying! I was only surprised to see you here!"

"And now you see me leaving!" he exploded in sudden irritation. He made a gesture of appeasement with his hand. "I'm sorry. I didn't mean to bite your head off, but I am out of sorts because of my stupid squabble with my aunt!" He walked out of the little dressing-room and they went downstairs together and by mutual consent into the drawing room.

Hugh threw himself down moodily on a window seat and stared out at the frosty garden. Susanna watched him a moment or two, debating what she should do. He looked like some caged beast which had been disturbed and now prowled restlessly, glowering at its tormentors through the bars of its prison, throwing itself down in a corner only to rise again, unable to settle, and begin to pace restlessly seeking escape. Though seated, Hugh was not relaxed. His fingers drummed at the windowpane, his black hair tum-

bled untidily in its natural curl—unlike Leo's—over a
scowling forehead and he held his body tense as if about to
spring. And at any moment he would, jumping to his feet
and turning angrily on anyone in his path.

Susanna knew she was not excluded and must choose her
words carefully. If she said the wrong thing it would be the
equivalent of jabbing at the beast with a stick and inviting
it to lash out with a huge clawed paw. As calmly as she
could, she asked, "Is Viola in some kind of difficulty? Can
I be of any help?"

Hugh's head snapped round and his dark eyes glinted at
her fiercely.

"It's not that I'm asking what it is—if she is!" Susanna
hurried on, wishing she had held her tongue. "I only want
to know if it will touch Papa."

The warlike gleam faded from his face, much to her relief. He said tersely, "I have been away, as you know, and
it's some years since I last saw Viola. I have no first-hand
knowledge of her actions during that time and as to what she
has done recently, I'm equally unable to supply you with
details!"

"Then she is in trouble," said Susanna disconsolately.
"But you don't know what she's done, either."

"I have some idea!" he said grimly.

"But you cannot tell me?"

Hugh looked up at her pale, serious oval face with its
fringe of hair and the clear grey eyes, watching him so honestly. He clambered to his feet, "Allow me to handle the
matter, Susanna! With luck I hope that there will be no need
for you to concern yourself about it." His voice was curt and
discouraged further questions. She watched him walk across
to the hearth which had been the scene of his rescue of
Sammy and put both hands on the mantelshelf, to stand
looking down between them at the dancing flames.

Remembering him amongst the clouds of soot and confusion and thinking how capably and easily he had taken charge in the crisis, Susanna, was moved to say sympathetically, "It must be very strange and difficult for you to come home to England after so many years in foreign countries and find yourself amongst such peaceful scenes. You are used to the excitement and hurly-burly of the march and of life around the campfires with friends and comrades who have shared in hardship, to say nothing of battle!"

Without raising his bent head, he said, "That's what you think a campaign is, do you? Excitement and adventure, good comradeship and noble hearts?"

Susanna flushed. "I suppose I sounded foolish. I'm sorry. I can only imagine such scenes and have no knowledge to base my imaginings on."

He turned round then and came a little way towards her. "Don't apologize. The picture you have of it all is shared by plenty of others. None of them has ever been near a battlefield either. I have heard more nonsense spoken about the recent wars since I arrived back in England than I would have thought possible. And not all of those spouting it have your excuse. Of course you can know nothing of it. How should you?"

"Then what is it like, really? Tell me." She sat down on the little striped silk sofa before the fire and folded her hands in her lap. After a moment's hesitation, he came to take the place beside her.

"Well, generally speaking, it is all a mess. Thoroughly confusing. No one knows where he is going or what he's supposed to do when he gets there. You arrive at a place at nightfall with perhaps a hundred or more men, not knowing where it is, to find you are not expected nor is there any shelter or food to be had, nor fodder for the horses. If you lay your hands on a map it is probably wrong. Local people, understandably enough, are more concerned to hide their food and hay than to surrender it to passing armies, even for ready money. It is all very well to put out orders forbidding pillage, but if the soldier is cold and hungry it's difficult to stop him forcing his way into the peasant's house and taking what he can find—or driving out the owners to warm himself at their fire! Flogging or shooting may discourage a few, but in the end one turns a blind eye.

"As for battle, I believe that more than anything it is a waste—a waste of all that is bravest and best. And as for noble virtues, such ideas are better crushed. Too often you must act against your better instincts." He gestured with a resigned sweep of his hand. "Your instinct is to help a wounded man, but your military judgement is to leave him where he lies, because you are more needed elsewhere. In Spain, where there was so much sickness besides injuries, it was a pitiful business to leave behind those who could not move out under their own power, leaving them to the tender mercies of the advancing enemy or a local population too poor and primitive to render much aid. I have seen men too desperately wounded or weakened to stand, who have crawled after their departing comrades, begging piteously that we should not abandon them. I think I shall never forget their cries!" Hugh glanced at her. She was listening and watching with a pale face. "No man goes soldiering because he loves it," he said gently. "But because he must. Sometimes it is the only life he knows, and then he's in a bad state indeed!"

"And you?" she returned, equally quietly, "What took you soldiering?"

He hunched his broad shoulders. "Want of fortune and lack of any other occupation. Most gentleman's occupations being barred to me, of course, by reason of my persuasion."

"Your persuasion?" She looked at him puzzled.

"Ah. . . ." he said softly. "So that is something Viola has not seen fit to tell Sir Frederick! Understandably, since he is a member of parliament!"

"You are a Catholic!" Susanna exclaimed loudly, divining the mystery.

"And Catholics are not allowed to sit in parliament—not as yet, anyway. It would not affect Sir Frederick directly, of course, but to be known to have married a Catholic wife would not be well viewed in some quarters and could well cause him some professional embarrassment! However, I doubt Viola is very religious and it probably doesn't trouble her. Whether you wish to tell Sir Frederick is entirely up to you. I shall not."

"Well—no, not unless it became necessary," said Susanna slowly. "After all, it is an altogether outdated law and there can be no good reason to stop Catholics being members of parliament. The Jacobite cause is surely lost for ever. As for my father's point of view, I have often heard him speak in favour of Catholic Emancipation. I know he was a supporter of Peel's bill in 1801—and although I was only a child at the time I recall his being very cross at King George bringing about its defeat. I don't think my father would mind as much as Viola obviously fears. I think she should tell him. But I shan't—not unless I must. She should tell him herself."

"Hmn," said Hugh. "Well, as for myself, I saw myself barred from more or less everything except the army. Had I been a peacetime soldier, then I dare say it might have blocked my preferment there. But in time of war, you know, it is more a question of whether a man knows his military trade, than of which language he says his prayers in—always supposing that he says any at all!"

A thought seemed to strike Hugh, and he went on earnestly, "But you mustn't think I nurture any particular resentment at being forbidden to take part in public life in my own country. I was brought up in full realisation of my situation and accepted it. One of the first things I found barred to me was being educated at an English public school. I had to be sent abroad for my education, as was my father before me. He was sent to France, but owing to the revolutionary troubles there in the seventeen-nineties, I could not be sent there but was dispatched to relatives of my grandmother, in Italy. I spent my boyhood at Pallanza on Lake Maggiore. It's a beautiful place and an idyllic climate. I swam in turquoise water as warm as a bath and as clear as crystal, I went out with the fishermen and explored the famous islands with their palaces and churches. I scrambled over the foothills of the mountains. I was indulged as a small boy can only be in a Latin country. No, I don't regret being denied the freezing dormitories, appalling food, Spartan rigours and brutal régimes of the average English school for the sons of gentlemen!" Hugh grinned at her.

"I see," said Susanna thoughtfully, turning all this over in her mind.

"So," Hugh continued, "this has not been the first time I have returned to England from a lengthy stay abroad! But when I returned as a young fellow—and found my own country a very wet and chilly place, I can tell you!—I found I must do something to support myself. As I told you before, ours is a large family and cannot support all its members in idleness! So adventuring I had to go! I've managed to keep myself in funds one way and another. There was formerly my army pay, of course. But I've always been tolerably lucky at cards. Besides, one comes by odd bits of good fortune on one's travels." He made a wry grimace.

"The prizes of war, you mean," she said. "Articles of value, large and small, like the musical box you won from Broughton and gave to me."

"Ah, that!" he said. "Do you still have it? I thought you were going to throw it away. You seemed to take a dislike to it. But don't misunderstand me. The British Army is by no means so avid a snapper-up of unconsidered trifles as the French! I've seen captured French infantrymen who had their knapsacks stuffed with silver candlesticks and the like! Anyway, one's priorities change in time of stress. A thing's value may be nothing if it's not immediately practical. I've known fine oil paintings cut from their frames and used to shield loads on a mule during a storm! That was their value then! But no, I can't say I am sorry my soldiering is over and done with.''

''But what will you do now that your soldiering, as you call it, is finished?'' she demanded. ''You can't play cards all your life!''

Hugh laughed aloud then. ''Luckily I don't have to, not now! I have come by way of inheritance into a small estate on the shores of the lake of which I told you, near to Pallanza. It will support me well enough if I choose to live simply and the house is a pretty one in the classical Italian style with very fine gardens full of pink and white oleanders. I remember it.'' He paused, perhaps thinking back to his boyhood. ''Yes, I shall go there.''

Susanna felt a curious sadness. ''So you'll go adventuring no more,'' she said aloud. ''But settle down and inspect the grapes in your vineyard and the cheeses in the store.''

''It does sound somewhat bucolic and remarkably tedious!'' he admitted. ''Especially all alone.''

''But you will get married no doubt!'' The words slipped out before she could prevent them and Susanna blushed furiously. At the same time, she thought: he will take an Italian wife and never return here again. His own country, whose flag he has served loyally, will lose him for ever and all because of a stupid law which cannot be repealed because the king is mad!

Hugh scratched his mop of black curls. ''Ah, but then I need to meet the right girl. Sadly, I've only ever met the wrong ones, and plenty of those!'' He leaned back and stretched out his long legs, the gleaming toes of his top-boots reflecting the leaping flames in the hearth. ''And what about you, Miss Harte? Don't you have plans to marry? Not to your cousin, of course, as you've already denied that! Just as well, if you don't mind my saying so.''

''Oh, Leo means well,'' said Susanna. ''There's no harm in him and he's really very kind, you know. His worst vice is laziness.''

Hugh grunted, obviously not sharing her opinion of Leo but not wishing to disagree with her. ''And is there no one else?'' He twitched an enquiring eyebrow at her.

''No,'' said Susanna simply.

''Were you not forced to run that dreadful gauntlet called the Season?''

''Yes, I was!'' declared Susanna with such deep emotion that he was surprised. ''And you describe it perfectly. It was awful! Yet I must confess I've always had a bad conscience about it, because my mamma and my Aunt Jessica, Lady Weston, both worked so hard on my behalf and spent such a lot of money. I was just eighteen. We went to London and stayed with my Aunt Jessica in Portland Square. She gave any amount of parties purely on my account, to launch me, you know, as if I were a boat.''

Hugh chuckled.

''But it was all such a waste of time!'' continued Susanna, growing more and more impassioned. ''And worse, it was degrading! All that dressing up and worrying about whether velvet bows would better trim a bonnet than false flowers... and learning to twitter amusing things and simper at young men... all in order to catch a husband. As if any man with an ounce of sense would want such a butterfly as a wife!''

''I agree,'' said Hugh. ''So you did not meet any suitable young man?''

"Oh yes, I dare say they were all suitable," said Susanna dismissively. "But I didn't want any of them. There was nothing wrong with them, you understand, but nothing right, either. So we came home at the end of it, and I wasn't even unofficially engaged. Mamma and Aunt Jessica were terribly upset and so disappointed, and I felt very badly because I had let them down. They had spent so much time and money. Aunt Jessica said I was obviously plainer than she had thought and my feet were too big—"

Hugh leaned forward and peered down at the carpet. Susanna obligingly lifted the hem of her gown an inch or two and twiddled a pair of long, slender feet in satin slippers at him.

"They look perfectly all right to me, quite elegant," he said, thinking privately that she also had very trim ankles.

"I dare say they are all right as feet. One is left and one is right. But they aren't small. Mamma said I did it all on purpose to vex her, and I had always been contrary, even as a baby. I was so sorry, truly sorry, and I felt it must be my fault, so when they produced Mr. Biggins, I really tried to like him."

"Who on earth is—was—Mr. Biggins?" exclaimed Hugh, receiving the new twist in the saga with rapt attention.

"He was the curate and a very respectable man and even very pleasant, if rather dull, but he had a lisp and I thought it really couldn't do, not with my name."

"Your name."

"Yes, I mean two 's' in one name. How could I marry a man who couldn't say either and would call me 'Thuthanna' all our married lives? Well, he would probably have called me 'Mrs. Biggins' because he was that sort of person. But even that would have come out at 'Mithith Bigginth'..."

Hugh put his hands over his face and uttered an extraordinary strangled gurgle.

"So you see," said Susanna, "it was no good and I had to refuse him. Mamma said I was obstinate and unnatural and had given her grey hairs. Aunt Jessica wrote to say she washed her hands of me and would not, after all, leave me her gold fob watch as promised, even though she was my godmother. She said I was ungrateful and didn't appreciate all they had done. So I'm afraid," concluded Susanna sadly, "That I was a dreadful failure!"

Hugh's shoulders stopped shaking. He took his hands from his face and sat upright with a jerk. "Now that I won't allow! Of course you were not a failure! You're a very sensible girl who knew better than to tie herself for life to a fool!"

"But I let everyone down, and they all tried so hard for me," Susanna argued. "And took so much trouble."

"Did they ask you first? No, I don't suppose they did. So what they did, they did entirely on their own account and of their own volition. If they were disappointed, that was their own problem, too, and not yours! You have nothing to reproach yourself with at all. They brought it on themselves."

She looked at him doubtfully. "I never thought of it like that. I suppose there is something in what you say."

"Depend on it. Nor, incidentally, do I think you plain!"

"Thank you," she said seriously, after considering this.

Hugh smiled and twisted in his place so that he faced her, his right arm lying along the back of the sofa. It had already grown dark outside, the early twilight of winter, but the servant had not yet come to light the candles. The room was bathed in the rosy glow of firelight and it played on her pensive face and gave her more colour than she normally had.

"In fact," he said quietly, "I think you are beautiful."

"Oh no!" She looked at him shocked. "Viola is beautiful."

"You are speaking of the shape of a nose or of a striking complexion. But that is only one kind of beauty. There is another kind. It comes from within. That is yours."

She gazed at him with such a comical expression on her face, at once so puzzled and alarmed, that he saw she really was unused to talk of this kind and had not the slightest notion what to do about it or how to respond. She opened her mouth as if she wanted to speak but no words came out. There was something so enticing about the soft fullness of her parted lips that before he had time to think what he was doing, Hugh had leaned forward and kissed them.

Susanna gave a gasp and started back in dismay. Her heart gave a tremendous leap in her chest so painful that she put one hand to her bosom, whilst holding out the other to ward him off and stammering, "Please—don't!"

No man had ever kissed her on the mouth and the sensation was both novel and exhilarating. The warm pressure of his mouth seemed to linger and tingle. She became disturbingly aware of the intimacy of their situation, alone together in this shadowy firelit room. Leo had warned her that Russell could not be relied upon to behave as a gentleman and it seemed that indeed he couldn't. She experienced an irrational fear that he might try to kiss her again or even try to do something much worse, although quite what she was not sure. The worse part of it was, she could not find his action dreadful, though she knew she should, but only really rather nice...

"I'm sorry," he said. "That was a very foolish thing for me to have done." He rose to his feet. "I have a letter to write and should perhaps do best to take myself off until dinner. Shall I ring for candles?"

"Yes, please do," Susanna whispered almost inaudibly.

He tugged at the bellrope and then walked rapidly towards the door. As he reached it, she called impulsively, "Hugh!"

He paused and turned, waiting.

"I was not quite gracious when you gave me the little musical box," she faltered. "But I—I shall keep it."

He drew a deep breath. "Perhaps you would do better to throw it away!" he said, and went out quickly before she could reply.

CHAPTER FIVE

LEO WAS RETURNING home from a leisurely hack across the downs. People who knew Leo well generally agreed that he was at his best when he was around horses. For all his dandified appearance, Leo was a fit and healthy young man, an excellent rider, no mean amateur jockey and genuinely loved the beautiful animals. It was all the more surprising that Leo had proved so bad at picking winners. He often reflected on it, puzzled, himself. The other reflection which still had the power to amaze him was that money could be lost so fast. But there it was. Leo had entered society as a young man of modest but respectable fortune and within three years had woken up one morning to find himself quite without credit and owing money everywhere.

One or two of his creditors had turned quite nasty. Leo had been obliged to appeal to his Uncle Frederick and his Uncle Frederick, to give the old boy his due, had come up trumps. There was no denying that, thought Leo to himself now. He clicked his tongue to encourage the bay and when its ears twitched in response, smiled and patted the animal's glossy neck. Sir Frederick had paid off his nephew's outstanding debts and arranged to make him a small annual allowance. Of course, Leo could not have afforded to live on the allowance, if he had not taken up his residence at the Hall. But with the cost of his daily board met as part of the family's general expenses and his lodging equally free and gratis, the money Sir Frederick allowed Leo went into that young man's own pocket to be spent on necessities, such as his tailor's bill and such general wants as a young man needs.

Well, some of them, thought Leo, swishing at a hawthorne bush with his riding crop. He could not afford a mistress for a start. His amourettes were restrained to village maidens who were not unwilling to grant their favours for a half-guinea and a length of ribbon. And he certainly could not afford to marry—although what he really needed was an heiress. Living as a poor relation was a far cry from owning his own establishment and having a future. Leo's future did not augur well. His uncle would not abandon him, but his uncle was sixty-five and when Sir Frederick was sadly no more, Leo might well find he had to shift for himself elsewhere. A wealthy wife would take care of it. But he was in no position to go courting with completely empty pockets and no prospects, so the whole thing turned in a vicious circle.

The way out was by marriage to his cousin Susanna. Until recently Leo had not been unduly worried by his uncertain financial situation because he had always assumed that he could, when he felt ready to do so, marry his cousin. Susanna was heiress to the Hall and all Sir Frederick surveyed. Through a marriage, Leo might yet be master of the Hall. But this sanguine prospect had received two serious setbacks of late.

The first had been the arrival of Viola and the alarming possibility that Sir Frederick in his old age might suddenly gain a son and heir, thereby diminishing his daughter's future prospects considerably and depriving Leo of a cherished hope. Even so, since a year had passed without Lady Harte announcing a happy event, Leo had begun to relax on that account. But now a second, unforeseen, and much more dangerous enemy had arrived on the scene.

"God rot Major Russell!" declared Leo aloud and struck out again at nearby bushes. "Why the devil can't he get what he came here for, and take himself off again? If I knew what it was he wanted, I'd help him to it myself!''

At this point Leo saw, walking along the track ahead of him, a comely damsel with a wooden yoke balanced across her shoulders, at either end of which hung a full pail of milk. Leo cheered up considerably, urged the bay forward and rode up beside her.

"Good morning, Bessie my dear!" He swept off his high-crowned hat with its ribbon and buckle and gestured widely with it as he bowed over the saddle.

"Go on with you, Master Leo!" retorted the maiden. "Don't you go making me laugh now, or I'll spill the milk and get into trouble!"

"Bessie my love, if you only get into trouble for spilling milk, you have nothing to worry about!"

She giggled. "Get away!"

"Those pails look awfully heavy," observed Leo, riding beside her and looking down at them with mild interest. He could also observe, with more interest, from this angle the delights revealed by a gap in her bodice. She really was a splendid figure of a young woman. She had a mop of curly fair hair, a glowing rose and white complexion, a bosom like a feather bolster and marvellous hips. Leo sighed. "Bessie, my dear child, you remember the matter we mentioned last time we met?"

"Yes, I do!" said Bessie sapiently. "You must think I'm daft."

"No I don't. I think you are very pretty. I like you very much. And I promise, I'll bring you a new petticoat from Newbury, if you'll do it. A silk petticoat, there!"

"Oh yes?" demanded Bessie. "And what's my Jem going to say when he sees me wearing a silk petticoat? Ain't he going to ask where I get 'un?"

"Jem?" enquired Leo suspiciously.

"Jem Bolger, as works with Mr. Grummit the black-smith. You know him, Master Leo. I'm been walking out with Jem six month."

"Oh, yes..." said Leo gloomily. Before his mental eye formed an image of Jem Bolger, a sweaty giant in a leather apron, with a remarkably low forehead and a notoriously powerful right arm. "Oh well, then, Bessie... Best forget about it." He touched the brim of his hat with his whip in salute and trotted off down the path.

When he reached home and had left the bay at the stableyard, Leo turned not towards the house, but towards the gardens. He pushed his hands in his pockets and wandered along, turning over the situation in his mind. Certainly, nothing was going his way. Possibly Russell could be bribed to go away, but Leo had nothing to bribe him with. A better idea would be to unearth some scandal involving Russell. That might be the answer. "I wager his reputation ain't altogether what it ought to be!" observed Leo aloud. "It shouldn't be difficult to fix something up!"

His wanderings had brought him to a little frequented part of the grounds. Over a hundred years before, when the fashion had been for water-gardens, someone had laid out such a thing here. But the fashion had passed and the garden had been abandoned. All that was left was a large rectangular pond fed by a channel from the nearby river. The pond was infested with weed. In summer its surface was green and smelly and in winter, as now, it was covered in a thin film of ice. At the far end of it was a neglected rustic bridge, a sight melancholy enough for the most romantic mind. Especially—Leo's eyes narrowed—especially as leaning over the parapet of the bridge and gazing down into the water was a graceful female form. Leo was not of a poetical turn. The charming scene simply caused him to exclaim, "What the devil does that woman want there?"

He walked briskly forward and, before she could observe him and escape, hailed her. "Good day to you, Lady Harte! This is a very wild spot in which to find you! And you'll take cold if you don't watch out!"

She was well wrapped up enough in a fur-trimmed pelisse but the cold air had caused the end of her nose to glow pink and this was altogether such an odd setting for her, that she obviously realised she had to offer Leo some explanation.

"Winter is such a tedious time. One is shut up in the house so. All the chimneys in that house smoke. The drawing room was just the worst. I get the most dreadful headaches. So I came out for a walk. It's very romantic down here, don't you think?"

"No," said Leo honestly. "But I ain't of that turn of mind. I never saw anything in that fellow Byron. Longwinded sort of chap. I tried to read something of his once— Suky gave it to me. It was dashed odd. The fellow himself sounds a trifle *louche* from all I've heard. I was talking once to a fellow who knew the family and he said they were all well-known for being cracked."

Leo leaned against the parapet with his back to the pond. He folded his arms. "Lady Harte, might I ask you something?"

"What?" she demanded suspiciously. Her gaze flickered over him, but he looked the picture of amiable inoffensiveness.

"Your, um, nephew—Russell. Charmed to meet him and all that. You don't know how long he plans to stay?"

"Not above another week!" said Viola sharply.

"Leaving as soon as that, is he?" Leo brightened up visibly. "Splendid! I mean, pity."

She glanced maliciously at him. "What's wrong, Leo? Are you afraid your cousin will fall head over heels in love with Hugh? She'll be wasting her time if she does. Hugh's career is scattered with abandoned lady-loves. He is extremely untrustworthy where women are concerned. Don't say I didn't tell you."

"Look here," said Leo anxiously, pushing himself away from the parapet and his good humour evaporating. "When you say untrustworthy, how far would he go? I mean, you know..."

She shrugged elegantly. "As far as the girl will let him, I dare say. Isn't that usually the case with most men? But Susanna is twenty-six, not seventeen. I suppose she doesn't still think babies are found under cabbages? I dare say, she can look after herself."

"I'm not so sure..." said Leo grimly, tapping the riding crop against his boot.

A spiteful gleam entered her eye. "Then you had better do something about it, Leo. Quite frankly, you've let the grass grow under your feet. Serve you right if she does run off with Hugh. You've had your time and opportunity."

"Well, yes," he admitted. "I've always intended to ask Susanna, you know...but, well, it's marriage... It's a very—very limiting sort of thing."

"You don't have to tell me!" said Lady Harte bitterly, glowering at the icy water beneath their feet. She looked up at him and added briskly. "By the way, Leo, don't think that if you don't marry her, I shall continue to allow you to sponge off Freddie! Your credit is about run out here, my dear."

He flushed. "See here, Viola—"

"No, you see here, Leo!" she interrupted. "There are going to be some changes at the Hall! Freddie is far too good-natured. You have been taking advantage of it shamelessly. If you want to marry the girl, do so...and take her away with you somewhere."

"Ah!" he said. "That's what you would like, isn't it? To be rid of Suky?"

"Yes. If you can rid me of her by marrying her, you will be doing yourself a good turn as well as me. I've only permitted you to stay on here because I've hoped you would do it. If you don't marry her, then you have no use for me. And that means, off you go. I advise you not to dally over it, Leo!" With that, she walked away and left him scowling at her retreating form. While this conversation had been taking place, another encounter was occurring in another part of the garden. It was a much less romantically secluded part. It was by the arched entry through the brick wall into the vegetable patch. Susanna and Mrs. Merrihew had been conferring with the head gardener over the question of winter vegetables. Details concerning potatoes, carrots and onions having been settled and the hothouse inspected to see what more delicate fare was still to be had, Susanna had turned back towards the house alone. It was much to her surprise to see that as she arrived at the archway from one direction, a familiar and stalwart figure in a plain grey coat appeared round the corner of a garden shed and approached it from another. Major Russell, it seemed, had also suddenly developed a curious interest in root vegetables.

Susanna waited for him to come up to her. "Good morning," she said. "What on earth are you doing here?"

"I'm a very keen gardener," he said promptly and grinned at her.

"Rubbish!" She peered at his left hand. "What is that you have there?"

He held the article up. It was a broken piece of glass pane about three inches square. "One of the gardeners has obligingly found this for me. It's a piece of cucumber frame."

"You do the oddest things," said Susanna seriously. "I wish I knew what you were really about. What can you want with a piece of broken glass?"

"Well, let us go up to the house and I'll show you," Hugh said obligingly. He offered her his arm which she took and they proceeded towards the Hall. "I've often thought," said Hugh, "that I should have liked to be a scientist. You know, fiddle with bits of things in glass tubes and pound things up with pestle and mortar. One can get very interesting results."

"Is that why you are so interested in minerals?"

He gave her a startled look. "How do you mean?"

"Wasn't that the book you took down from the library shelf? A book on minerals?"

"You're very sharp," he said with respect. "I wish I had realised how sharp you were. I should have been more careful. Yes, it was. Just for my own interest, you know."

Very likely! thought Susanna but didn't say it.

"One could discover things," said Hugh dreamily. "And make a fortune. Have you ever heard of Joseph Strasser?"

"No, good heavens, of course I haven't! Is he real? Does he exist?"

"Well, not now, I imagine he's well and truly dead now. But he did exist."

"I wish," she exclaimed with some exasperation, "that you wouldn't speak in riddles."

"I don't. But Strasser, he invented things by fiddling about with chemistry. I only name him as an example."

They had reached the Hall now. When they had divested themselves of their outdoor clothing and discovered that Sir Frederick was in the library, they took possession of a small morning room. There Hugh pulled out a chair for Susanna at a small table, first setting down the fragment of glass pane on the table top. Then he seated himself on the other side opposite to her, adjusted his cuffs and drew his handkerchief out of his pocket.

Susanna watched him curiously and without daring to speak. He seemed to be about to perform some kind of conjuring trick. He breathed on the glass and rubbed it vigorously with the handkerchief until it was clean and shiny and then put it down flat with great care. Next he tugged a gold ring from his finger and held it up. In the gold band was set a single glittering stone.

"You can tell me, I'm sure, what kind of stone this is," Hugh asked her.

"Yes, it is a diamond," she replied promptly, feeling ridiculously as though she had been transported back to the school-room.

Hugh nodded but seemed momentarily side-tracked. He contemplated the ring and murmured, "This belonged to my father. He showed me the trick—if you like to call it that—which I'm going to show you, using this same ring. Small boys, you know, are fond of any kind of novelty."

"And grown ones, too, it seems!" she retorted, and he looked up and grinned at her impishly which made her heart skip up into her throat.

"Now, then!" said Hugh severely, resuming his pedagogic manner. "Diamonds were found in India many centuries ago. The Hindu jeweller used to polish them by rubbing one gem against another. There was a good reason for that, for the diamond is the hardest natural substance known to man and how else should he polish it? Then, much later, in the middle-ages, the existence of diamond dust was discovered, here in Europe, and a new way of cutting diamonds perfected. Now you know as much about it as I do," Hugh concluded, "without going through the tedious business of reading it up. So I'll proceed to the practical demonstration."

He hunched over the glass pane and began to scratch on it with the diamond set in his ring. He looked so much like an earnest schoolboy, with a frown on his forehead and his hair tumbling untidily forward, that Susanna almost laughed aloud and thought to herself that he must have looked just so, those many years ago when his own father had demonstrated the property of a diamond.

Aloud she asked rather anxiously, however, "Are you sure it won't damage the stone to use it so?"

"No, no—there!" Hugh held up the glass pane on high so that the light from the window shone through it and clearly showed the "S" scratched on it. "A true diamond will cut glass. Quod erat demonstrandum!"

Susanna obligingly clapped her hands.

"Ah, but I haven't finished!" he said and began to scratch at the glass again. This time it squeaked shrilly and she put her hands to her ears in protest. Hugh sat back and surveyed his work with a satisfied nod. Then he held it up again for her to see it. Now the "S" was enclosed in the scratched shape of a heart.

Susanna blushed. "What nonsense!"

"The lady pours scorn on it and I thought it a pretty conceit—a Heart for a Harte, do you see?"

"Yes, I do see but I still wish you hadn't scratched it on the glass."

"Prefer me to go out and carve it on treetrunks, would you?"

"I should prefer you not to carve it anywhere!"

Hugh heaved a sigh. "Yes, I dare say you would. And very sensibly. But soldiers are sentimental, you know. Some of the worst brutes I've ever come across had a fondness for kittens and small children. Show a soldier a scrap of lace and velvet made up into a heart with 'Mother' embroidered upon it and he'll spend his last farthing to obtain it and tuck it away carefully in his pocket before he goes off to butcher his fellow men!" He spread out his handkerchief and put the glass fragment down on it. As he wrapped it up, he added, "I shall have this made up into a keepsake for you, when I have done with it—and when I leave, you shall have it and put it on your dressing-table and sigh over it. In that way, my work will not be wasted."

Yes, I dare say I shall! thought Susanna sadly to herself. "Thank you, sir," she said aloud with assumed cheeriness. "But have you not done with it? You have showed me what a diamond can do."

"Yes. But that was not the purpose of my obtaining it . . . to show you, I mean. I wish to try out something else but cannot at the moment." He had wrapped up the glass completely now and returned it carefully to his side pocket.

"Do you know, Major Russell?" Susanna said suddenly. "You bestow your gifts in the most careless and offhand manner, generally saying either you have no use for the item or, as in this case, I may have it when you have no further need of it."

"Bad manners, I fear."

"Not at all!" said Susanna calmly. "You do so because you are shy."

"What?" Hugh looked up startled. "My dear girl, I doubt anyone else would agree with you!"

"I don't care. I believe it's true. You fear I will not accept these things, so you make as though you didn't care twopence whether I did or no—and the item is nothing to you."

"I think," Hugh said slowly and seriously, "that if I had the time now for such a thing, I would be afraid of you. You are damnably sharp, too sharp. It makes me very nervous. Whether or not I was shy, as you term it, before—I assure you I am quite terrified now!"

"Of me? That I don't believe!" she told him severely.

"Don't you?" asked Hugh quietly. "Don't you, indeed?" He folded his hands together on the table-top. "You are quite right, Susanna—at least, in a way you are. I am not generally speaking a timorous fellow, but you are quite unlike any other young lady of my acquaintance and I have to confess, I am rather at a loss. I don't quite know what to say to you. I fear you will either think me impertinent or a fool. Possibly even both.''

"I am not in any way special," said Susanna after a pause. "It is because you have been so little time back in England and have not had time to meet many people." He made no reply to this and she went on, "Hugh—when you first came here, I asked you why you had come. I believed you had some purpose. I still believe it. I wish—I wish very much you would tell me what it was.''

He shook his head. "No, better not.''

"But I think you are very worried," she said gently. "Sometimes it is better to share a care. I think we are friends. Surely you can trust me?" She leaned forward earnestly towards him, putting out her hands in a little gesture of urgency.

"You have a true heart," he said, "and if you admit me to your friendship then I am indeed honoured. But I would prefer not to burden you with this matter. What makes you think I am so worried by it?''

"I don't know..." She frowned. "You have been here such a little while, and when you first came, I was not sure about you. But now I feel as though I had known you a long time, always.''

Hugh unclasped his hands and reached out to take hers in his and hold them lightly. They trembled a little in his grip but she did not try to remove them. "Perhaps you understand me, Susanna, because you and I are both somewhat oddities in our world. I, because I am not to be considered as good an Englishman as my Anglican neighbour, even though he might be a perfect scoundrel. You, because you would not sell your self-respect and dance to the tune called by empty-headed people frequenting what is known as 'good society.'''

He opened out his hands, still holding hers, so that he turned her palms upwards. In his broad sunburned clasp they looked very small, like a child's with a skin like rose-pink silk. "I cannot read your hand," he said ruefully, "because I am not a gypsy, even though I may look like one. If I could read it, I would wish to read much happiness in it. I hope you will always be happy, Susanna."

He sounded so sincere and at the same time so resigned and down-cast that she could only falter, "Thank you..."

He smiled at her and lifted her fingers to his lips. At that moment, there was a movement by the door.

A voice said curtly, "You forget yourself, sir! You will oblige me by releasing my cousin!"

Susanna gasped and spun round. Hugh dropped her hand and rose to his feet, pushing back his chair roughly so that it scraped on the polished floor.

Leo was standing by the door holding his hat and his riding crop in his hand. His face was flushed and angry with two spots of scarlet burning on either cheekbone.

"You might do better to announce yourself in the ordinary way," Hugh said coldly. "And not alarm the lady."

"Your solicitude hardly does you any credit," snarled Leo, "since you are probably more worried that you have been surprised than she has!"

A serious quarrel obviously promised to develop. Susanna jumped to her feet. "Don't be silly, Leo! You misunderstand—"

"I doubt very much that I do!" he interrupted.

"Miss Harte..." Hugh leaned forward. "Perhaps you would be so good as to excuse us for a few moments? I think Mr. Drayton would like to speak his mind freely and would do so better without your presence. I know that goes for me!"

She looked from one to the other of them in despair. Though Leo showed more obvious signs of anger, she was not fooled. There was a very dangerous look about Hugh altogether. His jaw was firmly set and he leaned forward in a way which was indescribably menacing. She began to be seriously frightened and begged, "You will not be foolish, either of you, promise me!"

"Run along, Suky!" ordered Leo brusquely. "This is men's business!"

There was nothing she could do but leave them and run upstairs to her own room where she sat down on the edge of the bed and wrung her hands impotently, exclaiming, "I am so stupid! I wish I knew what to do!" She then thought, Leo will do something stupid—or Hugh will, or both of them will! This led to a hardening of her mood and she exclaimed, "I declare, men are so difficult! I should have stopped there and knocked their heads together, that's what I should have done!"

But she had not, so she had to leave them to sort out their differences by themselves. Susanna picked up the little musical box which stood on her dressing-table and regarded it disconsolately.

"WELL, DRAYTON," said Hugh, when they were alone. "Don't tell me you are about to call me out? I thought you didn't go in for duelling? I recall your expressing yourself very bluntly about it the other day."

"No more do I," said Leo, scowling and stepping forward. "But I'm not a coward. And I'm not prepared to stand by and watch you play fast and loose with my cousin's affections. Stay clear, Russell! I won't have it, do you hear me?"

"I have not played fast and loose, as you choose to put it, with Miss Harte's affections," Hugh said quietly. "And I take great exception to your suggestion."

Leo surveyed him. "I don't know what you would call it. Amusing yourself, I dare say. Now listen here—Susanna is no flirt. She wouldn't know how to carry on in such a way. She's spent her entire life, apart from a few weeks here and there, buried down here in the country. She hasn't the slightest notion how the world goes on, and she certainly hasn't had any experience of dealing with fellows like you! Viola tells me, you plan to stay another week. You would oblige me—and incidentally, play fair by Susanna—if you left at once!"

"I am sorry," Hugh told him curtly. "I cannot."

"Why?" demanded Leo pugnaciously.

"Because I have not achieved what I came here to do. And don't ask me what that is—because it's none of your business. And that's all I have to say on the matter, Drayton! If you're not satisfied, I cannot help it. I can't say I place much value on your opinion, anyway."

For Leo, who had been rejected one way or another three times now in one day, this was too much. He lost his temper and with it his head, leaped forward with a roar of rage and struck out at Hugh's face with the riding crop.

The look in his eyes had forewarned Hugh fractionally in time. He flung up his arm to deflect the whip and clenching the fist of the other, struck Leo a solid blow in the midriff. Leo gasped, turned purple and doubled up. His feet slipped, the riding crop dropped to the floor with a clatter, Leo crashed into the table and sent it flying and slithered full length across the polished floor to finish some feet away.

Hugh stepped back and waited for him to rise. Leo scrambled awkwardly, panting, to his hands and knees and stayed there. Hugh, thinking him badly winded, went across and held out his hand. "Here—I'm sorry—but you cannot expect me not to defend myself."

But Leo was not as badly winded as appeared. Because he had been out riding, he was wearing the supporting corset which gentlemen often donned if they meant to spend any length of time in the saddle and which not only gave a trim appearance but supported the back. In this case, it had taken the brunt of Hugh's blow. Leo swallowed, struck aside Hugh's hand furiously and then grasped the ankle of one of Major Russell's shining topboots and tugged.

Hugh's feet shot from under him and with a horrific splintering of wood, he landed amidst the fragments of a chair behind him. Leo let out a cry of triumph and launched himself at his enemy. So blind was he with fury now that he had quite forgotten any gentleman's rules and had reverted more to the tactics of the prize-ring at which he had often been an enthusiastic spectator. He grasped Hugh by the throat and tried to throttle him. Hugh responded with a mighty crack at Leo's nose. Blood spurted out and scarlet spots appeared on Leo's neckcloth and Hugh's coat. At the same time, Leo felt a painful thwack on his back which could not have come from his opponent, beneath him. He looked up startled to see whence it had come.

"Get up, sir!" roared Sir Frederick, brandishing his stick. "On your feet, do you hear me? And you too, Major Russell! Get on your feet, the pair of you, or by Harry, I'll knock what brains you have left out of both your skulls!"

The gentlemen disentangled themselves and got to their feet, both out of breath and sadly dishevelled. Leo pulled out his handkerchief and mopped at his bleeding nose. The handkerchief seemed to prompt a memory in Hugh who swore and put his hand in his pocket. "Ouch!" he exclaimed and took it out, also stained with blood.

"Now what the devil have you done, sir?" cried Sir Frederick, puce with rage.

"I beg your pardon," said Hugh, "I had a piece of glass in my pocket. I'm afraid it's broken."

"It is my opinion," roared Sir Frederick, "that you have both taken leave of your senses! I don't ask the reason for this unseemly fracas. I would only point out to you that this is my house and not a tavern. Nor, in my day, did gentlemen settle their differences with their fists like a pair of grooms! Leo!'' He turned to his nephew.

"Yes, uncle..." mumbled Leo indistinctly through the blood-stained handkerchief he still held to his nose.

"Major Russell is a guest in this house. You will oblige me by not trying to strangle my guests!"

"I'm sorry..." mumbled Leo.

"And as for you, Major..." Sir Frederick turned on Hugh who was sucking his blood-stained thumb but snatched it away as he saw Sir Frederick's eye on him. "This may be commonplace behaviour in the army, but if so, I believe it more to be that of a drunken private of foot than of an officer and a gentleman!"

"I apologize!" said Hugh stiffly.

Leo took his crimson handkerchief from his nose and said unexpectedly, "I started it. I made to hit him."

Hugh gave him a quick glance. "I inadvertently offended Mr. Drayton, Sir Frederick. It was unintended."

"By which I take it you are making him an apology," said Sir Frederick. "Very good, sir. Leo!"

"Oh, all right," said Leo sulkily. "I accept it. No hard feelings, Russell." He held out his hand.

Hugh shook it briefly.

"You had better go and clean yourselves up, the pair of you!" ordered Sir Frederick. "Before the ladies see you. Give 'em both fits of the vapours. And look what you have done to the furniture!" He brandished his stick at the shattered fragments around them. "Kindling, gentlemen! You have reduced my furniture to sticks of kindling! Nothing but blood and destruction everywhere. It looks as though you have fought the confounded battle of Waterloo in here!"

CHAPTER SIX

SUSANNA WAS RELIEVED to find, when she came down to dinner that evening, that calm was restored and the gentlemen appeared—outwardly at least—to have resolved their differences. Leo's nose was a little swollen and red and Hugh's hand was bandaged. But otherwise there was no sign of their earlier dispute, the nature of which had been essentially conveyed to her by Mrs. Merrihew, in the housekeeper's own way.

"Some of the morning-room furniture came by way of an accident, Miss Susanna. The pieces will have to be sent to Newbury to be glued. If the cabinet-maker cannot mend them, I dare say he can make new to match. Jones the carrier will take them in on Friday."

"You don't know how they came to be broken, exactly?" asked Susanna in some trepidation.

"One of the gentlemen slipped and fell, Miss, I believe— or both of them did. I'll tell the maid not to put so much polish on the floors."

Down in the servants' hall there was no question of sparing the ladies' feelings and the fight had been the subject of much gleeful discussion. Leo's man put his own viewpoint on it to Charlie Treasure.

"Ere, your gent planted a facer on my gentleman! Mr. Drayton, I'll have you know, isn't one for fisticuffs!"

"Nor is the Major without being provoked!" retorted Charlie vigorously. "The Major don't go about presenting a bunch of fives to a another feller unless he's got reason!"

"He's 'armless as a babe in arms, is my gentleman!" protested the other, affronted.

"Come off it!" said Mr. Treasure sapiently. "I seen his sort before! Hangs around prize-rings and the turf and not too fussy who he rubs shoulders with! Not but he don't fancy hisself at the same time! Acts one way here in the boo-soom of 'is family and another when he gets away! Done up fer cash, ain't he?"

"We are a trifle embarrassed for the readies," admitted the other valet reluctantly.

"Spends other people's!" said Charlie Treasure. "That's what!"

But upstairs around the dining table the gentlemen were scrupulously polite to one another. Hugh, perhaps to avoid conversation with Leo, seemed very interested to engage his Aunt Viola in small-talk and Susanna, although pleased the two men were not scowling horribly at each other over the soup, felt a pinpoint of annoyance which anyone else would have accurately described as pique.

Much later on in the evening, when the tea-tray was brought in and the gentlemen reappeared distinctly more mellowed from brandy, cigars and the billiard table, Susanna saw Hugh again make a beeline for his aunt and corner her where they could not be overheard. But Susanna could see them clearly. Viola was wearing the Harte diamonds and they twinkled and sparkled as she fidgeted on her chair. She looked ruffled and fiddled continually with the little ivory fan she held. Hugh was leaning forward and speaking earnestly as if he pressed some argument. Susanna fairly itched to know what it was. Viola shook her head. Hugh argued more. Viola glanced nervously at Sir Frederick who was dozing off by the fire and then got to her feet and pointedly changed her chair to sit by Leo. Hugh glowered, got up and wandered off by himself.

"See that?" muttered Leo in Susanna's ear just before Viola changed her seat.

She gave a start as she realised that he, too, was watching the exchange on the further side of the room. "I'm sure I wasn't looking!" she lied.

"Yes, you were. And thinking what I'm thinking! What's he want? She ain't happy about it and rattled lest my uncle will notice! He's a dashed sight too interested in her, nephew or not!"

"Be quiet!" she said angrily.

Viola came to seat herself by Leo at that point, and Susanna moved away. But Leo's words had only fanned a flame already kindled. Susanna could contain herself no longer. Now that Hugh was alone, she chose her moment and went to join him where he was standing with his back to the company, studying a family portrait.

"My late mother," she said, coming up behind him. "Painted shortly after her marriage."

"Reynolds' work, isn't it?" he asked briefly. "I seem to recognise his brush."

"Yes. He managed to make Mamma look quite romantic, which really she wasn't. She was a very practical woman. I don't mean that in any disrespectful way. She just was. She was very English, if you know what I mean."

Hugh nodded and stared up at the young woman in the painting, a vision in muslin and voile, her hair dressed in an elaborate edifice of curls, poised slightly windswept against a landscape of trees and hills. Then he glanced towards Viola.

"Yes," Susanna said calmly, guessing his line of thought. "I have often thought so, too. Papa wanted a wife like that..." She pointed at the portrait. "And he married Mamma and she wasn't like it...except in Sir Joshua's painting. So when he married again, he looked for a wife he thought really was like that."

"And found Viola? Yes, it's possible."

She glanced up at his frowning profile. "Hugh, you and Leo had a fight, didn't you? A mean, a proper fight with your fists."

Hugh looked round and for the first time that evening, a hint of a grin touched his mouth. "Oh, that's a proper fight, is it, Miss Harte?"

"You know what I mean. Mrs. Merrihew said you both slipped and fell on the polished floor!"

"Ah," he said appreciatively, "the discretion of a good upper servant—nothing like it! No diplomat could do better!"

"You're not going to do it again, are you?" she asked anxiously.

"Not unless your cousin insists, and in any case, not in here... if you are worried about your furniture."

"I'm worried about you!" she said vigorously and when she saw his dark eyes fix on hers very directly in an unspoken question, added hurriedly, "And about Leo, too! Either of you might have broken an arm or—or something."

"Oh, Leo and I are fairly tough and not porcelain ornaments! We take some breaking and in any event, we mend without visible cracks..." he said carelessly. He held out his arm. "Shall we join the other two, Susanna?"

He was not prepared to discuss it further. She put her hand on his sleeve and they walked sedately back to the fire. Sir Frederick had gone to sleep altogether now and snored from time to time. Leo and Viola conversed in whispers so as not to wake him, but it seemed to Susanna that Leo's manner towards Viola was more reserved and cautious. He was not trying to make her laugh as he usually did. Perhaps he did not feel much like laughing. They sat for a little and made pointless conversation and then Sir Frederick awoke with a snort and a start and exclaimed, "Bless me, bless me! So late already?"

At that signal, the party broke up for bed.

VIOLA PULLED her muslin wrap around her and sat down before her mirror. The maid deftly removed ribbon and pins from her mistress's hair and began to brush it out. When it lay on her shoulders in long, black curls, Viola signalled to the girl to leave. Alone, she leaned forward and stared at her own reflection.

The candlelight flattered it. It made it difficult to see the tiny lines which had appeared around eyes and mouth. But she knew they were there. She touched her upper lip and smoothed it. Another three or four years and she would have become the sort of woman of whom people say, "She *was* a great beauty!"

Viola was afraid of losing her looks. The knowledge that one day she must, hung over her like a sword of Damocles. Every morning and night she carried out this inspection, looking for a new wrinkle, a slight sagging of the skin around the chin, a grey hair. On the backs of her hands were beginning to appear those pale brown freckles which no cosmetic preparation could bleach out. The skin was ageing, she was ageing. She was terrified.

So completely had she been concentrating on her own face that she had not heard the step behind her but now, to her dismay, she saw a figure reflected in the mirror as looming over her shoulder, and gave a cry, spinning round on her stool.

"Don't be alarmed," Hugh said soothingly. "I didn't mean to frighten you!"

"How long have you been there?" she demanded furiously. "And what are you doing here, anyway! This is my dressing-room and I'm not properly dressed!"

"You are quite decent," he said calmly taking a seat uninvited by her.

"You were watching me," she said bitterly. "I some-times think you read my mind, Hugh."

"I fancy I sometimes do." He put out his hand and took hold of hers and she did not pull it away. "My dear, you are as lovely as ever. Of course you don't look as you did when you were twenty!" Her hand twitched in his and his fingers closed on hers, preventing her snatching it away. "But that is not a crime, nor is it particularly a disadvantage! You are more mature, more gracious . . . not such a pretty butterfly. I like it better."

She sighed. "You mean well, Hugh. I can't pretend with you. I hate to think I am growing old. Freddie calls me 'dear child.' I suppose, compared with him, I must seem young. But I'm not a child or even a young girl . . . and I do hate it, Hugh!" Such genuine resentment and frustration broke out in her voice that he had to repress a smile.

"Your husband loves you," he said, serious again. "Do you quite realise it, Viola?"

"Yes, of course I do!" she said briefly.

"I wonder. He would forgive you just about everything. If you have been foolish, Viola, it would be best to tell him."

Now she snatched her hand away. "I have not been fool-ish! Go away, Hugh!"

"Not just yet. I want to talk to you about the dia-monds!" he said bluntly.

Her manner changed. Icy calm, she leaned forward, her black curls tumbling about her pale face. "I told you ear-lier this evening, Hugh, there is no reason for you to look at them any more closely than you have! And they are already locked away for tonight!"

"Viola," he said patiently, "If there is something you feel you cannot tell Sir Frederick, is it possible you can tell me?"

"No!" she cried furiously. She jumped to her feet. "Get out, Hugh! Get out of here at once!" She advanced on him like an angry tigress, her eyes gleaming with rage. "I won't talk about the diamonds, I won't talk about anything with you! I want you to leave! I want you to go away! If you don't, I shall do something to make you—there! I warn you, Hugh!''

He rose slowly to his feet and walked towards the dressing-room door. There he paused. "Don't push me too far, Viola. I came here because I wanted to help you. I'm your friend—a true friend of which you do not have many. Remember that!"

In response she snatched up a little china dish from the dressing table and hurled it at him. He ducked and it crashed harmlessly against the lintel and fell in fragments to the floor.

Hugh clicked his tongue. "Temper, Viola!" He went out before she could lay her hand on another missile. The dressing-room connected with her bedroom. He walked across it past the bed which had been already turned down and let himself out into the corridor.

It was as he closed Viola's door quietly that he realised someone watched him and looked up to see Susanna standing a little way from him holding up a candlestick.

"There was a noise from Viola's room..." The yellow light of the candle falling on her face and its flickering shadow prevented him from seeing the flush on her cheeks, but he knew it was there. "It sounded like breaking china or glass."

"She dropped an ornament," he said. "You won't leap to foolish conclusions, Susanna, about this?" He gestured towards the door out of which he had just come. "I wasn't there bent on seduction, only wanting to have a private word with her."

Now, even in the candlelight, he could see her complexion darken. Her eyes snapped warningly at him. "You have been trying to have a private conversation with her all evening!"

"Yes, I have," he admitted. "But I'm beginning to think I'm wasting my time. Well, I shall just—" he broke off.

"Leo thinks you—" Now it was her turn to fall silent, biting her lip.

"Yes?" he asked coolly. "Leo thinks what?" There was a new note in his voice, a faint hint of danger.

She pulled the shawl about her shoulders more tightly around her. "I have told him it's nonsense. Leo thinks you may once have been her—" Again she faltered.

"Her lover? No, never. Her friend—yes. And I hope I still am!" he returned.

She gave a sigh. "I am glad to hear you deny it, though I never believed it!"

"I shall be leaving within a few days," he said abruptly.

She gave a visible start. The candle tilted and the wax dripped onto the floor. "So soon? In such bad weather? Everyone says it will snow! The country people all expect it at any moment!"

"Then better I leave before it does and the road is blocked out of here." He moved forward as if he would walk past her but when he reached her side, paused. "I am sorry if I've caused you any distress by my presence here. I came here hoping to achieve—well, something which I haven't and I dare say, couldn't. It—it has been a great pleasure to have known you, Miss Harte. I'll say it now…though I shall say it again when I take my formal leave in public. But I want to say it now, in private, because it's not just a formula for politeness."

"I am sorry you are going . . ." she said in a small, lost voice. Her eyes gazing up at him and fixed on his face seemed luminous in the candlelight.

Hugh put out his hand and tilted her chin gently with one finger. "I am sorry too, but that is the time, you know, when it's best to go." He stooped and kissed her lips lightly. The candleflame jumped again and fresh wax pattered onto the floor. Hugh's arm slid round her waist and drew her towards him. She made no effort to resist, but pressed her slender, supple young body against his strong muscular one and reaching up with her free arm put it round his neck, drawing his head down towards hers.

All this she did spontaneously and easily. It seemed so right and natural and she wanted him so desperately to hold her close and never release her. He kissed her again, but this time it was different. The pressure of his mouth was fiercer, forcing her own lips apart. His grasp around her became rough and her heart leapt wildly and began to thump like a tom-tom in her chest, whilst every nerve in her body became alive and tingled. She pressed herself towards him, not merely yielding but with a surge of active desire of the kind she had never known...

And then he released her, pushing her back abruptly away from him. "No!" he said sharply.

Susanna felt her cheeks burn. Humiliation flooded over her. She was rejected. Perhaps he thought her forward. It had not been the way any lady should behave. He must have sensed the longing in her. She felt as she had been stripped naked, not in her body, but in her innermost thoughts and wishes. She had let him see how much she cared and how much she, or her treacherous body, had wanted him.

He saw the growing embarrassment on her face and the unhappiness in her eyes and added more gently, "I'm sorry, Susanna. That was all my doing and my fault. It is very late... I'm rather muddled in my own mind... And I'm rather given to behaving badly with women, I'm afraid."

"Are you indeed!" she burst out suddenly, anger replacing embarrassment.

"Well, you know how it is!" he said brusquely. "A soldier takes his pleasures where he finds 'em. Easy come and easy go! No time for anything else. He gets used to that sort of thing. It's got to be a habit with me. I apologize, of course!"

"Keep your wretched apology!" she stormed at him, stamping her foot and fighting back the tears. "I don't want to hear it! Yes, go away! Go away as soon as you like! We shall all be well rid of you!"

She turned and fled down the corridor, leaving him standing alone in the darkness, watching the bobbing glow of the receding candle-flame.

LEO GOT UP the next morning bright and early and dressed with extra care. He peered into his mirror as carefully as Viola and noticed with satisfaction that the application of cold presses had reduced his nose to its normal proportions. He tied his neckcloth three times before he was satisfied and demanded of his valet, "Did you clean those boots with champagne, Hill, as I told you?"

"Yes, sir," replied Hill, adding meaningfully, "I had a bit of trouble getting the champagne off the butler, sir."

"Oh, I'll slip the fellow half a guinea," muttered Leo, airily dismissing this quibble as he inspected the gleaming boots.

When at last he was entirely satisfied, Leo descended the stairs a very picture of the perfect swell, a walking illustration to aspiring devotees of "bon ton." Unbeknown to himself, he was observed from a shadowy corner of the main entrance hall by Charlie Treasure.

"What the well-dressed gent is wearing..." thought Charlie to himself with fine sarcasm. "And none of it paid for, I wager! Cor, I'd like to see a charge of grapeshot let loose in his direction! He'd be down on 'is face flat in the mud, fine rig-out and all, before you could say knife!"

Leo's object in all this preparation was his cousin Susanna, whom he found in the library with Mrs. Merrihew in attendance, checking the day's menu. He fidgeted impatiently in the background until they had finished and the housekeeper departed.

"I say," he said crossly and momentarily diverted from his purpose. "Ought that not to be Viola's affair?"

"The dinner menu?" she returned with a laugh. "I'm sure Viola prefers to leave it all to me!"

"Oh, well," he said. "That's not my business. I'm glad I've found you alone, Suky. I particularly want to talk to you."

Susanna put down her pen and sat back in her chair to study him carefully. "You look awfully fine, Leo. Very handsome."

"Thanks," said Leo artlessly and she hid a little smile. Leo disposed himself on a chair, arranging his coat-tails and fiddling with his cuffs whilst she waited patiently, wondering what all this was leading up to. "Now then, Suky," he said when he was finally satisfied with his general arrangement, "I want you to listen to me particularly well, because I mean to speak very seriously, you know."

"Yes, Leo," said his cousin obediently.

"I've lived here at the Hall some time and I think we know one another tolerably well, as well as we ever shall, anyway." Leo paused, frowned as if recollecting some mentally rehearsed speech and continued, "Very well, in fact. You know I am very fond of you, Suky."

"Thank you, Leo. I'm very fond of you, too," she assured him.

"There!" he exclaimed brightly. "That's just what I mean! But you're twenty-six, Suky, and I'm—well, I shall be twenty-eight next month, so it's high time we thought about putting things on a proper basis."

"Which is?" she enquired cautiously.

"Lor, Suky, don't be awkward! You know I mean marriage."

There was a silence. His cousin turned first pale and then red. "Leo," she gasped incredulously at last. "Are you, are you actually asking me to marry you?"

"Yes," said Leo simply. "Haven't I just said so?"

"Marry—you..." repeated Susanna as if totally disorientated by this novel idea. "Marry...you..."

"Suky!" he interrupted. "You can't be that bowled over! You must have expected it."

"No, Leo," she said frankly. "As a matter of fact, I didn't! After all, you've never mentioned it before and you've been here long enough."

"I didn't want to hurry you!" said Leo virtuously. "I wanted you to make up your own mind."

"And can you—can you honestly imagine us married, Leo?"

"Of course I can!" he retorted, flushing beneath the serious and enquiring look in her grey eyes and her tone of curiosity. "Or I shouldn't have asked."

"Why have you asked, Leo? I mean, now, today."

He hissed in exasperation. "I told you, I wanted to give you time. And you've had time. And it's New Year and—"

"And this is your New Year Resolution, Leo? One— marry Susanna. Two—"

"Stop that!" he ordered angrily. "You're making fun, Suky, and it ain't fair! I'm serious!"

She assumed a straight face. "Yes, Leo, you are. And I'm sorry to tease you. But it was a little unexpected, you know, for all you say. I do thank you, Leo. It is a great compliment. But I feel we should drive each other mad. So I must refuse, I'm afraid."

"Refuse?" He gaped at her. "You can't!"

"Yes, I can. I have."

"Now, look here!" Leo began to be very agitated. The Byronic curls, artistically arranged, became even more romantically dishevelled. "We haven't driven one another mad, so far. Why should we do it when we're married?"

"Because marriage isn't like any other arrangement!" Susanna burst out, beginning to sound agitated herself. "Honestly, Leo! You must realise that! It's not the same as just living here under the same roof, as cousins! I am very fond of you, Leo dear! But not that sort of fond! I mean, I mean, I'm not in love with you!"

"That's it!" shouted Leo, leaping to his feet heedless of the loss of elegant composure. He shook his fist, his face grew purple and he struggled for words. "That's it!" he repeated hoarsely. "You've gone and done it!"

"Done what, for heaven's sake? Leo, do calm down!"

"Calm?" yelled Leo, hopping about from one champagne-cleaned boot to the other. "Of course a fellow can't be calm when he's been cut out by someone else! And under his nose! I knew this would happen. You've gone and fallen for Russell! Lost your head. He's turned your brain!"

"Rubbish!" she exclaimed angrily, jumping to her feet.

"No, it's not! I knew this would happen! He's swept you off your feet!" Leo's expression grew grim. "Damn bounder! Ruddy military Romeo! Scarlet-coated rake! He found you an easy conquest!"

"That's very rude, Leo!" she shouted. "Besides untrue!"

"It is true! Face up to it, Suky!"

They stood facing one another, inches apart, crimson faces thrust close together and glowering at one another. Leo recalled himself to the situation first.

"Now listen, Susanna! And sit down!"

"I will not!"

"Yes—you—will!" thundered Leo with unexpected authority. "Sit down!"

Susanna sat down and stared at him amazed.

"Right!" said Leo masterfully. He tucked his hands under the skirts of his coat and began to stride up and down in front of her like a schoolmaster with a difficult pupil. "Pay attention to me, Suky. I'm telling you the truth! That fellow is no good! He's a rascal! We should have sent out and made enquiries about him when he first came! I wager we would have found out he's a wrong'un! We accepted him because Viola vouched for him, but Lord, look at her other friends!"

"I will not," interrupted his cousin in a stifled voice, her eyes sparkling with rage, "sit here and permit you to slander Major Russell, who is a guest in this house!"

He stopped pacing up and down and stared at her in some exasperation. Then the anger in his face faded and he came towards her, dropped on his heels in front of her and took hold of her hand, looking up at her with pleading in his eyes.

"See sense, Suky dearest! Please!"

He looked so honest and well-meaning and his agony was so real that her own anger disappeared.

"Oh, Leo, I know you mean well! But you are worrying about nothing! I know you are trying to protect me, and bless you, my dear—but I don't need protecting!"

"You do!" he cried out in anguish. "See here, Suky. I can understand it. I do see it from your point of view. Here you are, buried down here and along comes Russell, out of the blue. He's handsome, he's dashing, he's a bit of a rogue—Lord, you wouldn't be human if you didn't fall for the fellow! Yes, I do want to protect you. But so does he—only not in the same sense! He's had a few women under his protection in his time, I wager!"

Her cheeks burned scarlet. She removed her hand from his and ordered, "Get up, Leo! Stop acting like a spoiled child. You've absolutely no grounds for saying any of this."

"Don't I? I've seen 'em before, Suky, fellows like Russell! You haven't, because when you were in London years ago doing the Season, he was just the sort of fellow your Mamma and Aunt Jessica Weston—old dragon—made sure you didn't meet! Besides which, there were fewer of them around because they were all away at the war! Now they are all back again. There are Major Russells—put your money on it—all over England now! In every provincial town, knocking on the door of every house of any standing, wheedling their way in, all adventurers, all rogues and all on half-pay and looking for an heiress!"

Susanna leapt up so violently that Leo, still balanced on his heels, fell over backwards inelegantly and finished sitting on the floor with his knees under his chin and his hands behind him. She turned away in a whirl of skirts, the hem striking his face and then turned back as vigorously, causing him to duck hastily again, and demanded, "And you, Leo? Is it just possible that you are looking for an heiress also?"

Leo got up and dusted himself down. "All right, Suky. I admit I'm done up for money. There's precious little use in my denying it! But I am dashed fond of you, too. I don't want to see Russell break your heart! And I have always thought we would get married, one day..." His voice trailed away disconsolately.

Susanna came back to him and put her hand consolingly on his arm. "Dear Leo, I am truly very sorry if you thought that, especially if you thought it because of anything I did to encourage you. I didn't mean you to think I would marry you some day. I truly never thought of it. We were just such good friends. I hope and trust we still are. But even if Major Russell had not come here, I should still have refused you. I just can't marry you!"

"All right..." mumbled Leo, looking away from her.

She hesitated and drew a deep breath. "As for my feelings about Major Russell, I assure you there is no question of my running off with him or any such nonsense!" She saw the expression which leapt into his eyes and added hastily, "No! He hasn't suggested any such thing! In fact, he told me last night, that he will be leaving very shortly, in a day or two, and he made his goodbyes."

"Bounder!" howled Leo with fine inconsistency.

"No, he isn't!" she replied firmly. "He is an honest man who admits his faults. I—I do like him." She fell silent.

"Like him or love him?" demanded Leo grimly.

"I said 'like!', Leo. Now I am not going to discuss Major Russell or anything else we have mentioned here this morning any more." She smiled suddenly and put out her hand to twitch at his neckcloth and straighten it. "Poor Leo, all dressed up to go courting! And you do look so fine. You must go and find another young lady, Leo. I know you will find someone who will fall madly in love with you at first sight! And she will be a very fortunate girl."

"She won't be you," he said soberly.

"She can't be me, Leo. I'm sorry, really very sorry." Susanna picked up her papers and pen from the table. "Now I really do have a dozen things to do and must ask you to excuse me, Leo! Please cheer up!"

With that she was gone. Leo remained where he was alone in the middle of the library for some five or six minutes sunk in thought. Then he shook himself and muttered, "Well, all that remains is for my Uncle Frederick to order me out of the front door and I shall have a flush of rejections! Nobody wants me, it seems! Things look bad, Leo my boy! You are going to have to do something to change all that! And fast!"

SIR FREDERICK proceeded in a stately fashion down a gravel path through his gardens. He wore his warm coat buttoned up under his chin, a flat, old-fashioned three-cornered hat wedged well down over his ears, woollen gloves and gaiters. His stick was tucked under his arm and his hands folded behind his back. He looked the perfect English country gentleman, which was exactly what he was.

"Morning, sir!" said his head gardener deferentially touching his forehead.

"Morning, Barnes! Bad frost!"

"Tolerable bad, sir. But not so bad as yesterday. A mite warmer, sir, and tis a bad sign. We'll have snow within twenty-four hours!"

Sir Frederick paced on. "Tum-tum-tum!" he sang to himself, because although he liked "a good old-fashioned tune" he could never remember any words. "Tum-tum…" Sir Frederick narrowed his eyes and squinted into the glare of early morning sunlight which sparkled off the frost and made the bushes look as though they were hung with tinsel. "Good morning to you, Major Russell!"

"Good morning, sir!" returned Hugh who had approached from a side-alley and met with his host at the joining of the two paths. They fell into step beside one another. "Cold morning."

"Gardener forecasts snow!" said Sir Frederick. "Dare say he's right. It's a trifle late this year."

There was a pause as they walked on a little in silence, then Hugh said, "I am very sorry indeed, sir, about the fight with Mr. Drayton in your house."

Sir Frederick took his hands from behind his back, grasped his stick and waved it vaguely at the horizon. "No matter. Forgotten, forgotten! Young blood. But I hadn't thought my nephew had it in him! What'yer fighting over? No, no! Shan't ask! Don't want to know!"

Just as well! thought Hugh grimly, wondering how his host would react if told the subject of dispute had been his daughter. Probably with surprise bordering on amazement and indignation.

"Must be dashed dull for you nowadays," continued Sir Frederick. "What will you do with yourself now the war's done?"

"I don't know, sir," Hugh answered after a pause. "I may travel on the continent."

"Ah..." Sir Frederick prodded at a lump of earth with his stick. "Yes...of course. Difficult for you. I was a warm supporter of Peel's emancipation bill. Pity we couldn't get it through. Opposition, you know, from on high..." Sir Frederick pointed upward at the heavens as if some Protestant deity had directly intervened, but Hugh realised that what his host delicately referred to was His Majesty King George III.

As it was, he stopped in his tracks and exclaimed in surprise, "You know? About that? Did she—Viola—tell you about her religion?"

"No." Sir Frederick shook his head regretfully. "Others did. I've not mentioned it to my wife because I have hoped she would see fit to confide in me herself. Hoped she'd have enough confidence in me."

They began to walk again. "My aunt," Hugh began awkwardly, "Lady Harte...she's had a few bad experiences, sir. One way and another. They have made her slow to trust people. That is, they have made her slow to trust the right people. She's far too often put her trust in the wrong ones. She doesn't mean badly. I do believe, sir, that she has many excellent qualities and all that it needs, is for them to be encouraged."

Sir Frederick stopped and turned to face him. "Yes," he said. "I am of that opinion, too." He tapped Hugh on the chest with the knob of his walking-stick. "As for the Catholic Emancipation Bill—possibly I shan't see it passed in my lifetime, but I am certain, quite certain, you will see it in yours. Then you, and your children, will enjoy the same rights as any other English gentleman! Which is as it should be."

"Yes, sir," Hugh said quietly.

They parted ways, Sir Frederick continuing towards the house and Hugh making his way towards the paddocks. Reaching them, he leaned on a fence and stared out over the silvery grass, his breath rising into the air like smoke-signals. He had been there a few minutes, lost in thought, when he became aware of a dull thud of a footstep behind him making the grass, stiff with frost, crunch. A strange, coarse voice growled, "Be you the gen'leman from up at the big house?"

Hugh turned. A few feet away stood an extraordinary and alarming personage. He was massively built, with a low, beetle brow and long arms which swung either side of him and ended in ham-like fists which opened and shut in a threatening manner. He wore canvas gaiters and a homespun suit and an old, greenish-black felt hat. Small, piggy eyes glared at him.

"And who are you?" asked Hugh, sizing up this possible opponent. Whoever he was, he was bent on business.

"Bolger—Jem Bolger—is the name. Apprentice to Grummit the blacksmith."

"Oh, I see...a blacksmith," said Hugh, understanding now the massive build of the other. "What's your problem, Bolger?"

Jem took a step nearer. "Are you the gen'leman from the big house as has been messing with my Bessie?"

"I beg your pardon?" exclaimed Hugh.

"My girl!" growled Bolger. "Bessie."

"I see. I'm sorry, I don't know the young lady," said Hugh, thinking. I suppose this is some rival in love of Leo's. Lord!

"Ah..." said Jem fiercely, crinkling what brow he had and making himself look even more fearsome. He strug-

gled with some calculation and then pronounced triumphantly, "Then if'n it isn't you, tis the other one!"

"Does Bessie say who it is—was?" enquired Hugh curiously.

"Gen'leman from the Hall." Jem scowled. "Tis the other
one. I knows him. Come down the smithy a few times to
watch the shoe-ing. Tisn't you, at any rate," added Jem
generously. "I bid you good-day, then, master! Tis the other
one I wants!" With that, he turned and shambled away.

Hugh walked back to the house. In the entrance hall he
encountered Leo, mooching about with hands in his
breeches' pockets. He stopped and stared morosely at Hugh.

"Ah, Drayton!" said Hugh. "Glad to see you…"

"Why?" demanded Leo. "What do you want?"

"I just met an acquaintance of yours. He appeared to
harbour some grievance. A Jem Bolger."

"Oh, Bolger…" mumbled Leo. "Drat. Least of my
problems, though. Thanks for telling me. I'll stay away from
the smithy for a week or two. He'll have forgotten after that.
He don't remember anything for more than a couple of
weeks, Jem. Got no brains. Big fellow, ain't he?"

"Aggressive, too."

"Pity no brains," said Leo. "Or he'd have done well in
the prize-ring. I had the idea to enter him for a few fights. I
even took him to a mill to watch and learn. But he don't
have the talent for it. He can only hit a thing like an anvil
which don't move. A real pity because I could have won
good money on him."

"I'm sorry," said Hugh sympathetically, "that the en-
terprise didn't turn out well. Good idea."

"Nothing turns out well, not for me!" said Leo gloomily
and wandered away.

Charlie Treasure, hovering in the background, bobbed up
at his employer's side.

"It seems to me, Charlie," observed Hugh, "that Mr. Drayton isn't his normal cheerful self."

"No, sir. I expect, Major, it's on account of the set-down he had this morning." Hugh bent an enquiring eye on him and Charlie continued, "I happened to see him come downstairs this morning and he was all dressed up like he was going to a wedding. Hullo, sez I, what's he about, then? He goes into the library, sir, and start talking to the young lady."

"Charlie," said Hugh, "I know I asked you to keep an eye open but I didn't intend you to spy on Miss Harte. Please don't."

"No, sir, I know you didn't. I wasn't. Only they started shouting at one another so I overheard some of it. He was asking her to marry him, Major."

"The devil!" exclaimed Hugh.

"And she turned him down, sir. Flat. Felt a bit sorry for him, I did. Anyhow, I expect that's why he's going round looking like a feller what's lost a shilling and found sixpence. Thought you'd want to know, Major." Charlie, receiving no reply, peered up into his employer's face. "I said, Major, I thought you'd like to know!"

"What?" said Hugh, rousing himself from his thoughts. "Oh, yes, Charlie...yes, indeed. Well done. Um, you had better tell the menservants to watch out for a Jem Bolger. I think he means to knock Mr. Drayton's head off his shoulders."

"Been chasing petticoats, has he, sir?"

"Haven't we all?" said Major Russell wryly.

CHAPTER SEVEN

SUSANNA OPENED her eyes. A pale, dull light bathed the room. She turned over onto her side, tucked her arm under her head and wondered if it was worth getting up early. The maid had not yet crept in and lit the fire, but it did not seem quite as cold as it had been. Susanna's nose, peeping out of the covers, did not have that icy numbness that heralds a really freezing winter morning. On the other hand, all the local people warned that a sudden mildness of weather after a period of severe cold often betokened snow.

Susanna's mind drifted idly from one thing to another in an early-morning way and then her eye fell on the little musical box which sat on her dressing-table, directly across the room from the bed, and that brought her mind to thoughts of Hugh.

She had to admit that thoughts of Hugh were never very far away from it. But Hugh himself would soon be far away and she was going to have to get used to the idea. Whatever he had come to the Hall for, he had not obtained it. Susanna threw herself over onto her back and stared up at the ceiling. She wished she knew what it was. The lurking feeling of unease which she had had since he first arrived had never fully left her and this morning it seemed to have regained something of its first urgency. It was as if someone or something had called out a warning. The trouble was, she did not know who or what, or what it was about. Look out! shouted a voice in her head. But at what? At whom? In which direction?

She was suddenly unable to lie here any longer. To be in-active was intolerable. She jumped out of bed and scurried on bare feet across the room to the wash-stand. The water in the blue and white Staffordshire bowl was cold—last night's—but at least it wasn't frozen. The weather had in-deed turned a touch warmer. She splashed her face, tow-elled it dry robustly and dressed at speed. She was already brushing out her hair when the maid came with the coal-bucket.

"Lor, Miss Susanna, you up and about already? There was I, creeping about thinking I'd disturb you!" The girl put down the heavy bucket with a sigh and a clank of the brass handle as it fell against the side.

"I couldn't sleep, Mary." Susanna hesitated. "Is anyone else up?"

Mary was kneeling before the hearth and pushing coal into the kindling. "Well, Miss ... funny enough, everyone seems to be early today. There's Lady Harte—"

"Lady Harte!" exclaimed Susanna, turning from the mirror with a handful of hair clasped in her fist and held high above her head about to be pinned into a knot. "Dressed?"

"Yes, Miss. She said she slept very bad, Miss. Then Master Leo ..."

Wonders would never cease. What had got Leo out of his bed so early?

"He's gone down to the stable already, Miss," supplied Mary as if reading the unspoken question. "He says the bay is lame. he wants to send the stable-lad over for the veteri-nary. I haven't seen the master yet ..." Flames crackled up and Mary sat back on her heels, satisfied. "But the other gentleman has been down and breakfasted."

Hugh. Susanna threw a light shawl round her shoulders and went downstairs. As she came into the Hall, Leo appeared in boots and greatcoat, slapping his chilled hands and smelling distinctly of horse.

"The bay is spavined!" he said crossly by way of greeting. "I suspected it! Hatton would have it that it was only the frozen ground had done it, but that horse hasn't been sound in weeks. When the horse-doctor gets over here, he'll say the same, you'll see! My uncle should turn Hatton away! He's the idlest fellow and worst head-groom in the county!"

"Good morning, Leo!" said Susanna. "Hatton has worked here for years. Father's never complained."

"Because he's not interested in horseflesh! So long as the carriage horses are fit and able to work, he don't ask about the rest! Hatton has a crooked elbow! Why, he's down there now, scarcely sober! Had the effrontery to tell me, he only took a drop to keep out the cold!" Leo snorted. "Is there any tea?"

"I dare say." She watched him shrug off his heavy coat and stride noisily across the hallway into the dining room.

As she approached it herself, she heard Leo's voice again, relating his tale to someone else. Susanna pushed open the door, expecting and hoping to see Hugh, and found herself facing Viola who sat at the table, moodily pushing a piece of toast about her plate. Her step-mother glanced up and seemed momentarily pleased to see her. But then, Viola was not interested in talk about horses and even her step-daughter offered welcome escape.

"Mary said you slept badly," Susanna said to her.

"Very badly..." replied Viola irritably. "Leo—for goodness' sake! Couldn't you wash before you came in here! You've brought the stable with you!"

"Sorry..." said Leo. "But I didn't think anyone else would be here. Unless it was Russell. I mean, you ladies aren't usually about at this time of day."

Susanna wanted to say, Nor are you! But then she wondered if it was because he wanted to see Hugh alone that he had risen so early. If so, he had been thwarted. We are all up early! she thought, glancing again at Viola who looked distinctly out-of-sorts. And Viola, had she also perhaps hoped to see Hugh alone? The elusive feeling of unease returned. Susanna poured tea for herself and Leo and nibbled at a piece of pound-cake. Leo was demolishing a plate of cold beef. The sight of his robust masculine appetite seemed to annoy Viola even more. She rose to her feet suddenly and walked out without a word.

"Sulking!" said Leo indistinctly, waving his knife inelegantly at the door. "Depend on it!"

"What about?"

"Lord, I don't know! Something to do with Russell. She's not been happy since he came."

"Where is Hugh?" Susanna asked.

"Don't know. Around somewhere. Not out in the stable-yard while I was there. He had been there, earlier. Looking his own horse over. He told Hatton he would be leaving soon and wanted the animal given extra oats."

Susanna thought if she tried to eat any more pound-cake, it would choke her. She pushed the plate away. Leo observed her surreptitiously. Off her feed . . . he thought, his mind still running on equine lines. I can fetch the veterinary to the bay, and Lord, I'd fetch a physician to Suky if he could cure what ails her! But he can't, dash it . . .

His cousin got to her feet and made a mumbled excuse before leaving him to his breakfast. "Things are coming to a head!" said Leo to the teapot. "You'll see!"

The teapot was a perfect breakfast companion. It said nothing at all.

HUGH WAS IN THE SMALL morning room. The fire crackled up merrily in the hearth but Hugh sat with his back to it at an open writing desk and wrote energetically what looked like a letter. His hand was still lightly bandaged but did not seem to give him any trouble. His hair fell forward over his forehead as he concentrated on his work and she was reminded of him as he had sat once before, scratching earnestly at the piece of glass. Scratching her initial with the diamond in his ring. Her heart ached so badly she thought it really must break and wondered sadly why she had always thought the idea of broken hearts fanciful before. He looked up then and when he saw her, exclaimed in a surprised voice, "Susanna!"

She nodded, not trusting herself to speak. He put down his pen and folded up his paper without sanding it, so that the wet ink must have blotted hopelessly and rendered his work useless. It was as if he feared she might catch a glimpse of what he had written. He thrust it into his pocket nevertheless and stood up.

"We are all very early," muttered Susanna. "Leo has been down to the stable. He said that Hatton, the groom, told him you wanted your horse made ready."

"Yes," Hugh agreed, his dark eyes watching her face.

"You're going soon, then?"

"Today, I fancy. I may only go as far as Newbury and call by on Broughton again and go on towards London tomorrow. Charlie has packed my kit."

"Bags..." said Susanna automatically.

He smiled briefly in the way which always made her heart give a little hop. "Quite so. I must dissociate myself from army ways and army language."

"I'm sure Papa will be sorry to see you leave and Viola, too, naturally." She stumbled a little over her words. "And Leo and myself... You've been here such a little while and it's such a long journey."

"I'm accustomed to long journeys, Miss Susanna. I made one from Portugal to the Pyrenees once!"

"The war..." she murmured. "Yes, of course, it is nothing to you... But it might snow!" she added sud-

denly, grasping at the straw. "You might only get half way
to London and become stuck in some awful inn along the
road! Won't you wait here a few days?"

"And get marooned here instead? It's an attractive
thought, Susanna, but not a practical one."

"I suppose not," she said in a flat little voice. A shiver of
embarrassment ran over her. Here she was, as good as begging him to stay, which he plainly did not want to do! She
might just as well be a love-struck sixteen-year-old instead
of a mature young woman of six and twenty who ought to
know how to behave. More briskly, she said, "I will ask
Mrs. Merrihew to see you have food packed, in case you do
find yourself lost in the middle of nowhere."

"That's very good of you, Miss Susanna."

They were formal and awkward, both of them. Hugh
perhaps did not look so uncomfortable as she felt, but she
sensed that he was uneasy beneath his outwardly practical
manner. She asked, "What were you writing?"

"Oh, that—" Automatically his bandaged hand touched
his pocket. "Nothing of any consequence. Well, to tell you
the truth, it was a letter."

"It will be sadly creased and blotted now."

"I should have torn it up anyway," he said. "It was the
sort of thing written by an idiot." He turned away, walked
to the fire, pulled out the creased paper and dropped it into
the flames. It flared up and was gone. "There..." he said
softly, staring down at the blackened scrap of ash. "That's
that."

DESPITE EVERYTHING, his departure was delayed because
Sir Frederick did not appear until the early afternoon and
Hugh could not leave without bidding farewell of his host.
But his bags had been brought downstairs and lay on the
hall floor in readiness. Susanna gave them a mournful
glance every time she passed by.

"Going, are you?" asked Sir Frederick genially. "Coming on to snow, you know! Pity you have to be off so soon! Not much company here and the ladies get bored."

"I have business in London, sir." Hugh hesitated. "I'm very obliged to you for your hospitality. I hope you don't feel I forced myself on you and your family."

"Good Lord, my dear fellow, of course not!"

"There's just Viola..." said Hugh. "I know she's about somewhere but I haven't been able to find her. I particularly want to say goodbye. I have—I have something for her."

"I'll send a servant to fetch her," offered Sir Frederick. He moved towards the bell-pull but even as he put out his hand, a piercing scream rang through the house.

Hugh threw up his hand and a curious expression crossed his face. Sir Frederick paused with his hand still outstretched and exclaimed, "Upon my soul! What the devil was that?"

Running feet sounded outside the room. The door burst open and Viola appeared, her face drained of colour. "Freddie!" she cried and flew across the room to him.

"My dear girl!" cried Sir Frederick, clasping his wife's out-stretched hands, "Whatever is amiss?"

Hugh had moved a little to one side, a wary look in his dark eyes. A light footstep at the door heralded Susanna. He turned swiftly and as she opened her mouth to enquire what was wrong, signalled to her to be silent. She tip-toed across the floor to stand by him. Viola had burst into floods of tears and flung both arms round her husband's neck. She was sobbing hysterically on Sir Frederick's bosom. Sir Frederick looked both alarmed and dismayed, but at the same time, so Susanna thought, rather as though he liked it. He patted his wife's back and repeated, "What's amiss, eh?"

Leo arrived with a clatter. "What's wrong?" he demanded loudly.

Viola wrenched herself away from her husband's consoling arm and whirled around. "I've been robbed! That's what's wrong! *We* have been robbed! Oh, Freddie! They are gone! The drawer has been forced open and the box is gone!"

Hugh let go a long deep sigh. Susanna, for some reason, stepped closer to him. It struck her suddenly that they seemed to have formed themselves into a balance of alliances, Viola with her father, she with Hugh—and Leo standing in between as if uncertain on which side to throw his weight.

"The Harte diamonds!" Viola cried out passionately. "Someone has stolen the Harte necklace!"

There was a moment's silence and then pandemonium broke out. Leo and Susanna both spoke at once, questioning whether this really could be so. Viola burst into tears again and only Hugh folded his arms and stood back a little observing them all.

"Quiet!" roared Sir Frederick, making more noise than any of them! "Hold your tongue, Leo! You too, Susanna—just wait a little! Don't you see Lady Harte is distraught! Go and fetch some smelling salts or something!"

Whatever else she had done, Viola had not fainted, but Susanna fetched the smelling salts and when she returned, Viola had been led to a chair and sat there, wringing her hands, her lovely face tear-stained and her long black curls tumbling in confusion onto her shoulders. "Oh, Freddie!" she wailed. "I took such good care of them! I locked them away faithfully every night! Hugh knows I did! I told him and I showed him the drawer, didn't I, Hugh?" She flung out a hand appealingly towards him.

A cold little shiver ran up Susanna's spine. A picture leapt into her mind. Hugh, standing in Viola's dressing-room be-

fore the walnut chest, with one hand reaching into the cav-
ity formed by removing one drawer and tugging
experimentally at the locked one above.

"Yes, you did," Hugh said expressionlessly.

"You see?" cried Viola wildly. "It's someone in the
house, Freddie! It's a servant! They all knew the jewels were
kept in that drawer! No one else did!"

"Hang on!" objected Leo. "The diamonds would be no
use to a servant. They couldn't get rid of 'em! They'd have
to take 'em at least into Newbury and even there, there's not
a jeweller who wouldn't recognise the Harte necklace! I
mean, it's not like London which is full of fences! Getting
rid of stolen goods is child's play in London—but not out
here!"

Hugh glanced at him quizzically as if amused by Mr.
Drayton's familiarity with the disposal of dubious items—
information presumably gained from the gossip of others
and not first-hand!

"That's true!" declared Sir Frederick, suddenly taking
charge. "For once in your life, Leo, you've spoken sense.
But first things first. We shall inspect the scene of the crime,
just in case there has been any mistake!"

"How can I be mistaken?" asked Viola emotionally.

"Now, now, my dear child..." he said patting her
shoulder. "Leave this all to me."

He led the way upstairs and they all followed, Viola leaning on Leo's arm.

The top drawer of the walnut chest had certainly been
forced open and gaped empty. Susanna's heart had not
seemed able to grow heavier, but now it sank into her slippers.

"Bad business!" said Sir Frederick, shaking his head.
"Bad business, indeed!"

He led them all back downstairs again like a flock of
sheep and they reassembled in the library. Sir Frederick took

up his stance in the middle of their circle and stuck his cane on the floor. "Now, see here! I have to speak bluntly and if any one here should take offence, I apologize beforehand. But this is a serious matter! Viola, my dear! You're sure the diamonds were there last night?"

"Yes, Freddie, of course they were! I wore them at dinner and I locked them away afterwards as I always do!" she burst out.

"Calm yourself!" He held up his hand majestically. "Where do you keep the key, my dear?"

"On my person, always!" Viola stamped her foot in frustration. "Freddie, why must you always spend time talking? This isn't the House of Commons! Call the servants!"

"Not yet." There was a note of authority in her husband's voice which silenced Viola. She fell silent and began to twist her hands nervously together. "And this morning, when you got up, the drawer was not damaged?"

"No, Freddie! I should have noticed at once!"

"So," continued Sir Frederick inexorably. "At some point during the morning, someone entered the dressing-room, forced the lock and took the box containing the diamonds." He paused. "It seems to me it is unlikely to be a servant. They have all been employed here for some time and even if any one of them had done it, he, or she, would surely have realised that the servants' rooms would be searched."

"They have to be searched, anyway!" cried Viola wildly. "Freddie, I think I shall go mad if you don't order some action!"

"And they shall be searched," said Sir Frederick calmly. "As will our rooms be."

This time the following silence was a thunderstruck one.

"Ours, Papa?" gasped Susanna. "Surely no one of us...?"

"I trust not, my dear. But if the servants' quarters are to be searched, we must submit to a search of our own apartments. It is only fair and just and avoids a natural resentment on the part of the staff whose loyalty is questioned. Susanna, I think perhaps you should take Lady Harte out for a while. Perhaps you could wait together in the library?"

Viola opened her mouth as if she would object but then thought better of it. Susanna bit her lip, threw a quick glance at Hugh who stood stony-faced a little way from her and took her step-mother's arm. Viola shook off her hand and walked out unaided. Susanna could do nothing but follow.

IN THE DRAWING ROOM, Sir Frederick turned to his nephew and Major Russell.

"Now then!" he said crisply. "Leo! I dare say you owe money all over the place! This ain't your doing?"

Leo's face turned turkey-red. "No, it damn well isn't!"

"Not playing one of your stupid tricks? Some dashed idiotic practical joke? You've done such things before! If you have, own up now, sir!"

"I swear—" Leo said hoarsely. "I didn't do it. The Harte necklace? I'd have to be out of my mind! You can search my room straight away, if you want! You can search me! In fact, I insist on it!"

"I shall do so, sir, if necessary, depend on it!" Sir Frederick turned to Hugh. "Major Russell? It pains me to have to question a guest. But you are no fool, sir, and must be aware your position looks dashed suspicious. You are about to leave this house for London. As my nephew says, a servant could not dispose of the diamonds. Nor is it likely that outside of London could a buyer be found. I must ask you, did you do this?"

Hugh took a deep breath. "No, sir. I did not."

"My wife says she showed you the drawer in which the diamonds were kept."

"Yes, sir, she did. She assured me she kept them locked away."

"Didn't see her unlock it at any time?" Sir Frederick pushed his face forwards like a stubborn bull terrier.

"She unlocked it once, sir, to show me the necklace."

"Hum..." Sir Frederick tapped his cane on the ground. "Normally I should have asked for your permission to search your room in the same way as others will be searched. But you have already packed your bags. I must therefore ask permission to search your baggage."

Hugh took a deep breath. "And I must refuse it, Sir Frederick."

His host gave him a stunned look. "What, sir?"

"I must refuse. I am sorry. I can't agree."

"Oh, come on, Russell!" Leo burst out. "This isn't the time to stand on your dignity! Let someone take a look and then it's all over and done with and you can be on your way!"

"Quiet, Leo!" ordered his uncle. "Now then, Major. I understand your point of view. Of course it's dashed insulting and no one is more aware of it than I am! I assure you, sir, I am deucedly embarrassed! I beg you, do not make my embarrassment worse by forcing me to insist!"

"I have told you," Hugh repeated quietly. "I did not break open the drawer. You have my word."

Sir Frederick looked even more unhappy. "Dash it, sir! I ain't questioning your word! You are a gentleman, sir! As I am—and a gentleman takes another gentleman's word! But since all our rooms—mine too, mind you!—are to be searched, surely you can see that it's only proper someone should take a quick look at your baggage! Just a glance, you understand, for form's sake!"

"I can't agree, sir."

Sir Frederick paused. "Why?" he asked bluntly.

"I can't tell you. It—it involves another matter."

Sir Frederick took a turn up and down the room. "You place me in a dashed awkward situation, sir. I am sorry. I must insist. Leo—bring Major Russell's bags in here!"

"Look here..." began Leo nervously, glancing at Hugh. But seeing Hugh did not object any further but only folded his arms and stood waiting, he added, "All right, if you say so..."

There were only two bags. Leo put them both on the floor between his uncle and himself.

"Perhaps you would care to open them, Major?" Sir Frederick asked.

"Let Drayton do it!" Hugh said tonelessly.

"I don't like this!" Leo muttered, squatting on his heels and pulling at the straps securing the first bag. "Mark it, Russell, this wasn't my idea!" The usual collection of linen was revealed. Leo gave it a perfunctory search. "Dashed bad form..." he mumbled.

Sir Frederick pointed at the other bag with his cane. "Keep your comments to yourself, boy!"

Leo unbuckled the second bag and thrust in his hand. A curious expression crossed his face. He glanced up quickly and enquiringly at Hugh.

"What's the matter?" asked his uncle sharply.

Leo bit his lip and pulled out his hand. It held a small bundle, a handkerchief wrapped around something oblong with sharp corners. Leo stood up and put the object on the table, opening out the handkerchief. It was revealed to be a small ebony box.

"Will you open this, Major?" Sir Frederick asked.

Hugh moved at last. He stepped forward and flicked back the lid of the box with a disdainful hand.

"Good Lord..." whispered Leo. "The Harte diamonds!"

The necklace lay on its bed of purple velvet, winking up at them. It looked both beautiful and cold and there was no denying its almost magical aura, its power to attract. All three men stared down at it. Then Leo murmured, "The damn thing is evil..."

Hugh looked at him and opened his mouth as if he would have agreed, but then closed it firmly.

"Sir," said Sir Frederick. "You told me a moment or two ago that you did not force the drawer in my wife's dressing-room. I ask you again, did you do it?"

"No, sir."

"Look!" Leo began but fell silent as his uncle directed a furious glare at him.

"Let me put it another way, Major Russell," Sir Frederick pursued. "Is this the Harte necklace?"

"Yes, sir, it is," Hugh said.

"Ah, now, we are getting somewhere!" Sir Frederick struck his cane on the floor. "It is the necklace but some other hand placed it in your bag!"

"No, sir, I put it there," Hugh said.

This time even Sir Frederick was bereft of speech. Abruptly he turned away and began to stride up and down the room. Eventually he came back to them. "Major Russell! I am an old man but not a fool! I do not believe you to be a common thief! There is more in this than meets the eye! Will you tell me, sir, how you came to be in possession of my wife's diamonds? You may rely on my discretion. And on that of my nephew! Not a word of what you say shall be repeated outside this room. Your reputation will not suffer."

"I won't blab!" said Leo loudly.

Hugh shifted his stance slightly but replied in the same even and unemotional voice, "No, sir. I cannot."

"Why?"

"I cannot tell you my reason. I have nothing more to say."

"Dash it!" cried Sir Frederick. He stared at Hugh baffled and perplexed. "Well, then, sir, you put me in a situation which I very much regret. I must ask you, sir, to leave my house at once. You were about to do that, anyway, and so it's no hardship, I dare say. But I must ask you never to return nor to communicate ever again in any way with any member of my family—"

Hugh looked up quickly.

"Including my wife!" added Sir Frederick.

Leo leaned forward and touched Hugh's sleeve. "Russell, dash it! Tell him!"

Hugh only shook his head, and Leo, with an oath, turned and walked over to the window.

"Your bags are packed, sir. Be on your way!" ordered Sir Frederick brusquely.

"That might be difficult!" said Leo's voice from the window.

They turned towards him and he pointed wordlessly at the panes. Outside a thick white veil was descending over the world. Snowflakes fell soft and rapid against the glass, sticking to it like scraps of lint. Both the other men joined Leo and looked out. Already the ground was covered in a thick white carpet which had fallen silently and unobserved as they argued.

"Snowed in, by Harry!" exclaimed Sir Frederick. He heaved a sigh and turned to Hugh. "Then you must remain with us, Major, for a little longer. We have no choice. This sorry matter will not be mentioned by anyone during that time. Leo! Go and tell the ladies—as much as you must."

LEO FOUND BOTH WOMEN in the library. Susanna stood at the window and watched the snow drift down and Viola sat by the fire, her fingers pulling nervously at a scrap of lace-trimmed cambric. When Leo came in, she looked up, her fingers gripping the handkerchief tightly, but Susanna darted towards him.

"Oh, Leo! What has happened?" She held out her hand imploringly and he took it in his and squeezed her fingers. "Hold up, Suky. You're not going to like any of this. Don't go to pieces, now!" He turned towards Viola and still holding to his cousin's hand, announced loudly. "Lady Harte! Your diamonds are recovered, you will be pleased to hear!"

Viola's face turned as white as a ghost's. "How..." she stammered. "So soon? W-where? W-who?"

In response, Leo took his hand from Susanna's and transferred his arm to her shoulders. "They inadvertently found their way into Major Russell's bag." Beside him he felt Susanna sway and press heavily against his supporting arm. "In view of the weather, Major Russell has had to postpone his departure. My uncle asked that for the rest of Russell's stay, we none of us mention this matter."

"But he wouldn't—couldn't..." Susanna whispered. She pulled herself away from Leo's arm. "He didn't do it!" she repeated fiercely.

"Look here, Suky," he said in a low urgent voice with a glance at Viola. "I don't know what all this is about any more than you do! But I do know I don't want you involved! The whole thing is dashed fishy. Now you will stay away from Russell—I mean it! He doesn't deny he put the necklace in his bag himself. He does deny he forced the drawer! But he won't offer any explanation."

"That shows he didn't do it!" she said vehemently. "All he had to say was, that someone else put the necklace in his bag! Someone who was afraid of it being found in his possession! If Hugh says he didn't force the lock, he didn't! I don't know how he came by the necklace!"

"He had no business to be in possession of it by any means!" Leo said fiercely. "However he got his hands on it, he put it in his bag—that's not contested! You and I,

Suky, are going to do just as my uncle says. We behave—if we can—as if nothing had happened. We do not mention the necklace! And you don't go bothering Russell about it! Or about anything else, do you hear me?''

They had forgotten Viola, but now by some shared intuition, they both remembered her. The cousins turned towards Lady Harte who still sat before the fire. She did not seem to have heard any of their argument. Her face was that of a puzzled child, both perplexed and naive.

''You have got it wrong, Leo,'' she said simply. ''The necklace couldn't be in Hugh's bag.''

''I'm afraid it was, Lady Harte. I found it there myself.''

''Not Hugh,'' said Viola patiently as if he were deaf. ''Not Hugh. It couldn't.''

Susanna ran across the room and dropped onto her knees before her step-mother. ''Viola! You are Hugh's relative and you know as well as I do, he didn't do it! If you know anything more about this—about why Hugh came here—''

Viola's expression changed. The childlike simplicity left it and was replaced by the shrewd and defiant look of a woman to whom self-preservation was all. She no longer looked beautiful but only hard. She pushed Susanna away from her physically and Leo, seeing the gesture, strode forward and took his cousin protectively by the shoulders, assisting her to her feet. The look he gave Viola was no friendly one.

''I don't know what you're talking about!'' said Viola shrilly. ''I don't know anything! I don't know why Hugh came here! Hugh does what he likes! I'm glad the necklace is found! If you ask me, it's that horrid little man, Treasure! He's behind it! He took my necklace and put it in his master's bag because his own might be searched. He didn't think they would search Hugh's!'' She jumped to her feet and surveyed them as they stood together before her. ''I shall go and find Freddie and tell him so!''

Viola walked to the door and there turned and looked back at them. "Freddie loves me," she said triumphantly. "I shall go and tell Freddie I'm very pleased they have found my necklace. Freddie will be happy because I am happy. It's nothing to do with you, either of you! I'm the one Freddie loves!" She went out.

"She is a hateful woman!" Susanna said shakily.

"She's a jealous one," he said. He patted her shoulder. "She's afraid of you, Suky. She sees you as a rival. See here, my dear, the next few days are going to be pretty bad for you. But you must see it through."

"I know it," she said quietly.

CHAPTER EIGHT

THE REST OF THAT DAY seemed to Susanna as if it must be the worst in her life. The atmosphere in the house was indescribable. They mumbled essential conversation at one another and were all scrupulously polite, but otherwise remained silent. Dinner was a gloomy and formal meal. It was as if a death had occurred in their midst.

But if it was bad enough for her, it was far worse for Hugh as she realised. He sat in stony silence and after dinner retired to his own room. When he had gone the embarrassment appeared, if anything, to increase. Viola claimed a headache which for once was probably genuine and went to bed. Sir Frederick pleaded parliamentary work and retired to the library. Leo and Susanna tried to play draughts but neither could concentrate and finally Leo picked up the pieces and returned them to their box.

"The Newbury road is completely blocked, let alone the London one beyond it," he said. "Barnes came and said so."

She said, "Yes," in a cold little voice.

"Tomorrow will be worse," Leo continued, watching her. "Perhaps you'd better plead sick and stay in your room."

"No!" his cousin looked up at him her eyes blazing with sudden passion. "I should feel I was deserting Hugh!"

"Deserting him!" Leo stared at her in something like despair. "Lor' Suky! You can't do anything to help him. He's brought it all on himself. Besides which, I don't know that he wants help. He's dashed independent. Those sort of fellows are very awkward. You can't do anything for them. They resent it."

Susanna got up from her chair. "Papa said we weren't to talk about it and we shall not, Leo."

"This confounded snow!" he burst out, leaping to his feet and striking one clenched fist into the palm of his other hand. "He was on the point of taking himself off, and good riddance! And now, here he stays which no one—not even he himself wants!"

Susanna cried out, "Please, Leo!" in such a wretched voice that he was silenced for a moment before coming to drop on his heels in front of her and plead,

"Don't torment yourself, Suky! He isn't worth it! That must sound pretty rich, coming from me! But he isn't—I know it!"

"I won't talk about it!" Susanna said obstinately. "Goodnight, Leo."

He watched her go in silence, but when she had left the room burst out to the empty air, "The devil take the Harte necklace! It is the cause of all this! It brought Russell here and it prevents his leaving! I wish the damn thing were—" Leo broke off and a stupefied expression crossed his face. "I wish it were . . ." he repeated. "Good Lord, and so it is! Of course! What numbskulls we all are! And especially me!—I'm a fool!" Leo chortled and then gave a little caper on the hearth rug. "But now," he muttered, coming to a halt. "What do I do now? Sit tight or speak up?"

As SUSANNA MADE her heavy-hearted way across the hallway on her road to bed, the library door opened and to her surprise her father appeared in the aperture.

"Ah, Susanna," he said. "I heard a step and thought it might be you. Come in a moment, my dear."

Surprised, she followed him into the library. He offered her a chair and when she had taken a seat, stood before her with his hands folded behind his back, his bluff red face puckered in some concern but his eyes beneath the bushy overhanging brows, shrewd. "This is a difficult business, Susanna!" he began rather pompously. "I'm not unaware..." Here Sir Frederick's pompous manner evaporated and his sentence trailed away unfinished. He mumbled instead, "Ho-hum! What's to be done, eh?" he addressed this question to himself and not to her but Susanna chose to answer it.

"We can all stop treating Hugh—Major Russell—as if he were a thief! He is not one. You know that, Papa, as well as I!"

"Dare say I do, my dear! But see here, I've given the fellow every opportunity to clear his name and he don't choose to take it, so what's anyone to make of that?"

"I don't know!" she exploded, clenching her fists and beating them impotently on her own knees.

Sir Frederick observed this sign of pent-up emotion. "Formed something of a liking for the fellow, have you? Well, well, so had I. I'm sorry, dashed sorry! But there. I don't doubt the fellow is following some code of honour of his own. But it's a deucedly wrong-headed one! He's obstinate! And he ought to know better! He's a military man. I dare say stubborn adherence to a position sometimes wins a battle, but occasionally so does a tactical retreat!

"Won't you talk to him again, Papa?" Susanna begged.

He stared thoughtfully at her pale face and earnest grey eyes. "Like your mother..." he said suddenly. "Dashed like your mamma. I dare say, you think Viola isn't much like your mamma, eh?"

She flushed. "No, Papa, she isn't. But we are all different, I suppose."

"Mmn... You've done well, Susanna, this past year. Made your step-mother welcome, put aside your prejudices against her. Please don't think I haven't noticed your effort and don't appreciate it! Only natural that you should have prejudices in the circumstances. You think, no doubt, that my remarriage is in some way a disloyalty to your late mamma. It is not. She was an excellent woman and we spent many happy years together. But a man grows accustomed to having a wife about the place... Of course, I have you, my dear. You have been a great consolation, great consolation... and I wouldn't have you think otherwise. I should have said so before, and thanked you for welcoming Viola before now, but there..."

He cleared his throat. "Your late mamma and I sometimes discussed what we should do, either of us, in the event of, ah, one of us departing this mortal world. Your mamma was quite insistent that I should remarry at once—as indeed, I was for her to do the same. It don't do to be alone. Naturally we knew we had a devoted daughter in you, my dear. But the day will surely come when you marry and have a family of your own, and then where would poor old Papa be, eh? No, no, far better I remarried, as I did."

Susanna got up and kissed him. "It's all right, Papa. I only want you to be happy. If Viola makes you happy, then that is all that's necessary."

"And you?" he returned shrewdly. "What would make you happy? Or who? That's the thing—who, not what! Not Leo, at any rate. Has the boy ever suggested marriage?"

"Leo? Yes, Papa. But I refused him."

"Wise thing. I should forbid it anyway. Silly young puppy. If he weren't my own sister's son... Throw him out..."

"Leo isn't so very bad, Papa!" Susanna was moved to defend her cousin.

"Bad? No, not bad. Useless! Worthless!" Sir Frederick was growing choleric. He began to stride up and down waving his hand to emphasize his words. "Causing trouble

in the village, too! Can't let the girls be! Village lads don't
like it!''

"Leo?" Susanna gasped. "I didn't realise... Oh..." She
fell silent and thoughtful.

"Well, don't look so shocked!" said her father irritably.
"You're not just out of the schoolroom. You must have
learned something! Not that that ridiculous charade of a
Season did you much good! Your Mamma was all for it and
Jessica Weston—a woman I never could abide! Then there
was that fellow, Billings or some such—"

"Biggins, Papa, Mr. Biggins, the curate."

"Complete idiot. But the fact is, my girl, you ought to
have a husband!" Sir Frederick stopped pacing up and
down and observed his daughter's distress. He sighed. She
was in love, of course, and it made a bad situation worse.
He really had not the slightest notion what to say to her. It
was a woman's matter and Viola should do the talking but
the circumstances, the fellow being her nephew, he could
hardly expect her to do so. "Your happiness is of some im-
portance to me, my dear." He took his daughter's hand and
patted it with clumsy tenderness. "So—ah—don't break
your heart over this, will you? Nothing to be gained by it.
Some other fellow will come along some day! Ah—hum!"
He pinched her cheek. "Run along, now!"

THAT NIGHT SUSANNA hardly slept at all and the following
day was worse. The snow lay deeper and had frozen form-
ing a hard crust. Every able-bodied manservant both in-
door and outdoor was organised into a snow-clearing party
and shovelled energetically to clear the main drive and essential paths around the house and between house and
stableyard. Hugh borrowed an old coat and went out and
joined them. Watching him surreptitiously from the window as he attacked the snow with furious energy, Susanna
realised that he was burning off his frustration and anger

with physical hard work. At one point he stood up and
wiped the sweat from his forehead with a muscular fore-
arm. He glanced up at the windows of the house as he did
as if by chance, and she wondered if he glimpsed her,
watching him. But if he had, he made no sign of it.

Apart from that, Leo stuck to her side with a devotion
which would have bordered on the embarrassing in any
other situation. Her cousin had cast off his customary in-
ertia and haunted her foot-steps about the house. When not
literally at her side, he watched her like a hawk. She would
not have been surprised if he had set up camp outside her
bedroom door, but fortunately even Leo had not thought of
this. She was not so taken up with worry for Hugh, however, that she did not notice Leo had a very odd manner
about him. Every so often a curious satisfied smile would
cross his face and he would give a little nod.

Eventually she could stand this no longer and demanded, "What on earth is it, Leo? You look—smug! Is it
because Hugh is in trouble?" Her voice gained a threatening note and her eyes sparkled warningly.

"Lor, Suky!" he said, holding up a protesting hand.
"You look as if you'd set about me if you thought such a
thing! No, it's not. It's just that something was puzzling me
and I've worked it out. Or I fancy I have! Just my simple
pleasure, my dear. You must excuse me!"

"What nonsense you do talk!" she exclaimed in exasperation.

But Leo could not be persuaded to relax his vigilance and
when she retired to her bed that night, Susanna still had not
succeeded in exchanging one word privately with Hugh. She
slept fitfully until well past midnight and then awoke again
and sat up in the darkness with her arm wrapped about her
knees to consider the situation.

It was very cold in her room. The fire had all but gone out
completely. Susanna shivered. The morning, when it came,

would begin another dreadful day such as the previous one had been. She would not be able to get anywhere near Hugh, although she had once or twice caught his eye, and she desperately wanted to tell him that she believed in his innocence and beg him to tell the truth and clear his name as she was sure he could. She firmly believed he wanted as badly to talk to her. But it will be no good, she thought. Leo dogs me like a shadow. I shan't be able to shake him off! The only time he isn't watching me, is now!

At that, Susanna unwrapped her arms and sat up straight. Yes, now... Now in the middle of the night. Everyone was asleep. She could creep along to Hugh's room and tell him all she wanted to without anyone being the wiser.

Of course, going to a man's room in the middle of the night was inexcusable behaviour in a young lady! But desperate times called for desperate measures. Susanna scrambled out of bed and flung a shawl about her shoulders. She thrust her feet into her slippers and after some fumbling managed to light a candle. The corridor was dark and unfriendly. All kinds of strange noises whispered and creaked out of the wainscoting and although the other doors she passed were all shut, she still had the unpleasant feeling that unseen eyes watched her. Before Hugh's door, at the far end of the corridor, she hesitated. Then, glancing once quickly over her shoulder, she put out her hand and turned the handle.

The guest room which he had been given was furnished with heavy, old-fashioned pieces. The bed was a four-poster. It stood in the middle of the room with its curtains drawn about it because this was a draughty room. Susanna crossed the floor, put out her hand and nervously drew back the curtain from the head.

The flickering glow of her candle showed her Hugh, sprawled out on the pillows and fast asleep. So soundly was he sleeping that she even felt a moment's resentment that he was not suffering the tormented sleepless nights she had done. But men, she supposed sadly, were different in that way. They didn't lose sleep over things which couldn't be altered. Hugh, too, had learned over the years to sleep against the noise of an army encamped about him, in filthy and uncomfortable billets, in tents, probably even out in the open, with battle looming over him, often hungry, thirsty and unwashed, drenched to the skin or freezing cold. What seemed to her a tragedy of overwhelming proportions, perhaps only appeared to him a minor inconvenience to be taken in his stride.

With these thoughts running through her head she began to wish she had not come and to think she ought to creep away again. But she found herself standing and watching him as he slept with the desperation of knowing that soon he would be gone for ever and she would never see him again. He looked younger, asleep. The lines which weather and hardship had engraved on his skin were softened. He had long, dark eyelashes which rested lightly on the skin. As she leaned over him, the eyelashes fluttered—the heat of the candle had perhaps disturbed him or a subconscious awareness that someone was there. His eyes opened, saw the shadowy form of a figure by his bedside and into them leapt a look of ferocity she had not anticipated. He pushed himself up on the pillows and snarled, "What the deuce do you want? Haven't you done enough?"

Susanna gave a little cry and stepped back but at the sound of her voice, uncertainty entered his manner. He put up a hand to shield his eyes against the glare of the flame and asked incredulously, "Susanna?"

"Yes..." she whispered.

"I thought it was—" He struggled up into a seated position. The neck of his nightshirt was unfastened and it dragged open to reveal his brawny shoulder and the tangle of dark hair on his chest. The golden candlelight emphasized the skin's shiny coppery hue. "I'm sorry, I thought it was someone else."

"Viola . . ." she said dully. "Perhaps you would prefer it were."

"I most certainly would not!" he said belligerently. Then he squinted at her in the dull yellow light and added with a return of his uncertainty, "What are you doing here?"

"I wanted to talk to you—" She began forlornly but then the words suddenly came tumbling out as if a dam had been released. "Oh, Hugh! Leo follows me about all day and I couldn't come except now! I know you didn't steal that wretched necklace and I so wanted to tell you! Is it Viola you are shielding? You can't leave here with your reputation in shreds! It's so unfair!"

Her voice had been rising on a tide of emotion and he put out a hand and hissed, "Hush! Someone will hear you!" When she fell silent, he added with a touch of humour, "You do realise that this visit of yours won't help this reputation of mine you are so worried about, and would completely ruin yours!"

"I don't care!" she said obstinately. "Oh Hugh, what are we to do?" A chill draught blew across the floor from under the door and she shivered.

Hugh saw it and said abruptly, "Here, I'll get out and you get in!"

"W-what?" she stammered, startled.

In reply, he threw back the covers and swung his bare legs out of the bed. "You get in, before you freeze. I'll sit out here!"

They exchanged places. Susanna first put down her candle on the bedside table and then hesitantly clambered into the place vacated by Hugh in the bed. It was blessedly warm. She wriggled her chilly bare toes in the heat left by Hugh's body and settled down in the dent on the feather mattress where he had been lying. Hugh obligingly piled up pillows behind her back as a support and then retreated to sit on the end of the bed by her feet with his back against one of its posts and surveyed her. He was only wearing his nightshirt and she was equally lightly clad, but in the dusky intimacy of the candleglow it did not seem to matter so much. All the same, she began to wonder if coming here had been such a good idea and how Hugh might view it. She was experiencing something of the same feelings she had when she had watched him stripped off and washing under the stableyard pump. No other man affected her like this. But then, for no other man would she have come here.

"Sir Frederick has forbidden me to communicate ever again with any member of this household, once I have left," Hugh said suddenly, interrupting a disturbing train of thought.

"Yes, I know," she replied unhappily. The reminder spurred on her resolve. This was indeed her only chance to let him know how she felt. In for a penny, in for a pound...she had come this far. Susanna put out her hands. "Hugh, take me with you when you leave! I want to go with you, be with you! Please don't go and leave me behind!"

He took hold of one of her outstretched hands but he was shaking his head and said gently, "No. Such things don't work out, Susanna! I've seen them before, these affairs—elopements or whatever you care you call them!"

"I am of age!" she protested.

"Yes, yes, I know! But that's not it. Girls are apt to lose their hearts to a red coat, you know, and as I told you, I've seen these runaway matches and how they turn out. At first all goes well, for a few weeks. Then the novelty wears off and the girl gets homesick and misses her family and friends. There are all the usual problems which any close relationship brings and quarrels. The disputes get worse—the girl starts writing pathetic letters home begging to be forgiven. Sometimes the family does forgive her—but it never forgets! The rift is always there. It's a miserable business and no one is happy. I won't let you do it.''

"What all that means,'' she said fiercely, "is that you don't want me!"

"Of course, I'm flattered," Hugh said.

"Flattered!" She was so angry and so mortified that she dragged her hand from his and struck out at him with it. But she was too far away and he simply leaned to one side so that the blow, miserable feeble effort that it was, sailed harmlessly past him. "Flattered!" she repeated. "You—you wretch! Is that all you can say?"

"No,'' Hugh said. "I could say a great deal more—but I won't, because it wouldn't help either of us."

Susanna let her hand fall on the coverlet and leaned back against the pillow with a despondent sigh.

Hugh watched her. Her long red-brown hair framed her oval face with its classical features and its look of innocence which has somehow been betrayed. He thought she looked like a Magdalene such as the Spanish painter Murillo might have depicted her. There she lay in his bed in her thin cotton nightgown through which the tantalising outline of her soft little breasts were clearly visible, though she was quite unaware of it, and yet she paradoxically deprived the scene of any of the debauchery it ought to have suggested, just by the invisible veil of her own honesty.

Hugh looked away from her, down at his hands. "You ought not to have come here, Susanna."

There was a different note in his voice. It roused an answering tremor in her breast. She whispered, "It was because I wanted so much to see you alone."

"You see,'' he said, still not looking at her. "I'm not—I'm not the sort of gentlemanly fellow you're used to. I'm not even Leo."

"I'm beginning to learn things about Leo!" said Leo's cousin sapiently. "He seduces the village girls."

Hugh looked up then and grinned briefly. "Did whoever told you that, also tell you he's currently hiding out from one of their infuriated swains? Do you know a Jem Bolger, a blacksmith?"

"Bolger? Oh, yes, a frightening fellow! Goodness," said Susanna, in awe, "Leo hasn't annoyed him, has he?"

"Just a little, but it seems Bolger's brain doesn't retain anything for very long and he can be trusted to forget soon."

"Trust Leo to do something so silly!" she said unsympathetically.

But at that Hugh suddenly became animated. He leaned forward and said urgently, "No! Not silly! Natural! That's the way men are, Susanna! Nor, incidentally, is your cousin a fool. He takes endless trouble persuading people that he is, for some reason best known to himself. He deceived me for a while. But in fact he's perfectly sensible. What's more, he's a healthy and normal young fellow and of course he goes chasing after village girls! See here, how can I explain it?" Hugh glared at the guttering candle-flame as if it might offer some help. The wax had burned down to a stub. "Young ladies," said Hugh, "might assuage their natural feelings and energies with romantic novels. Men don't— that's it. They're of a more practical turn."

"I'm six and twenty!" said Susanna with some force. "And nor do I want to sit and read about it, either!"

"Don't you, now?" asked Hugh softly. At that moment the candle flame gave a last despairing flicker and went out.

In the velvet blackness, the weight which was Hugh sitting by her feet was lifted as he stood up. Her eyes had not yet become accustomed to the gloom but she could hear the rustle of his nightshirt and sense that he had come to stand beside her. The covers twitched and Hugh slid into the bed beside her.

Automatically, she moved over to make room for him. Her heart seemed lodged somewhere in her throat, she was perspiring and her skin had become ultra-sensitive so that her whole body had leapt into a new, strange life of its own. In the very pit of her stomach there was a curious quivering sort of ache. Hugh's arm slid across her, pushing her back into the pillows beneath him.

"It's all right," he whispered huskily into her ear, his breath tingling her earlobe.

"Yes..." she mumbled, reaching up her arms to wind them round his neck. Hugh's mouth closed over hers, his tongue touched against her parted teeth and then encountered hers. She gave a shuddering gasp and thrust herself towards him, her fingers digging into the muscles of his shoulders, both frightened and excited by the proximity of that powerful body and the animal aura of aroused masculinity which it exuded. His hand slipped over her shoulders and downwards to close lightly on her breast. He was breathing heavily and muttering something by her ear into the crumpled, sweat-stained pillows which she did not understand. The gently exploring hand moved down from her breast across her stomach and rested on her hip where its touch became firmer. His fingers wrestled with the recalcitrant folds of her night-gown and his bare leg brushed against hers.

She was not ignorant of the general idea of the process but she was ignorant of its details. She was not sure which way to move. She hesitated, waiting for him to give her some indication. It was that hesitation and its reminder of her innocence in the matter, which brought Hugh abruptly to his senses. He swore luridly and pushed himself away from her, flinging himself over onto his back.

Susanna waited for a moment but he did not speak. He was panting and seemed in the throes of some violent distress. She sat up and bent over him in concern and whispered, "Hugh?"

He said in a strangled voice, "Wait!" and then without any warning, he sat up so that their heads clashed and she gave a cry of pain. "Out!" Hugh ordered hoarsely.

"W-what?" she stammered, at a loss.

"Out!" he repeated in a tone of suppressed fury. "Out of my bed and out of my room! Now!"

"But—" she began, bewildered.

Hugh leapt out of the bed and caught hold of her shoulders. He dragged her bodily from the pillows and out of the bed and shook her vigorously until her head rattled and she cried out, "Stop, stop!"

He did stop but only to repeat in a breathless, angry voice, "Out of here! You're a little fool, Susanna! You've no business here! You don't know what you're doing! You've taken leave of your senses!"

"But I thought you wanted me!" she wailed.

"I'm human, confound it!" he shouted at her and then as if he recalled they might be overheard, lowered his voice and went on hoarsely, "Of course I wanted you! If a girl comes offering herself, I'm not the man who usually says no! But neither am I in the business of seducing innocent maidens! You can surrender your virtue to somebody else, not to me! In the morning you'd only be crying your eyes out and feeling sorry for yourself!"

"I won't!" she protested.

"Yes, you will! And I'm too old a hand to fall into that trap!"

"Trap?" she cried, dismayed. "You think I wanted to trap you?"

"Out!" ordered Hugh again, ignoring this. He dragged her across the floor and opened the door. "And don't ever do anything like this ever again, do you hear me? Another fellow, not me, won't stop where I did. Now, get out!" He thrust her unceremoniously out into the cold, dark draughty corridor and shut the door in her face.

Humiliated, bewildered and dismayed, Susanna felt her way in the darkness back to her own room. In its privacy and in her own bed again, a burning flush of embarrassment swept over her, engulfing her from her toes to the crown of her head. With it she experienced a jumble of other feelings, dissatisfaction and frustrated longing mingled with outrage. She had been prepared to make for him the ultimate sacrifice, that of her honour. How could she have been so stupid? As Hugh himself said, she must have taken leave of her senses! How could he now consider her anything but a trollop? But no, at least a trollop would have given him some satisfaction in his bed. The encounter would not have ended a miserable failure. He thought her just a foolish, infatuated and ignorant girl. Worst of all, he just didn't want her. Susanna thumped her fists on the pillows as if she wished she pummelled Hugh, and then burst into sobs of despair.

"TEN O'CLOCK, MAJOR!" said Charlie Treasure, dragging back the curtains about the four-poster. "Blimey..." he added when he saw the state of the bed. "Lor..." he added to that as his eye fell on an object lying across it. He bent forward and delicately picked it up.

Hugh opened his eyes and squinted at the daylight which fell through the windows Charlie had unshuttered. "Did you say ten, Charlie?"

"Yessir. I would have woke you earlier, but no one else seems to be about much this morning excepting the old gentleman, Sir Frederick, and he's talking with his bailiff about snow damage, sir... They're digging out the sheep on the downs. Blessed if I know how they finds 'em." Charlie's voice expressed all the contempt and wonder of a confirmed Cockney sparrow for country-dwellers and their ways. "Arrangements being what they are, none too friendly," said Charlie diplomatically, "I thought I might as well leave you where you was. But they reckons it's thawing a bit and the road will be open tomorrow or the day after, and we can move out of here!''

And not, thought Charlie, eyeing the object he had retrieved, before time!

Hugh rubbed his hands over his face. ''Lord, Charlie, I feel like death.''

''Oh, yes?'' said his henchman. ''Thought you might be feeling quite the opposite, full of the joys of Spring, as they sez.'' He held out the object. ''What should I do with this sir?''

Hugh took his hands from his face and saw Susanna's shawl which Charlie obligingly pushed under his nose. ''Damn!'' he muttered. ''I'll return it, if I get the chance. Leave it there, Charlie!''

''Major,'' said Mr. Treasure. ''You knows me. I speaks my mind. There ain't no one got your interests more to heart than I has. We been in all kinds of tight spots together, Major, and got out of 'em. We're in one here on account of that there necklace and I hopes we gets out of it. But, Major...'' Charlie brandished the shawl. ''Nothing what happened in Spain, nothing what happened at Waterloo and nothing what's happened here as yet, will hold a candle to what will happen if this gets known! Think again, Major! That's all I ask!''

''Thank you, Charlie,'' said his master. ''I hope that concludes the homily? I haven't quite taken leave of my senses. Put the shawl down and mind your own business. And go and see if you can organise me a bath!''

''All right,'' mumbled Mr. Treasure, stomping away. ''Bath—a blooming cold one is what you needs!''

Susanna also rose late and left her room with reluctance. Now, in addition to facing a trying day, she had to face Hugh with the awareness of the previous night's fiasco foremost in both their minds.

Hugh was not at the breakfast table to her great relief, but Leo was. The idea of having Leo patiently dogging her footsteps all day was no more welcome than any other of her problems. She bid him good morning in a lacklustre way and poured herself a cup of tea.

Leo studied her closely over his plate of ham. "You look peaky. Not still worrying about Russell, are you? You needn't. He's the sort of fellow who always lands on his feet. Well able to look after himself. No matter how many knocks life gives him, he'll bounce back and make his way by hook or by crook."

Yes, Hugh would. But what about me? thought Susanna. Aloud, she said, "Please don't talk about it, Leo. And please don't follow me around all day! It's very tiresome. I know you mean well, but it isn't necessary." She put down her cup. "I'm going to the small morning room now where I shall be quite safe!"

Leo, torn between duty and his breakfast, said, "Fair enough. I'll join you there later."

Susanna peeped nervously into the morning room through a crack in the door. It was empty. She sighed with relief and went in. To avoid both Leo and Hugh all day was not going to be easy. She peered out of the window at the garden. Water dripped from branches and the roof, and channels had appeared in the smooth surface of the snow. It was thawing. The road would soon be open and Hugh gone. The thought, once so dreaded, had become welcome. She would have done anything now to hasten his departure. Or would she?

There was a noise at the door and a step behind her. She turned quickly, exclaiming, "Really, Leo!" But it was Hugh.

He stopped a little way from her. His coat was buttoned up and seemed to bulge slightly on one side by the armpit. He said quickly, before she could speak again, "I don't mean to disturb you. But I realised you were alone for a moment or two and I thought I had best return this myself."

He pushed his hand between the lapels of his coat and produced her shawl folded into a neat square. He handed it to her and she took it wordlessly. "Well, then . . ." he said awkwardly, and turned as if to go.

"Hugh!" His name slipped out from her mouth before she could prevent it. He turned back, his eyebrows raised enquiringly.

"About last night—" she began in haste.

He interrupted her, shaking his head. "That's all best forgotten, Miss Harte." He hesitated. "And I'm best forgotten, Susanna." He pointed at the window and the scene of thaw beyond. "I shall be able to leave tomorrow. Not before time. It was not my intention in coming here to do any harm, but I seem to have done a great deal."

"It was not your fault!" she mumbled.

"It certainly wasn't yours," Hugh said, suddenly gentle. She looked up at him, her eyes glistening with unshed tears. He stepped forward and took her hands. "Don't cry, my dear. Not over me, at any rate. I really am not worth it!"

She said miserably, "You are kind and honourable and loyal and I love you."

"No, you don't. I don't know what it is you feel, but you'll get over it."

Stung, she burst out, "Kindly allow me to know what I feel!"

"And kindly allow me to know better! I—I do have a great respect of you and liking. You should know that if that were not so, I should not have stopped when I did last night. As it was, it is because I like you, that I behaved as I did and put a stop to things. Please try and understand."

There was a distant clatter and the sound of Leo's voice approaching the morning room.

"Here comes your faithful watchdog!" said Hugh with a grimace. "It will save further argument and more broken furniture, I dare say, if I take myself off now!" He released her hands and walked quickly out of the room.

He must have passed by Leo in the hallway and she heard a brief exchange of voices. Then Leo appeared in the door. At the sight of his cousin, standing clasping her shawl in her hands and as immobile as a statue, he said quietly, "I'm too late, I see! Well, I tried . . . Are you still going to tell me you aren't in love with the fellow?"

"No," Susanna said almost inaudibly. "I am in love with him, but it won't make any difference."

Leo hunched his shoulders. "It might, my dear, it might. At least, it makes up my mind for me. Excuse me, won't you?"

He disappeared out of the room before she could stop him and left her crying out anxiously, "Leo! What are you going to do?"

CHAPTER NINE

HILL, LEO'S VALET, opened the door of his master's room and exchanged stares of veiled hostility with Charlie Treasure, who stood outside in the corridor. Then he turned and announced majestically, "Major Russell's man is here, sir, as you requested."

"Fine!" came in Leo's voice. "Show him in here. Treasure!"

Both gentlemen's gentlemen sniffed, Hill because he disapproved of Charlie, and Charlie because he disapproved of Leo. Charlie sidled into the room in his shuffling fashion and stood peering down critically at young Mr. Drayton.

Leo was comfortably established before a roaring fire. He lounged in one chair with his feet up on another, wrapped in a dressing gown of startling crimson hue and peeling an orange.

Looking like the blooming Sultan of Turkey, observed Mr. Treasure silently to himself. Idle young imp. Aloud he said, "You wanted me—sir?"

Leo ignored the appreciable pause before the 'sir' and waved a hand affably at Charlie who looked, if anything, even more mistrustful and contemptuous. "Yes, Treasure. You and I must have a little talk. No one hanging about out there in the corridor, is there, Hill?"

"No, sir," said Hill lugubriously. He picked up Leo's coat and went to hang it up, every line of his body bristling with affronted dignity.

Leo threw a piece of orange peel towards a waste-paper basket and missed. "Your guv'nor is in a bit of a pickle, ain't he?" he asked carelessly.

"He might be!" snapped Charlie.

"Come along, Treasure. You know he is. Good name tarnished, thrown out of the house..."

"I don't," interrupted Charlie vehemently, "discuss the Major's business wiv no one. And specially not wiv you. You ain't, as I sees it, the Major's best friend in this house."

Leo had finished his orange. He swung his feet down from the chair, swivelled round and jabbed a forefinger at Charlie. "Now that, Treasure, is where you are wrong! I am, possibly, about to prove myself the best friend he has! Major Russell is in a very tight spot and you and I together are going to get him out of it, with a little luck and always supposing I'm correct in my deductions. You do want to help your guv'nor, I suppose?"

Charlie's wizened countenance, which so far had expressed nothing but open scorn, now became wary. He eyed Mr. Drayton from top to toe as if studying him anew. "But why should you want to do that, sir? Seems to me, the Major is a bit in your way here—not mentioning the lady's name—and you'd like to see him go."

"I don't deny it. But there are other considerations. It's a question of putting my money on the right horse, you see."

Charlie thought he was beginning to see. However, since Mr. Drayton's history was littered with instances of putting money on the wrong horse, he was not encouraged. But he was intrigued.

"You mean," he said bluntly, "you fancy there might be something in it for you, if you was to help the Major."

"Yes, Treasure. You put it exactly."

Charlie relaxed. If Leo had protested that he had nothing but Major Russell's good name at heart and a desire to do the right thing out of a sense of duty, Charlie would have stomped away in silence without waiting to hear any more. But Leo's honesty impressed him. The young blighter was by way of a bit of a twister, but at least he knew it and owned up. There are situations in life in which a rogue is sometimes worth two honest men. Charlie, who was desperately worried about his master, felt a twinge of hope.

"And what, sir, did you have in mind?"

"We have to act quick, Treasure, and on the quiet. I hope you don't mind catching a chill, because it's out of doors we're going. So wrap up warm, my good fellow...and go and get the gardener to lend you a rake with a long handle and I'll dig out a fishing net."

Charlie's eyebrows twitched but he made no comment on this curious set of orders. He merely turned and stomped away to carry them out.

A LITTLE LATER a curious duo set out across the rapidly thawing snow. Leo, wrapped up to the ears in a greatcoat, carried a fishing net on a pole of the kind used by anglers to land salmon. Charlie, almost invisible beneath layers of mufflers, carried a long-handled rake and for good measure, a boatman's hook. Leo was particularly anxious not to be seen from the house, so they followed a roundabout route and arrived at last by the bridge over the lake in the abandoned water garden.

No one who did not know the layout of the park would have been able to identify it beneath its covering of snow. As before, however, it presented a picturesque scene. The icicles which hung from the parapet of the bridge dripped a tinkling series of droplets onto the thin film of ice below which covered the lake. The melting snow rustled down from the tree and every so often a loud crack marked the disintegration of ice somewhere. A flash of scarlet signalled a robin, hopping from branch to branch and curious to know what the humans were doing here. The sun shone brilliantly from a clear blue sky with the startling brightness of winter, reflecting blinding flashes of light from the snow layer as if the ground were strewn with diamonds.

Leo stopped and slapped his chilled hands together. "There's a punt, Treasure. It's always been kept under the bridge, tied up to the stonework. I hope it's not holed. I don't suppose anyone has used it in years. Suky—Miss Harte—and I used to fool about in it as children. It might be rotten and that will give us a problem."

Charlie set down his burdens and went to search under the stone arch of the bridge. "It's here, sir, and just about in one piece. It will float, but I wouldn't like to say for how long."

"Fair enough," said Leo. "If we do a little groundwork first, we should not have to be too long on the water. Follow me." He led the way up onto the bridge and began to mutter, half to himself and half to Charlie beside him.

"This is where she was standing when I saw her. Let's see...She's not as tall as me and her shoulder would be at about this height... She's about as tall as you, Treasure... Come over here... Yes, but she couldn't throw as well as you. Women don't play cricket, Treasure."

"No, sir."

"Rotten throwers. Ever seen a woman try and throw a ball?"

"No, sir. I've seen a couple of 'em throw an empty gin bottle pretty accurate."

"I am not speaking of your harridans, Treasure, I am speaking of ladies! Let's see, if she stood here—and she'd be in a bit of a hurry... I wish it had snowed before she came and then we would have had a set of footprints. Bit of luck, from her point of view, it snowing after she came... She stood here, all of a to-do and agitated, looking around in case she was spotted and she threw..." Leo made a weak motion with his arm. "You try it, Treasure, you are more her height, only not too hard...you're a gently nurtured female, remember!"

"Yes, sir," said Charlie without blinking. He made a feeble throwing movement.

Leo, shading his eyes against the brilliant sun, watched an invisible trajectory. "Good. So it must have landed about out there..." He pointed.

"There's a hole in the ice, sir!" said Charlie suddenly with scarcely suppressed excitement. "Look there, sir!" He pointed towards a spot short of the middle of the pond where the thin layer of ice was broken by a round dark circle.

"Right! Come on, Treasure!" ordered Leo briskly, suddenly sounding as excited as his companion.

They ran down to the punt, threw in their implements and scrambled unsteadily into their rather unseaworthy craft. Leo grasped the punt pole and pushed off from the side, propelling them towards the spot on the ice. Charlie crouched at the other end, peering down. "Here, sir!" He threw up a hand. "Stop here!"

Leo thrust the pole down into the mud. "Go careful, Treasure. It may have sunk into the mud on the bottom. Try the rake."

Charlie stood up, balanced insecurely in the punt, and gently lowered the rake through the hole in the ice. For some minutes he prodded around and drew it across the bottom of the lake. Then he gave a low whistle. "Something down there, Mr. Drayton!"

"For pity's sake!" exclaimed Leo in agony. "Be careful! Try the net!"

Charlie grasped the salmon net and began a highly difficult manoeuvre with the rake in one hand and the net in the other, rather like a housemaid with a dustpan and brush, but trying to operate both on the end of poles.

"Got it!" he squawked suddenly.

"Careful!" howled Leo again, as Charlie began to lift his discovery towards the surface.

"Dropped it!" said Charlie and swore colourfully.

"Let me..." urged Leo.

"No, you stay there, sir, and stop us floating away! Here, I got it again!"

With agonising slowness, he manoeuvred his catch to the surface and swung the net over the punt. Water and weed dripped from it and when he lay it down on the floor of the punt, a large puddle began to form. In the middle lay a mud and weed covered object.

"Well done..." said Leo very faintly.

"I takes it all back, sir," said Charlie.

"What?"

"I thought you wasn't up to snuff, sir. But you are. I takes it back."

"Thank you, Treasure, a generous admission. I say," said Leo with a grin, "you are aptly named, aren't you?"

Charlie looked up at him and his dour lined face creased into a rare smile and he chuckled. "Reckon I must be, sir!"

"Right, home we go!" Leo pushed the punt towards the shore. As they reached it, however, they suddenly became aware that they had an observer. Unnoticed by them both as they concentrated on their task and in their subsequent glee, he had come out of the trees and stood by the edge of the pond, waiting.

"Oh, Lor..." said Leo dismally. "Bolger..."

"I bin looking for you, master," said Jem, eyeing Leo. His huge hams of hands, hanging loosely by his side, opened and shut menacingly.

The punt touched the bank. Charlie, who had thrust their catch into his pocket, jumped ashore and stood, holding the reversed rake ready as a weapon. Leo still stood in the punt, unwilling to trust himself to land and his opponent.

"See here, Jem," he said placatingly. "I haven't touched her. I swear it! I don't know what she's told you—but I didn't do a thing!"

"You asked her," said Jem sullenly. "You said you buy her a petticoat! Then she comes to me and sez, You don't go buying me no petticoats, Jem! Gentleman at the Hall offers me a new petticoat. I don't never hear you offer me no new petticoat, Jem!"

"Yes, well, she would..." said Leo hastily. "You ought to have bought her a present, Jem. Ribbons or something. Girls like that. But I was only fooling, Jem, I swear!"

"You got Lucy Bagshot into trouble Christmas afore last," said Jem accusingly.

"You're not walking out with Lucy as well, are you?" asked Leo apprehensively. "I did pay old Ned Bagshot off, pretty generously I might say!"

"I ain't walking out with Lucy," said Jem carefully, "I'm walking out with Bessie. Mr. Lucas is putting the banns up at Easter and I don't want you messing with her before that. That's my right, that is."

Leo thrust his hand into his pocket. "See here, Jem, how about a couple of guineas to buy yourself a wedding coat and we'll call it quits, no hard feelings!"

Jem stared at him. Then he stepped forward. Leo thought he had come to take the money and relaxed his guard. But without warning, Jem stooped, grasped the end of the punt and lifted it easily clean up in the air with his blacksmith's arms. Leo toppled out with a resounding splash and a yell into the lake.

"Now we're quits!" said Mr. Bolger with some satisfaction, as he turned and tramped away.

Leo sat gasping and spitting water in the shallow but freezing edge of the lake, weed festooning his hair.

"Give us your hand, sir!" urged Charlie from the bank, reaching out first with his hand then with the rake. "You'll catch your death!"

Leo rose to his feet, rivers cascading from him and his coat pockets bulging with trapped water. He grasped the end of the proffered rake and stumbled to land, coughing and spluttering. "T-Treasure!"

"Yes, sir?"

"You m-mind you tell your guv'nor what I've s-suffered on his account! Oh Lor...." He shivered. "Let's get back, th-that confounded ape, Bolger..."

HUGH WAS SITTING in his room before the fire, unmoving. His dark eyes watched the crackling flames but his swarthy features showed no expression. Eventually a spark flew out and landed on the carpet. He stirred then and rubbed it out with the toe of his boot and sighed. There was a tap at his door and he called out wearily, "Come in!"

He did not look up as it creaked open and the draught blew across the back of his neck. But when a female hand was lightly laid on his shoulder he glanced up, only to look away again.

"I looked all over the house," Susanna said. "I was afraid you and Leo might have gone out for some awful purpose."

"Pistols for two?" Hugh reached up and patted her hand where it lay on his shoulder. "Not Leo's style. Nor mine, come to that. I don't know where your cousin is. I can't even find Charlie."

Susanna sank down onto the carpet by his feet with her hands in her lap and stared in turn into the fire. "You weren't downstairs and I suppose you feel you can't come down and sit with us, so I came up here."

"To keep me company in my disgrace? I appreciate it, Susanna, but we have said our goodbyes."

She said obstinately, "You have said yours, I have not said mine, and if you are going away so soon then I at least want to be with you for the short time you are still here."

Hugh touched the top of her head and then withdrew his hand.

"You are still determined to leave tomorrow?" she asked in a muffled voice.

"Yes. Even if I wished otherwise, your father would insist on it. I am in disgrace and have been shown the door, remember!"

She struck her hands together in frustration. "It is so silly! I wish you would tell the truth, Hugh! Why can't you? At least, tell me!"

"I tried to write you a letter," he said. "I wanted you to have some idea what it was all about, but then it seemed to me it was only making things more difficult."

She sighed and leaned her head against his knee. After a moment, he reached down his hand and gently caressed the nape of her neck. "Susanna? When you came here last night, it wasn't that I didn't want you, you know..."

"Yes, I know."

"I ought to say," Hugh said ruefully, "that I hope you meet someone else. Just at the moment, however, I can't say I hope anything of the sort." She looked up quickly and he went on, "But that is just my male vanity, you know! No man likes to think another gains what he has missed out on! But you will meet someone else, and so you should."

"No, I won't!" came in a muffled, obstinate voice.

"Come along," he said gently but firmly, taking her arm. "Get up off that carpet. Ladies don't sit about like that."

"They don't get stuck in the mud and they don't go climbing into men's beds, either." In a spurt of independence she added crossly, "And stop being so nice to me! If you cared twopence about me, you'd tell me the truth!"

Hugh said, "Oh, Lord..." so wretchedly that she immediately scrambled to her feet and onto his knee and threw both arms tightly about his neck, pressing her face into his shoulder.

"Oh, Hugh, dearest! Why is it?"

He hesitated for a moment and then put his arm round her and said quietly and with some difficulty. "I—can't tell you. Not because I don't want to, but because other people's happiness would be destroyed. No one can build their own happiness on the misery of others."

"And what if I am miserable, and you, too?"

Hugh took his arm from her and commanded, "Sit up!"

She took her arm away from his neck and her face from his chest and sat up straight on his knees, gazing mistrustfully at him and sniffing a little.

Hugh asked, "Haven't you a handkerchief?" and when she obediently produced a small scrap of lace-trimmed nonsense, added, "Good Lord, what good is that?" and dragged out his own capacious handkerchief.

Susanna blew her nose unromantically and wiped her eyes and said, "What is it? Don't start telling me about all these people you know of who eloped and lived wretchedly ever after, because I don't believe it always turns out that way."

"Not always, but enough times to make anyone think twice. I've told you, Susanna, I intend to go to Italy. Yes, I know!" he went on quickly when he saw her mouth open. "I'm sure it sounds idyllic and you would love to see the Italian lakes and the Alps and all the rest of it. Who wouldn't? But I'm not talking of the Grand Tour at the end of which you would return home laden with diaries and sketch-books and souvenirs ready to bore your friends to tears for a twelve-month! I'm talking of making your life permanently in a land which isn't yours, learning to speak another tongue and follow other customs. Your father would be horrified and quite rightly. If any daughter of mine proposed doing such a thing, I'd be furious. There is another matter, too.''

Here Hugh broke off and looked both embarrassed and obstinate.

''What is it?'' she asked with sinking heart.

''I may be an adventurer,'' said Hugh, ''but I've never been a fortune-hunter. Thanks to my Italian inheritance, I'm not without some fortune of my own, but that is the sum total of it. Before I had that, I had nothing. You will be your father's heiress, as he is unlikely to have children from his marriage with Viola. You could do a great deal better than me, Susanna, and so you should!''

''That is utter nonsense!'' she exclaimed. ''If by 'better' you mean 'richer,' then you should know yourself what rubbish you are talking!''

''Besides money, there is reputation. Mine has always been slightly questionable and now I am reputed a thief into the bargain, or have you forgotten the Harte necklace? No—I didn't steal the wretched thing! But I stand accused of doing so and I shall leave this house under that cloud. It's impossible that you could leave with me. I will not drag you around Europe with my reputation clouding yours, tied to a bad marriage of which you would eventually wish to be free! There it is, and don't, please, argue with me.'' There was a pause and he added more quietly and uncertainly, ''I wish it were otherwise, but it isn't.''

There is nothing I can say, thought Susanna sadly. It's no use and we both know it. He accepts it and so must I. She put her hand on Hugh's chest in a gesture of understanding, and felt his heart beating against her finger-tips. She had to accept his notion of honour. She could not force him into a course of action he believed strongly was wrong. As for his secret, whatever that was, he believed he could not tell her. It was his decision and she must respect it.

The door creaked again. Charlie Treasure put his wizened face through the crack and surveyed the scene before the fire, Hugh seated with one booted foot propped on the brass fender and Susanna perched on his knee, mournfully twisting her handkerchief in her fingers. *She's found out he's going off wivout her,* thought Charlie resignedly. *Just when I was beginning to think that this time he wouldn't cut and run.* He cleared his throat.

"Begging your pardon, Major—and you, Miss—and not being one to interrupt where I'm not wanted unless it's urgent—"

Hugh twisted his head towards the door. "What is it, Charlie?" he asked sharply but it seemed to Susanna with some relief in his voice. The interruption was not unwelcome.

"I think you should come down to the drawing room, Major. And the lady, too. Mr. Drayton has got something to say. He'd have said it an hour ago, only he had to 'ave a bath first. Best come down sharp-ish, Major!"

THEY ARRIVED in the drawing room to find they were not the only ones summoned. Sir Frederick stood before the fire, his hands behind his back and a suspicious look on his face.

"This had better not be one of your pieces of nonsense, Leo! I warn you, boy! If you have brought everyone down here on some fool's errand, by Harry, I'll turn you out of this house today!"

"A-tchoo!" came from Leo by way of reply. "I swear, Uncle..." He dragged his handkerchief from his pocket and blew his nose noisily. "Oh, there you are, Russell, and you, Suky..."

There was a movement from the far side of the room. Viola turned from the window and stared coldly at them all.

"I don't like practical jokes and I don't like to be teased. I wish you'd tell us what all this is about quickly, Leo."

"Well," said Leo boldly, "I don't know that I have much to tell *you*, Lady Harte..."

She started and paled and Sir Frederick said sharply, "What's this, Leo?"

Leo's reply was delayed by his being obliged to take his handkerchief again.

Hugh said, "Think twice, Drayton. If you're doing this to clear my name, forget it. That's my business."

"Your trouble," said Leo belligerently, stuffing his handkerchief into his pocket. "Is that you are damn self-centred! What about Suky? What about me, come to that? Anyhow, Uncle Frederick, did you bring down the Harte necklace?"

"I did," said Sir Frederick. He took his hands from behind his back and removed the familiar black case from his side pocket. "I echo Major Russell's words, young man, and say, think twice! No jokes and no tricks, now!"

"It's not—a-tchoo!" Leo's protest was drowned in another shattering sneeze. He gestured towards the table. "Be so good, sir, if you would...I've caught a confounded cold. If you would open the jewel case."

Sir Frederick narrowed his eyes beneath his bushy brows but said nothing. He opened the jewel case and laid it on the table. The necklace winked up at them all, glittering coldly in its purple nest.

"This isn't a trick," said Leo, "although it may look like one." He reached into his own pocket and produced an identical case, rather stained with water.

Susanna gasped and caught at Hugh's hand. He squeezed her fingers warningly. Viola gave a low moan and sat down abruptly on the nearest chair as if her legs had turned to jelly.

"Here we go," said Leo with some satisfaction. He opened the water-stained case.

"Good Lord!" exclaimed Sir Frederick. There was a stunned silence all round. Then Sir Frederick walked slowly up to the table and stared down at the two open cases, side by side. "But, dammit, there are two of them! Two Harte necklaces! Identical, by Harry!" He glared at his nephew. "What's this, Leo? What's going on? Which of these is the Harte necklace?"

"Ah, which indeed?" said Leo. "I fancy Major Russell can explain that."

Sir Frederick swung round and glared at Hugh. "Major? I'd be obliged!"

Hugh sighed and released Susanna's hand. He moved towards the table but before he spoke, he looked down the room towards his aunt's pale figure, in silent question.

Viola said in spiteful tone, "Tell them, Hugh. I'm sure you can explain it perfectly."

He nodded. "Well, Sir Frederick...there are two, as you see. One, of course, is real. The other is made of *strass*. That is to say, paste. The technique, as you may know, was perfected by Joseph Strasser, a German jeweller and chemist in the last century."

Susanna said involuntarily, "So that is Joseph Strasser!" and then bit her lip and fell silent.

"There have always been imitation stones made from glass," Hugh went on, "but Strasser found a way of backing faceted glass 'jewels' with quicksilver and launched a whole new business in paste imitation gems. The very best, and one of those two necklaces is an excellent example, can fool the untutored eye quite easily. No jeweller is fooled, naturally. And, of course, paste gems don't last indefinitely. They lose their sparkle eventually, unlike the real thing. But for a while, they can be passed off as the real thing with great success."

"Then how are we to tell which—?" began Sir Frederick, bewildered. He looked all at once much older, not only his sixty-five years but more. Susanna went to him and put her arm on his. He did not seem to be aware of her presence, but only looked at Hugh.

"A diamond is very hard, the hardest natural substance we have," Hugh said. "I've demonstrated all this to Miss Harte so what I show you now, is old hat to her. See here, I'll do it differently..." He dug in his pocket and produced a penknife. Taking up the necklace in the clean box, he opened the blade of the knife and scraped at one of the stones. Then he held it out to Sir Frederick. "You see, the knife makes no impression. Now this one," Hugh put down the necklace and took up its fellow which lay in the water-stained box. He repeated the action with the knife and this time, when he held it out, said, "You will observe, it is scratched. Paste stones are quite soft in comparison with the real things."

"Now wait!" exclaimed Sir Frederick. "Which of these was retrieved from your bag, sir? This one, surely, the one I have just brought downstairs!" He touched the first necklace. "But you have demonstrated the stones to be real. You, sir, had the real necklace in your bag! Where has this other imposter come from?" He pointed at the necklace in the water-stained case.

"From the lake in the old water-garden," said Leo indistinctly from his handkerchief. "Charlie Treasure and I fished it out a couple of hours ago."

From the other end of the room, Viola said very quietly but distinctly, "You had better begin at the beginning, Hugh, and tell them everything."

He said soberly, looking at her, "I didn't know Drayton had discovered the other one. I had no idea it was in the lake."

She sighed. "I had no idea you had the real one, Hugh. I swear it."

Looking at her stepmother, Susanna thought Viola had never looked more beautiful. She stood as still as a statue, her lovely face impassive and appearing carved out of ivory. There was a dignity about her that had never been apparent before.

Again Viola said, "Tell them, Hugh. Tell them all of it."

"As you wish," he said quietly.

CHAPTER TEN

HUGH STOOD FOR A MOMENT frowning and with his eyes
narrowed as if he squinted at some distant, dust-laden horizon. He turned over in his mind how to begin now as once
he would have assessed enemy strength and battle lines.
How out of place he looks in this comfortable country
drawing room, thought Susanna sadly. With his burly
frame, he would have dominated the room even if all their
eyes had not been fixed on him. She could not help but draw
a comparison between Hugh and the unfortunate Leo.
Hugh's tanned and weatherbeaten skin, practical manner
and unruly black curls touched with grey at the temples drew
unfavourable attention to Leo's good but weak features,
indolent manner and artificially curled hair. Not that poor
Leo looked his best just now, the end of his nose red and his
eyes watering.

Hugh looked up at last, finally bringing his gaze back to
the immediate circle of watching faces and said briskly,
"Well, to begin at the beginning is best, I dare say. But some
of what I say must of necessity be unwelcome." He turned
to Sir Frederick. "I am sorry, sir. I shall not, of course,
speak a word unless you agree."

"Out with it!" growled Sir Frederick hoarsely. "Every
damn thing! No fudging! I wasn't born yesterday!" He
stamped his cane on the floor.

Susanna sat down on a nearby chair. The emotional im-
pact of their conversation in Hugh's room had not left her,
but now it was temporarily pushed into second place by the

drama unfolding before her. Viola was in her direct line of sight. Her expression as she watched her nephew was a curious mixture, flitting from resigned if apprehensive to mocking and back again. However fraught her own situation, she was not beyond enjoying Hugh's obvious unwillingness to wash family dirty linen in public as he was now being forced to do.

Hugh nodded at Sir Frederick in acknowledgement but turned back to Viola. "Viola, dear aunt . . . if you want me to stop, shout out. I shall and wild horses won't drag out another syllable!"

She only gestured impatiently. "Why waste time? Get it over with, Hugh!" She turned in a swirl of silk skirts and put her back to the company and Susanna felt an involuntary spark of admiration for the defiance in every line of Viola's slim figure. She recalled the gruesome account of a prize fight Leo had once witnessed and chosen to regale her with despite her declared lack of interest. He had described one of the combatants as being 'down but not out'. Viola had retired to her corner, but was still able to come out fighting.

"Very well. I shall have to go back to the time of my aunt's first marriage. She will not disagree with me now, I think, if I say it was a very unwise match. One ought not to speak ill of the dead, but Harry Devaux was a wrong'un in every sense. We all knew it but couldn't get Viola to see it. So she skipped out and married him secretly." Viola's shoulders moved very slightly in a shrug. Hugh caught Susanna's eye and looked away.

So that is partly what preys on his mind, thought Susanna. Viola eloped and it all went wrong. Hugh's family has seen one bad marriage in it and doesn't want another. But heavens above! I am not Viola and I don't believe Hugh is another worthless Harry Devaux!

"I shan't go into details," Hugh was continuing. "But Harry was a gambling man. He ran through his own fortune and Viola's. I have to say that his influence on Viola was always bad. She became addicted to gaming almost as badly as he was and got used to frequenting the same fast company. After Harry died, she set about running up debts on her own account and became involved in one scrape after another. When we heard, that is, when the family heard—because I was away soldiering so it was all news to me when I came home! So, then, when the family heard Viola had married Sir Frederick, it was seriously alarmed. Viola had never shown any sign of appreciating how foolish her behaviour was and if she were to involve someone of the standing of Sir Frederick in her scandals...well, I don't need to expand on that.

"When I arrived back in England, I thought I was coming back to a little peace and quiet after several years of war. Instead, I found myself in the middle of battleground of a different kind. The family held a conference to which I was summoned. I went very unwillingly. I was asked if I would make enquiry about Viola, to establish how she was behaving and if there was any matter which—which, oh dash it, which would need hushing up. You see, we all suspected Viola had debts of which she had said nothing to Sir Frederick."

"Did you, my dear?" asked Sir Frederick mildly.

"Yes, Freddie..." came in Viola's voice, almost inaudible.

He walked slowly and stiffly down the room to where she stood and took her hand. "My dear child, why did you not tell me?"

She turned slowly and gracefully with a beautiful gesture of despair which would not, thought Susanna, have disgraced Drury Lane. "I was so afraid, Freddie. You would think me such a flibbertigibbet. They were nearly all gaming debts. I didn't dare to tell you of them. I thought, you wouldn't marry me."

Sir Frederick muttered, "Tsk, tsk, tsk!" reprovingly but said nothing more, only glanced at Hugh and nodded for him to continue.

"I must state frankly," Hugh said, "that the family set me to track down Viola on the principle that a poacher makes a good gamekeeper. I knew all the right places to enquire and whom to ask. I say this because I don't want it thought I was chosen because I was a model of propriety and clean living myself. Quite the reverse. In addition to that, Viola and I had always been friends, and I hope we still are, and they thought she would be more likely to listen to me. In that they were wrong!" A touch of asperity sounded in Hugh's voice and Viola cast him a quick, apprehensive glance.

Susanna thought, I do believe he is the only man of whom Viola is afraid. He understands her too well. At one time, this observation would have made her jealous, but now she was able to view it with detachment.

"I discovered the debts, of course," Hugh was saying, "that wasn't difficult or a surprise. But I discovered something else which was ... They had been paid. Not, however, by Sir Frederick. They had been settled by Lady Harte. But how could Viola have come by such a large amount of money, all at once and suddenly without anyone's knowledge? Well, the answer, as I eventually discovered, lay with a couple of rogues by the names of Tobias and Josiah Clay. These two fine fellows would protest they were respectable businessmen. They are, in reality, pawnbrokers. Although I dare say they don't call themselves that! They operate discreetly from unmarked premises—nothing so vulgar as a pawnbroker's sign for them—and at a good address. Not anyone may go to them. They deal only with clients who have been recommended. Their speciality is advancing money on family jewellery and silver to help out impoverished gentry. Discretion is their byword.'' Hugh paused. ''Lady Harte had pawned the Harte necklace.''

''Good Lord!'' exclaimed Sir Frederick.

''Well, sir,'' said Hugh hurriedly. ''It wasn't lost. Pawning isn't like selling outright. The Clays still had the necklace although if Lady Harte did not redeem it, they would eventually have disposed of it, very profitably. But they still had it so the family and I got the money together somehow and we redeemed it. I put it in my pocket and rode here, intending to return it to Viola with a stern lecture!''

Hugh pulled a grimace. ''Imagine my surprise when I walked in here on New Year's eve and saw my aunt apparently wearing it! It took no great amount of brain power to work out that the necklace she was wearing was a paste replica. She dare not let Sir Frederick see the real necklace was missing. But I couldn't show that unless I got my hands on it and tested it in the manner I've demonstrated to you. But it was obvious Viola had no intention of letting me examine it. So, what was I to do? Just give Viola the real necklace and demand the return of the other?

''I needed time to think and went to Newbury and stayed with Broughton. He told me that he had heard a rumour back in the summer that one of Lady Harte's guests at the Hall had undertaken a secret commission for her in London. This, presumably, was the making of the replica and the disposal of the real necklace. I made up my mind that this time, Viola must be brought to see how foolish—even mad—was her behaviour. I wanted her to realise how stupid it was to keep her acquaintance with her dissolute friends. I wanted her to face up to what she had done, to admit it in her own voice. She never would, you see. She would never admit that anything she did was wrong or take responsibility for any mayhem she caused.''

Hugh looked down the room at the lovely sculpted profile of his aunt, averted in classic pose. "I'm sorry, Viola, but it had to be done." He turned back to his audience. "So, when I returned from Newbury, instead of handing over the real necklace, I tried to force Viola to admit to me what she had done. But she wouldn't. What I did not realise was how much my presence here and my obvious suspicions had panicked her. She decided that the time had come for the 'Harte necklace' to disappear. She staged a robbery. The idea was, that the necklace would be supposed lost for good and the truth never come out. How Drayton worked out it was in the lake, I don't know."

Hugh ceased speaking and everyone looked expectantly at Leo, who hovered by the fire snuffling miserably into his handkerchief.

"Oh, that..." said Leo nasally. "Bit of luck, really. I chanced to meet Lady Harte on the bridge a few days ago. Thought it was a bit odd, her being out there on a cold morning. She was already planning the robbery and looking for somewhere to ditch the wretched necklace, but I didn't realise it then, naturally. When the necklace disappeared, I still didn't catch on, until I was cursing the thing to myself and wished it at the bottom of the lake, as one does... Then I realised, that's exactly where it was. Bit of a chance, but worth taking. Treasure and I fished it out. And then," concluded Leo gloomily, "Treasure fished me out. I think I've caught pneumonia."

"Drink some brandy and hot water!" said his uncle unkindly. "Nothing wrong with you. Young healthy fellow ought not to mind a dousing in cold water! How d'you come to fall in?"

"Slipped..." said Leo unconvincingly and his uncle snorted.

"I had decided I was wasting my time trying to get my aunt to see sense," Hugh took up the tale. "So I packed my bags with the intention of handing over the real necklace privately to Viola just before I left. However, the robbery caught me on the hop. My bag was searched before I could return the real one and it was found there. That's just about it . . ." Hugh finished and fell silent.

"I am so very sorry, Freddie," said Viola in a quiet little voice. "It was very bad of me, all of it. I didn't mean to get Hugh into trouble. I didn't know he had the real one. I thought, he just knew about it. To pretend it had been stolen seemed such a good idea." For a moment, Viola almost sounded wistful. "But then, when I did it, it wasn't snowing. When it snowed I got frightened."

Susanna frowned. "Why?"

"No tracks," said Hugh. "No tracks on the snow together with the roads being blocked meant the thief was probably still in the house, not miles away as Viola hoped we would all think."

"But I still didn't know it would be found!" Viola said in a burst of spirit. "I didn't know either of them would be found. I didn't know Hugh had the real one and I didn't know Leo would go fishing about in that lake for the paste one!" She threw Leo a look of intense dislike. "I don't know why he had to go meddling!"

"If he had not," said her husband firmly, "none of this would have come to light. Your nephew would have remained branded a thief, my dear."

"Oh, yes . . ." Viola heaved a sigh. "I suppose so. Freddie . . ." She turned her large, dark-lashed eyes beseeching up at him. "I've behaved so badly but I'm truly sorry. I'll never, never do anything so awful ever again! I promise! I shan't invite any of my old friends here again and if they come, I shall send them away! I shall turn over a new leaf and tell you everything! Please do forgive me, Freddie!" Her eyes filled with tears which brimmed pathetically on the lids but somehow managed not quite to spill over.

She's done that trick a few times, thought Susanna unkindly. I wonder how she manages it? She glanced at Hugh and saw a cynical expression on his face. His thoughts mirrored hers. He had probably witnessed the tearful scene a few times before.

"There, there..." said Sir Frederick gruffly. "No tears, eh? It's all over and done with. The necklace is back and no harm's done. Come along..." He put his wife's arm through his and led her away.

The door closed on them and the remaining three people stayed where they were in silence. Hugh glowered morosely into space. Susanna thought gloomily, Papa has obviously forgiven Viola everything. I suppose he would do anything to keep her here. But if he is still in love with her, at least it is not a blind love. He is aware now of what she is capable. Perhaps he will keep a closer eye on her in future. Leo sneezed and broke the silence at this point. Susanna, seeing that both necklaces lay forgotten on the table, observed aloud, "I had better put those away! Although if I had my way, I should like to throw them both back in that lake!" She picked them up and took them out.

Now that the two men were alone, Hugh stirred. "I am sorry if you've caught a chill, Drayton. It was in my cause and I should thank you, I suppose."

"It was that blasted clodhopper, Bolger!" explained Leo, aggrieved. "He was waiting on the bank and pushed me in!"

For the first time, a hint of amusement appeared briefly in Hugh's eyes. "Bad luck!"

"Well, at least, he'll forget about it now," said Leo optimistically. "As for the necklace, I was a bit doubtful, you know, that we'd find the thing. I had Charlie scraping along the bottom of the lake with a rake. We were just lucky, really."

"Tell me," Hugh asked curiously, "Just why did you take so much trouble on my account? I should have expected you to be quite pleased at the idea I was about to be thrown out in disgrace."

Leo sniffed loudly. "I wouldn't have shed any tears for your sake," he admitted frankly. "But I'm not an idiot. Suky's head over heels in love with you—" Hugh's face flushed but Leo either did not see it or pretended not to. "And so I thought, it wasn't fair on her in the first place. Then, I didn't like the way Viola treated Suky. Hang it, Suky is the daughter of this house and is here by right! Thirdly, I didn't like the way Viola treated me—although I don't have any right to be here. That last one is the nub of it, really." Leo paused. "You see, Uncle Frederick wouldn't throw me out, left to himself. But Viola might have got him to do it. So I thought, time to spike Viola's guns. Make everyone obliged to me. They can't throw me out now—not knowing what I do! They'd all be scared I'd go telling everyone!"

"Do you know?" Hugh said seriously. "You are an utter young scoundrel. If I weren't obliged to you myself, I'd punch you on the jaw, even given your sad condition!"

"That's good, coming from you!" said Leo snappily.

Hugh considered this. "Fair enough, I suppose. I'm not the one who should be casting stones. See here, though, haven't you ever wanted to get out in the world and make something of yourself? Stand on your own feet? You're perfectly capable. Don't you want to be independent?"

"No," said Leo simply. "I like it here. It's very comfortable."

"Well, I'm damned . . ." said Hugh, for once completely at a loss.

Leo stuffed his handkerchief in his pocket. "Are you going to marry Suky?"

"No!" Hugh said sharply.

Now it was Leo's turn to look aggressive. "You damn well should!"

"No, I shouldn't. Susanna and I have already discussed all this. I'm going to Italy to live. I don't intend to wrench her away from her family and tie her to my extremely uncertain future."

"What will you do, now?" Leo asked after a pause. "Just go away?"

"Yes—and as soon as I can. Right now, in fact. The snow has thawed enough to open the road and my bags are still more or less packed." Hugh hesitated. "You'll have to keep an eye on her for me, Drayton. I'd be obliged. If any other unsuitable character such as myself shows his face, send him packing. I'd like to think someone was watching out for her."

"Oh, I'll keep an eye on her," said Leo. "Although you ought to be doing that yourself. You want to slip away without anyone knowing, I suppose?"

"Yes." Hugh held out his hand and Leo grasped it. "Goodbye, Drayton. I'm sorry our acquaintance wasn't more amicable. You are by no means the fool you try so hard to appear."

"You are," said Leo rudely. "You're a complete and utter jackass. That's the trouble with honour and scruples and all the rest of it. They make a fellow act like an idiot."

"I'll bear it in mind!" Hugh promised ruefully.

Leo sneezed. "You won't get far today."

"I can get as far as Newbury and Broughton's house."

SUSANNA RETURNED both necklaces to her step-mother's dressing room and retired to her own room to compose herself and think things over. At least Hugh's name was now cleared, but she still did not know what he would do. She hoped he would stay. Susanna glanced towards the window. Water ran down it in rivulets as icicles on the eaves

thawed in the afternoon sunshine. There was no chance that
a further snowfall would lock them all in again. She rose to
her feet and set off downstairs.

Half way down, she met Leo comping up, handkerchief
in hand.

"I'm going to bed," he explained.

"I'll send Mrs. Merrihew up with some tea," she said
sympathetically. "I'm so sorry you've caught cold, Leo, and
very grateful, truly, for what you did."

Leo flushed crimson. "I didn't do it just for him, you
know. He knows that and so should you." He paused awkwardly. "He's gone, Suky."

Susanna's heart seemed to wither in her chest. She whispered, "Already?" Leo made no reply and she burst out,
"Why didn't you stop him?"

"Couldn't have done if I'd tried. He'd made up his mind.
He's set off for Newbury and that friend of his, Broughton." He eyed her white, stricken face and added roughly,
"Look, it's not that he doesn't care about you, Suky. It's
because he does. He's trying to protect you. You won't talk
him round because he's obstinate. He's that sort of fellow.
He believes what he's doing is right and no one will shake
him. Let him go, Suky. It's best."

He still received no reply, cast her an agonised look,
mumbled some further apology and stumbled past her up
the staircase to his own room. Susanna went downstairs to
the now deserted drawing room and sat down. In her mind
she peopled it again with them all as they had stood here less
than an hour ago. She could see Hugh, his tall, strong em-
battled frame and sunburned hands moving in expressive
gestures as he spoke, Leo hovering by the fireplace, her father grimly determined to hear the worst and Viola equally
determined to wriggle out of the tight fix in which she found
herself. Susanna no longer cared about any of them but
Hugh. To go on living here in this house, seeing the others

every day and being reminded of what had happened was an unbearable prospect.

The door opened, but she did not look up until Viola's voice asked, "Susanna? Do you mind if I come in and talk to you?"

Susanna turned her head. Lady Harte, taking this as acquiescence, came into the room. She held in her hands a flat, familiar ebony box which she put on a table near Susanna. Then she sat down and folded her hands in her lap.

"You think me heartless," she said. "But I didn't know Hugh had the real necklace."

"Possibly," Susanna replied coldly. "But when you did know, you still did nothing. You could have spoken up at any time and cleared Hugh's name. You didn't. If Leo had not found the paste necklace in the lake, you would have let Hugh ride away from here totally disgraced. Papa might forgive you, Viola, but I never shall."

A pink flush touched Viola's ivory cheekbones. "I understand that. Are you in love with Hugh? I suppose you are. Women generally are. I wouldn't waste time sighing over him, if I were you. If you knew as much about men as I do, you'd know none of them is worth breaking your heart for." She gave a bitter little grimace. "I dare say, you fancy I don't love Freddie. But I do, in my way. Freddie was kind to me when the rest of the world wasn't. Of course I don't love him in the way I loved Harry, my first husband. That was a marriage of passion, but I don't suppose you would understand that—you are such a, a cold sort of person. A perfect ice-maiden. Perhaps that's what took Hugh's eye, the challenge... Well, I have mediterranean blood. I do know what it is to suffer for love."

"And I don't?" Susanna said evenly, her eyes sparkling.

Viola hesitated. "But you're not like me, Susanna." She seemed to think this a sufficient explanation and gestured now towards the ebony box. "The Harte necklace. The real one. Freddie has taken the paste one and is going to supervise its destruction. A pity, because it's a very good copy. Freddie and I have discussed the real one." Viola hesitated. "Freddie thinks I should give it to you. It was your mother's and she meant you to have it. I wasn't able to look after it very well. So you had better have it, as Freddie says."

"I don't want it!" Susanna's anger flared up.

"Oh, don't be silly," said Viola, unmoved. "Of course you do. Any woman would."

"I—am—not—any—woman!" breathed Susanna.

Viola surveyed her. "You shall have it, anyway. Freddie insists."

Susanna cast the ebony box a weary glance.

"Freddie says, if you had had it from the first, this would not have happened," Viola said thoughtfully. "But I dare say it would... I'd have pawned something else. I had to. I was desperate for money. But you wouldn't understand that, either. Living down here, buried in the country, of course you are virtuous! You've never had the chance to be anything else!"

Susanna opened her mouth in surprise and outrage and then closed it again.

"You need to get out in the world!" said Viola calmly. "You need to find yourself alone and cut off from your family as I was—then see how you would get on! I know what I did was wrong, but if I were in the same situation again, I'd do it again. Only I shan't be in the same situation again. I'm not that stupid!"

She rose to her feet. "Freddie is quite right and you should have the necklace. I'm sorry to lose it, naturally, but I do agree with Freddie." For the first time Viola gave an unforced smile of genuine wry humour. "It takes temptation out of my path, you see."

She walked serenely out of the room and left Susanna contemplating the ebony box. After a moment she stretched out her hand and took it up. Opening it on her knees, she stared down at the glittering gems. "Before Hugh came here," she thought, "I did want this necklace. Of course I wanted it. I hated seeing Viola wear it and I told Leo so. If I don't want it now, it's because I want something else more—I want Hugh." She touched the diamonds with her finger tips. They were hard and unfriendly.

"But this shall help me get Hugh back!" Susanna declared suddenly.

A new resolution fired her as a plan formed incoherently in her mind. Hugh had gone, but only as far as Newbury. It was still light. She jumped to her feet and opened the door. One of the maids was crossing the hall outside. It was Mary. Susanna beckoned to her.

"Mary! I want you to do something for me, but you mustn't let anyone else in the house know!"

"Goodness, Miss!" said Mary, goggle-eyed and eaten up with curiosity.

"Go down to the stableyard and tell Hatton to saddle my horse."

"Bless us, Miss!" exclaimed Mary. "you can't mean to go riding out now! Tis very unpleasant outside, Miss Susanna. The snow has turned to all slush and mud and you'll be that dirtied!"

"Never mind!" Susanna said crossly. "Go and tell Hatton to be ready in twenty minutes!"

She left Mary to go on her errand and ran upstairs to change as quickly as possible into her riding habit. She pushed the necklace case into her pocket and taking a heavy woollen cape, hurried downstairs again.

She was able to reach the stableyard undetected but there saw to her annoyance and dismay that Hatton had saddled two horses.

"You need not come with me, Hatton!" she said crossly.

"And what'll the master say, if I let you go alone?" retorted the groom sourly. "There's young Master Leo been telling Sir Frederick all kinds of tales about me and getting me into trouble. All on account of the bay being lame, what isn't my fault! He'd like to see me turned away, would Master Leo. Well, I ain't running no risks of Sir Frederick's displeasure. If I was to let you go alone, it would cost me my place."

Susanna heaved a sigh of frustration but had to submit. Hatton was a disagreeable man and his company was the last she would have chosen, especially as she was about to do something of which her father would not approve and it was possible Hatton would cause trouble. But she allowed him to help her into the saddle, wrapped the woollen cloak warmly about her and set off, Hatton following behind.

The groom's suspicions were not aroused until they reached the main road, or what could be made out of it. It had disappeared during the snowfall, but now a narrow track had been opened up, deep in slush and mire which splashed up to the horses' bellies.

"Where be we going, Miss Susanna?" Hatton reined up and indicated the difficult going. "'Tis bad enough here and will get worse."

"We are going to Newbury, Hatton," she retorted calmly.

"Why, us shall never get there before dark!" exclaimed the groom truculently. "We should turn back now, Miss."

"You can, Hatton, if you want to. I shall go on."

"Now see here, Miss Susanna!" argued Hatton, riding up alongside her and putting his horse's head across hers to force her to stop. "Sir Frederick wouldn't go along with this!"

"Don't be impertinent, Hatton!" she said sharply. "It is my wish to ride to Newbury, and your task to escort me. I don't require your opinion."

"Tis my job to see you don't come to no harm!" said Hatton obstinately. "Road is unsafe up ahead, they sent word down and told us this morning. 'Tis open, but half crumbled away with the mud."

Susanna exclaimed, "Get out of the way, Hatton!" and brandished her whip at his horse so that it flung up its head nervously and she was able to push her own mount past and take the lead again.

Hatton followed behind grumbling mutinously. Secretly, Susanna was afraid Hatton might be right. Early January twilight was already closing in. The road was difficult to pick out, being in places no more than a single track between high banks of muddy snow. Despite the woollen cloak she was chilled by the cold wind. But she pressed on making as much speed as she could, although twice the horse slipped badly and she was almost flung from the saddle.

Hatton's lamentations grew worse, especially when they arrived at a picket of red flags.

"There, Miss, see what I mean? Now we must go back."

There had been a landslip caused by the thaw and the road had collapsed completely on one side. The surviving track was so narrow it hardly seemed possible a horse could safely traverse it. Susanna reined up to take stock of the situation.

"If we do get past," said Hatton discouragingly, "*If,* mind you! There's no saying we can get back again, certainly not in the dark. We might get to Newbury tonight, but we shouldn't get home again."

"Then we shall find an inn in Newbury, Hatton." Susanna urged her horse forward. Her heart was in her mouth, but the animal picked its way slowly and hesitantly across the muddy slope and arrived safely on the better stretch of track beyond.

Hatton followed successfully but only a quarter of a mile further on they came across the sad and alarming sight of the mail coach from Newbury, stranded. It lay tilted on its side in a deep gully. All the packages on its roof had been thrown off and lay scattered in the snow and mire. The passengers huddled together keeping warm as best they could in the slush and three horses stood, unhitched from the traces, heads drooping dejectedly. Enquiry informed them that the coachman had taken the fourth horse and ridden back to Newbury to fetch help. It was doubtful he could bring any before nightfall now. The passengers were gloomily debating whether to manhandle the coach upright themselves, so that they could at least shelter inside it until morning.

Susanna and Hatton left these unfortunates and pressed on towards the town. It was dark when they arrived. They halted and Hatton enquired sarcastically, "What now, Miss?"

"I want to find the residence of a gentleman named Broughton," Susanna said, realising belatedly that she had no idea whether Hugh's acquaintance lived in the town itself or outside. "Where should I enquire, Hatton?"

"If he's a gentleman he'll buy in his groceries from the best shop in the town," said Hatton. "He'll have an account there. That's the best place to ask."

She was grateful for this practical advice but suspected that Hatton was more anxious to secure shelter for himself for the night than to help her. It was now about six o'clock and quite dark although the streets were still busy. Enquiry at the high-class grocer's in question told them that Captain Broughton lived on the outskirts of town, but fortunately not in the countryside beyond. Susanna and Hatton arrived at last before the house, a pleasant double-fronted dwelling of prosperous appearance with well-lit windows.

Susanna's satisfaction at having arrived in one piece was now tempered with deep apprehension. It was possible Hugh was not here, which would be highly embarrassing. It was probable that he was—which was worse. Hatton helped

her from the saddle and she stumbled, so stiff and cold was
she, to the door and knocked loudly.

After a few moments, it was opened by a butler. He
looked understandably startled at seeing a travel-muddied
lady, blue with cold, on the step.

"Good evening," said Susanna with as much aplomb as
she could muster and trying to keep her teeth from chatter-
ing. "I am seeking Major Russell. I understand he is a guest
of Captain Broughton. I am Miss Harte."

"Yes, Miss..." said the butler and she felt her heart rise.
The man stood aside. "Won't you come in, Miss?"

He left her in the hall. Susanna's momentary euphoria
vanished and was replaced by extreme nervousness. She
looked about her. The house was comfortably and prettily
furnished. It did not have the robust masculine air of a
bachelor gentleman's dwelling. A gentleman would not have
chosen those ruched drapes. A sudden prickle of alarm ran
up her spine. At that moment a light step sounded and a
woman's voice asked, "Miss Harte?"

CHAPTER ELEVEN

SUSANNA TURNED. Before her stood a very pretty and becomingly buxom young woman in a blue gown. A lace cap was pinned atop a profusion of fair curls, the silk strings twisting enticingly about her white neck. Seeing her visitor's confusion, she smiled again and repeated, "Miss Harte? How nice to meet you. Hugh has told us so much. I am Louise Broughton."

Susanna mumbled, "Oh..."

A look of concern crossed the other's smooth brow. "Oh, but my dear Miss Harte! You are quite frozen! Do, please, come into the small parlour immediately by the fire!" She hastened forward and stretched out a neat little hand on the third finger of which gleamed a gold band.

"Oh!" repeated Susanna but differently. "Oh, I see! Mrs. Broughton! yes, how—how kind of you. I'm so sorry to disturb you unannounced at such an hour. You must think it excessively odd!"

But Mrs. Broughton was chivvying her into a nearby room and making tut-tut noises of concern. "Do sit down, Miss Harte, and let me give that damp cloak to Harper. I'm sure, if you sit about in that, you will take a dreadful chill on the chest. I'll have Harper fetch some tea."

Susanna found herself settled before a merrily crackling fire in a comfortable and untidy little room. An open sewing box on the floor, coloured silks tumbling out of it in profusion, two ladies' magazines abandoned on a couch and a small stack of novels of the kind lent out by circulating libraries pronounced this to be Mrs. Broughton's private sanctum. As if to confirm this, Louise said brightly,

"I'll go and tell Hugh you are here. He and William are playing billiards in the study. I'm sure, I don't know how they can see what they are doing for cigar smoke. William was so pleased to see Hugh back again. I think he finds this settled provincial life very tedious after so many years campaigning, and I must confess, so do I."

"You accompanied your husband to the wars, ma'am?" asked Susanna, surprised and not a little envious.

"Heavens, yes! William is quite hopeless at looking after himself. He's all right in army matters, you know," said William's obviously doting wife, relegating the conduct of the war against Napoleon to its proper place second to domestic issues, "but when it comes to replacing worn linen and such things, I'm sure the poor man has no idea even how many shirts he owns. Hugh, of course, is quite a different proposition, very practical. Hugh is the sort, you know, who no matter the circumstances, always makes out. I'm sure, one could put Hugh down on a desert island, like Robinson Crusoe, and he'd manage perfectly well to make himself comfortable. Why I remember before Salamanca, when we were without shelter of any kind and provisions of all kinds very short, Hugh managed to find—but there, you mustn't let me start prattling on. I'll go and tell him you are here."

"Mrs. Broughton!" said Susanna apprehensively. "It's possible Major Russell might not be very pleased to hear it. I mean, he's certainly not expecting me."

"Of course he will be pleased!" said Mrs. Broughton airily and, as it turned out, inaccurately. She disappeared on her errand and Susanna was left nervously contemplating her hostess's unfinished embroidery. The Broughtons were obviously old friends of Hugh's and knew him well. She both longed to talk to them and learn more about Hugh, envying them the shared experiences and adventures, and was appalled at what had already been said. Louise's cheerful description of Hugh as "always making out" and being able to fend comfortably for himself as well on a desert island as on the plains of Salamanca, was not encouraging. Why should such a man want to encumber himself with a wife? He didn't need one. He probably didn't want one. Susanna regretted bitterly her impulsive decision to follow him.

But it was too late to do anything about it. A heavy male footstep sounded in the hall outside, the parlour door flew open and Hugh, in waistcoat and shirtsleeves presumably straight from the billiard table, appeared like an avenging fury, filling the doorway and towering over the seated Susanna.

"What the devil are you doing here?" he demanded before she could speak a word in explanation or defence. He shut the door quickly behind him and advanced on her. "Are you out of your mind? That road is scarcely passable! I take it you didn't come alone?" He thrust a red and angry face with jutting jaw and scowling brow at her.

"No, Hatton has come with me," she stammered, quailing before such open rage and grateful that the groom had accompanied her after all. "He—he is still outside and, I dare say, very cold and cross."

"He's going to get colder and if he fancies himself out of humour, he's yet to hear what I have to say to him! He'll have to go back tonight and tell Sir Frederick you are safe. There is no question of your returning tonight. You can go back tomorrow!"

"But how can Hatton return in the dark?" she faltered. "With the road so bad?"

"He can take a closed lantern and how he makes his way is his concern. He is a damn fool to have brought you!" Hugh snarled.

"It is not Hatton's fault!" she was impelled to defend the luckless groom. "I ordered him."

"Hatton is employed by Sir Frederick and not by you, Miss Harte! Sir Frederick would certainly not approve this ridiculous escapade and Hatton must be aware of it!"

Fortunately Harper arrived at this moment with the tea and provided Susanna with a respite in which to gather up her wits and steel her resolve. Hugh had fallen briefly into a smouldering silence and when Harper had left, she began to speak at once before he could start again.

"I know you are angry, Hugh, and I did expect it! But you have said your piece and now it is my turn to say mine!"

"Speak on, then!" he said uncompromisingly.

"You should not have slipped away like that," said Susanna, conquering the tremor in her voice with some effort, "I'm sure Papa must be very distressed—after all the, the trouble. I know he'd want to apologize to you."

"I don't need Sir Frederick's apology, nor does he owe me one! You may tell him so."

"Well, what about me?" returned Susanna, forgetting her nervousness and growing aggressive in turn. "I won't be left behind like an unwanted portmanteau! I am coming with you, Hugh! I don't care where we go or what you say, I am coming too!"

He sighed in exasperation. "Now, look here, Susanna, we've been through all this—"

"No, we haven't. Not now things have changed. You are no longer in disgrace and there is no question of your reputation tarnishing mine! We shall not end up like Viola and Harry Devaux, how could we? We are neither of us so stupid. I know you say you have only a modest fortune but we shall be quite all right, because, you see, I have brought this." The time had come to play her trump card and take a desperate gamble. She pulled the ebony box out of her pocket triumphantly and displayed it before his nose.

She thought Hugh was going to have a fit. His face drained of colour beneath the bronze and then flooded with crimson. The veins in his neck swelled and he swallowed in a constricted throat, his lips moving soundlessly. "Susanna..." he said hoarsely when he was able, his voice sounding as if he were being slowly strangled, "Is that, by any chance, the Harte necklace?"

"Yes, and I haven't stolen it. It's mine now. Papa made Viola give it to me. So it is mine and I can do what I like with it."

"You've gone out of your mind," said Hugh simply. "How could you possibly imagine I would take you with me with that—!" He flung out his hand and pointed at the jewel case. "With that wretched thing in your pocket! What makes you think I want ever to see it again? As for living off the proceeds of it, which is what I imagine you mean..." He fell silent, bereft of speech. Susanna waited. "Susanna," said Hugh at last. "I shall take you back to the Hall myself tomorrow, together with the necklace, and explain, if it's possible, to Sir Frederick. I dare say Louise will find you a bed for the night."

"Yes, Hugh," said Susanna meekly.

A sudden light showed in his dark eyes. "So that's it!" he exclaimed. "Good Lord!" He leapt towards her and for one dreadful moment she thought he was going to attack her physically. "You knew very well that is what I would say! You knew I would insist on taking you back to the Hall myself. You knew there wasn't a chance I'd agree to go on with the necklace in our possession." He shook a clenched fist under her nose. "All this is a trick to get me back to the Hall! Once there, I suppose you fancy you could wheedle me around to changing my mind about going!"

"Yes, I know it's a shabby sort of trick, but I didn't know any other way!" said Susanna defiantly. She stood up and

flung up her head proudly, her grey eyes meeting his unflinchingly.

"Well, it won't gain you anything!" Hugh said shortly.
"I'll take you back, explain to your father, and leave again.
And you, my girl, will do as I say this time and stay be-
hind!"

WELL, IT WAS WORTH A TRY, thought Susanna sadly to herself later that night. But I can't say it has worked. She did
not know quite what she had expected, other than as Hugh
had correctly guessed, he would be obliged to take her home
himself. She had vaguely imagined he would be impressed
by her initiative and devotion. He was not.

They had spent a curious evening. Both the Broughtons
seemed blissfully unaware of any tension in the atmosphere
or to find it in any way strange that Miss Harte had dropped
out of nowhere to land on their doorstep on a winter evening—like the orphan of the storm, thought Susanna ruefully. Their cheerful kindness contrasted starkly with
Hugh's lowering countenance and monosyllabic conversation. Broughton himself had proved a good-natured young
man who obviously liked his comforts. It was a little difficult to imagine him suffering the hardships of campaign life,
but then, he had taken along his briskly efficient little wife
to cosset him. Meeting him, Susanna understood why.

Louise Broughton had happily fussed over her, too. Susanna was established in a comfortable little bedroom and
even a nightgown had been laid out for her ready on the bed.
As she surveyed it rather gloomily, a tap on the door heralded her kind and voluble hostess herself.

"I came to see if you have everything you need, Miss
Harte."

"Yes, thank you very much. You are very kind," said
Susanna dolefully.

"Now, my dear!" said Louise, darting forward and taking her hand. "You must not give up, not now!" Susanna looked at her a little startled and she went on, "You are just what Hugh needs! A woman with some spirit who won't be browbeaten and content just to do whatever suits Hugh! He needs someone who can stand up to him! I'm sure I've told him so a dozen times. The clinging vine sort of woman wouldn't suit Hugh at all. That is the mistake all the others have made!"

All? Susanna began to wonder how many lady-loves had passed through Hugh's life, legions probably. Louise proceeded to confirm this dismal calculation. "We've known Hugh for years and I've seen so many of them, women I mean, just come and go. They think, you see, that a very—very masculine sort of man like Hugh will take to some pretty little doll of a woman, but of course, he just gets tired of them and off he goes! What he needs is someone like you. He couldn't possibly get tired of you, because he would never be knowing what you were going to do next. It would keep him on his toes and he wouldn't have time to get bored! Hugh needs a challenge."

"Thank you," said Susanna unconvinced. "I'm sure you mean it kindly, but it's possible, you know, that Hugh sees it differently."

"Nonsense," said Louise airily. "Why, as soon as I set eyes on you downstairs, I knew you were the girl for Hugh. I told him so. Anyway, we knew it already, from the way he talked of you. Not so much what he said, you know, but the way he said it. Hugh admires you, Miss Harte!"

It would be nice to think Louse was right, but if this were the case, Hugh showed precious little evidence of it the next morning. "Hurry along!" he said uncharitably, "We have to take advantage of what little light there is. It will be a very unpleasant journey but don't complain to me, because you have brought it on yourself!"

The thaw had continued overnight. The melting snows had broadened out the accessible road surface but rendered it even more slippery and soft. The horses' hoofs sank deep into the mud and came out again with sucking noises, fetlocks caked in mire. The going was tediously slow and few other travellers had ventured out on the road. Hugh kept a forbidding silence except when issuing orders on how best to negotiate difficult patches. The sky was overcast, grey and dismal, a chill damp wind seemed to blow right through Susanna's clothes to her skin and she did not know when she had felt more downhearted. But she did not dare utter a word of complaint, knowing that it would be ill-received and more than likely call up another stern lecture.

The abandoned mail coach of the previous day was still in the same place with a gang of sturdy fellows now digging it out. The passengers had struggled through snowdrifts the previous evening to a singularly primitive hostelry where they had all passed a miserable night. They had now returned and were sitting silent and frozen in a depressed group, perched on pieces of rescued luggage. The foreman of the gang of labourers, hailed by Hugh, stopped shovelling snow to look up and wipe his brow with a brawny wrist.

"'Tis even worse up ahead, sir! 'Tis fallen away all on one side and what's still there is very soft. We shall have to dig out a whole new path for the mail here, and if you care to wait, you can follow on behind us. But we'll be an hour or more."

Hugh cursed under his breath and glowered at Susanna as if it were all her fault. She was looking very cold and miserable muffled in her cloak with her white face fixed on him in silent despair, but he hardened his heart. "We'll go on. A horse can get through where a wheeled vehicle can't!"

After a while they reached the picket of red flags and Hugh reined up. The road surface here had certainly deteriorated since the previous day. Large chunks had simply slid away down a gully and the remainder was a sea of churned mud. Hugh twisted in the saddle to face Susanna riding behind him and called out, "We may have to turn back, after all, and wait for the man to dig through. This is dangerous."

He looked worried and for the first time since the previous evening, his anger had disappeared, overcome by more immediate concerns.

"I came through with Hatton yesterday," she replied, shivering. The wind blew across the downs like a knife. She had begun to feel that if they did not reach the Hall soon, she would simply tumble from the saddle with cold. The idea of waiting like the mail's unfortunate passengers until a new route could be cut through the drifts was not to be contemplated. "I'm sure we can do it."

"H'm..." muttered Hugh. "I might, I don't know about you."

"I'm a perfectly capable horsewoman!" she said sharply, which was true. "I'm not afraid!"

"I'll go first," he said. "Follow after well back."

She sat and watched him pick his way over the mud. When he reached firmer ground he reined up and turned and signalled to her to follow. Susanna shook the reins and spoke encouragingly to her horse. Despite her professed resolve, she had to admit she was terrified. The horse hesitated, sensing the uncertainty of the ground. Hugh shouted, "Come on!" Susanna urged the horse forward again. For some reason, she did not know why, she put her hand to her pocket at that moment to check that the jewel case was still safe. Her fingers touched it and as they did, the path beneath her horse disintegrated.

There was a rush of cascading rubble and a strange creaking noise as earth parted and they plunged into nothingness. The horse neighed shrilly and made a wild leap for safety but in vain. Susanna was flung from the saddle, her hand still grasping the jewel case, and found herself sliding uncontrollably down a steep slope of slush and mud. Scrabble desperately though she did for a hand or toehold, there was none. The earth beneath her was moving inexorably and with terrifying speed, and she began to tumble faster, too. Rocks and clods of earth began to bounce past her, whilst she was powerless to protect herself from their assault and one must have struck her on the head because everything went black.

She came to, it must have been minutes later, to the sound of Hugh's voice, shouting out her name. She had come to rest at the bottom of the landslip. Her arm was twisted beneath her and when she tried to move, a blinding pain shot through it. She was in any case, trapped. A heavy weight of mud lay across her legs, but she was, thank God, lying on her back and staring up at the grey sky, and not face down in the stifling ooze.

There was a noise of someone slipping and sliding down the slope to land beside her. "Susanna?" came breathlessly in Hugh's voice. His anxious face appeared above her, smeared with mud and hatless.

"I'm all right..." she managed to falter. "But I can't move."

"I'll get you out of there..." He scrambled past her and began to dig frantically at the mud covering her legs with his bare hands. Eventually he got her free and took hold of her shoulder to drag her up. She gave a cry of pain and he exclaimed, "Is it your back?"

"No—no, only my arm..." she gasped. "The—the left one..."

"Here, put your right arm round my neck..." She managed to do as he asked and somehow with his support, although slipping and sliding and occasionally going backwards when trying to go forwards, they eventually reached the top of the slope.

Susanna's horse had rolled over and miraculously scrambled up covered in mud but unharmed. It stood with lowered head, shivering in the wind. Hugh dragged out his handkerchief and folded it into a triangle. "This is the best I can do for a sling. I fancy you've broken your arm. Can you get up in the saddle?"

He grasped her about the waist and lifted her up. She scrambled somehow into the saddle, fighting back waves of pain. It was when she was perched aloft at last and grasping at the reins and pommel with her good hand that she remembered the necklace. She gave a gasp of dismay and fumbled at her pocket.

"What is it?" asked Hugh sharply.

"The—jewel case..." She stared at him wildly. "It must have fallen out!" She looked frantically about her. "Where is it? I had it in my hand when I fell..."

"In that case," said Hugh, "it is somewhere under all of that!" He pointed at the mound of mud which had fallen from the road. "It might be found when the road is repaired in the Spring. But I fancy they will bring in a new load of rubble to make a foundation and lay it over that. I'm afraid, Susanna, the Harte necklace appears to be lost."

Susanna put a mud-stained hand to her face.

He said gently, "I'm sorry..."

"I am not!" came the fierce reply. She took her hand away, her grey eyes sparkling at him in her grimy countenance. "I'm glad! I'm glad the wretched thing is lost! Leo said it was evil, and so it was! It was certainly unlucky! I'm glad it's gone!"

There was a pause. "Come along," Hugh said hoarsely. "Time to be getting home." He stretched up a hand to touch her elbow and a crooked smile crossed his muddied features.

THEIR ARRIVAL and desperate appearance caused consternation in a household already alarmed. A cold, tired and vindictive Hatton had returned in the middle of the night taking his revenge by maliciously informing all at the Hall that Miss Harte had run off with Major Russell. Leo, who had developed a raging fever, had been forcibly restrained from rising from his sick bed and setting out in hot pursuit and Sir Frederick was about to send out messages by courier to every magistrate and militia post for miles around demanding the fugitives' immediate arrest.

All this was now forgotten and the surgeon sent for to set Miss Harte's arm. He did this as she lay on the sofa in the morning room and although she tried not to, she could not prevent herself crying out in pain, while Hugh sat by her, ashen-faced himself and still wearing his muddy coat and boots, and doing his best to comfort her.

After that she was helped up to bed by Mrs. Merrihew and Mary. Hugh remained sitting at the table in the morning room in his mud-stained coat, with his face in his hands.

After a while he was aware of someone else's presence. Sir Frederick put down a bumper glass of brandy beside him and ordered, "Drink that down, my boy! Settle your nerves."

"I think," Hugh said quietly, lifting his face from his palms, "I was never so frightened in my life . . . not even at Waterloo. Only a fool claims he's never been frightened, but when Susanna went over the edge down that gully in a landslide of mud, it was the worst moment of my life. I thought she—"

"Yes, yes. . ." interrupted Sir Frederick. "But she wasn't and isn't and you are both back in one piece."

Hugh said soberly, "I'm very sorry, sir. It was all my fault."

"Hum!" said Sir Frederick.

"The necklace is lost," went on Hugh. "it's under a ton of mud, sir."

"Best place for it," said Frederick calmly.

"Yes," Hugh said.

"Glad to see you back, both of you," continued Sir Frederick. "I did wonder if you would bring her back. You hadn't struck me as the sort of fellow who headed for Gretna Green with an heiress and a fast post-chaise, given half a chance. Now that you are here, and if you have pulled yourself together, I fancy you and I have something to discuss. I imagine you have a request to make of me, and if you haven't, sir, I should like to know why! You may make it, Major Russell, you may make it. It will not be viewed unsympathetically."

SUSANNA, also well plied with brandy, had fallen into a restless sleep. When she awoke it was evening and a candle had been lit by the head of the bed. As she opened her eyes she saw that Hugh sat beside the pillows, hunched on his chair in the dull golden glow, waiting and watching for her to awake. She turned her head on the pillow and smiled faintly at him. He reached out and took her right hand where it lay on the coverlet.

"How is the arm?" he asked huskily.

"Throbbing a little, but not too bad."

"The surgeon says it's a clean break and will mend well," he answered awkwardly, his voice sounding thick and unnatural.

"Did you tell Papa about the necklace?"

"Yes . . . it's all right. He is of a mind with me that it's in the best place, lost under a hill of mud and rubble. I hope it stays there for ever. You know, Susanna, when you said you were glad it was gone, I was, even in that awful situation, I was so happy to hear you say it, almost as happy as I was to see you safe and up on that horse again—" Hugh's voice broke off in a choked sound and then he burst out wretchedly, "Oh Lord, Susanna, forgive me . . . !"

"Oh, Hugh darling, please don't!" she began, dismayed to see him break down, a thing she had always thought unimaginable. She tried to move on the pillows and reach out to comfort him, but the broken arm gave a sharp stab of pain and she was obliged to fall back. "It was my silly nonsense," she said miserably, "riding after you like that and forcing you to come back!"

"I shouldn't have left," he said vehemently. "But I'm here now and won't go off and abandon you ever again, I swear."

She fixed her eyes on his grim countenance. "I won't make you stay, Hugh, if you don't want to. I don't have that right. I should not have tricked you into coming back."

"I should have come anyway, eventually . . ." he said quietly. "I could not have stayed away for long. I love you, Susanna."

Her heart gave a little leap of joy and her fingers gripped his. "Really, Hugh? I mean, I don't want you to say it if you don't mean it. That would be far worse than your not saying it at all. I don't want you to say it because you feel guilty about the accident or the necklace being lost. Neither of those things matter!"

"I do feel guilty about both those things," he admitted. "I thought you were going to be killed, Susanna. It was the worst experience of my life. I thought the whole damn lot was falling down on top of you and you'd be buried alive. I think I shall have nightmares about it for the rest of my life. But I think I loved you from the moment I first came, even if I didn't altogether recognise it. It was when I realised—or when I thought I realised that you had begun to care for me . . . You do still care for me, Susanna? I shouldn't blame you if you never wanted to see me again."

"Of course I care for you!" she said energetically. "I should have thought that was obvious!"

He gave her a rueful smile. "Well, it was—and very alarming at first. You see, I knew then that the time had come for me to go. I've always done that in the past. I'm afraid, cut and run when things looked like getting serious. Only, this time, I found I didn't want to. That's when I knew you weren't like anyone else, and frankly the idea rather scared me at first. I fought against it in my stupid, muddle-headed way. You see, it was a little like the two Harte neck-laces. All my life I'd dealt in a paste kind of love, not the real thing, only an imitation which lost its lustre after awhile like all paste gems. But this time I knew I'd fallen head over heels in love for the first and only time in my life, and there would never be anyone else for me, only you. For the first time, I had the real thing in my possession and didn't quite know what to do about it. I was proud of it and somewhat in awe of it. I both wanted to keep it with me all the time and was frightened I should spoil it and destroy it. That was the thing which frightened me most, Susanna. I thought I could so easily take you away from all the people who loved you and had cherished you all your life, and only make you unhappy myself."

"As if I could know any kind of true happiness without you!" she said reproachfully.

"I certainly could not hope to find any happiness anywhere ever again without you," he confessed. "And in the end I had to admit it to myself, I had to surrender, after all. Haul down my colours and hand 'em over to you for safe keeping, together with my heart."

"Oh, Hugh," she said, "I do love you so much!"

He put the little hand which lay in his to his lips and kissed it gently. "Your father says he has no objection to our being married. If you'll have me, that is."

She whispered, "Oh, yes..."

He leaned forward eagerly, "And I shall take you to Italy on our honeymoon trip, Susanna! You shall see the lake and the gardens and the house and all the rest of it! You will make it complete. Then we shall come back here, because that is your father's wish... But we shall go back to Italy to visit regularly if you don't mind spending your time travelling back and forth across Europe and dividing your days between two homes."

"Wherever you are, that is my home," she said softly.

He stood up and bent over the bed to kiss her mouth. "No victory we ever won against the French can hold a candle to this. And I'm not even the victor this time. I'm your prisoner for ever, my own dearest little mudpie."

Harlequin Intrigue®

QUID PRO QUO

Racketeer King Crawley is a man who lives by one rule: An Eye For An Eye. Put behind bars for his sins against humanity, Crawley is driven by an insatiable need to get even with the judge who betrayed him. And the only way to have his revenge is for the judge's children to suffer for their father's sins....

Harlequin Intrigue introduces Patricia Rosemoor's QUID PRO QUO series: #161 PUSHED TO THE LIMIT (May 1991), #163 SQUARING ACCOUNTS (June 1991) and #165 NO HOLDS BARRED (July 1991).

Meet:

**Sydney Raferty: She is the first to feel the wrath of King Crawley's vengeance. Pushed to the brink of insanity, she must fight her way back to reality—with the help of Benno DeMartino in #161 PUSHED TO THE LIMIT.

**Dakota Raferty: The judge's only son, he is a man whose honest nature falls prey to the racketeer's madness. With Honor Bright, he becomes an unsuspecting pawn in a game of deadly revenge in #163 SQUARING ACCOUNTS.

**Asia Raferty: The youngest of the siblings, she is stalked by Crawley and must find a way to end the vendetta. Only one man can help—Dominic Crawley. But will the son join forces with his father's enemy in #165 NO HOLDS BARRED?

Don't miss a single title of Patricia Rosemoor's QUID PRO QUO trilogy coming to you from Harlequin Intrigue.

HARLEQUIN Romance

This June, travel to Turkey with Harlequin Romance's

THE JEWELS OF HELEN by Jane Donnelly

She was a spoiled brat who liked her own way.

Eight years ago Max Torba thought Anni was self-centered—and that she didn't care if her demands made life impossible for those who loved her.

Now, meeting again at Max's home in Turkey, it was clear he still held the same opinion, no matter how hard she tried to make a good impression. "You haven't changed much, have you?" he said. "You still don't give a damn for the trouble you cause."

But did Max's opinion really matter? After all, Anni had no intention of adding herself to his admiring band of female followers....
